# HERO
## OF ORIA

BENJAMIN OSGOOD

*Hero of Oria*
Copyright © 2024 by Benjamin Osgood.

**MILTON & HUGO L.L.C.**
4407 Park Ave., Suite 5
Union City, NJ 07087, USA

**Website:** *www. miltonandhugo.com*
**Hotline:** *1- 888-778-0033*
**Email:** *info@miltonandhugo.com*

Ordering Information:
Quantity sales. Special discounts are granted to corporations, associations, and other organizations. For more information on these discounts, please reach out to the publisher using the contact information provided above.

Library of Congress Control Number: 2024915926
ISBN-13:      979-8-89285-144-2    [Paperback Edition]
              979-8-89285-145-9    [Hardback Edition]
              979-8-89285-143-5    [Digital Edition]

Rev. date: 07/09/2024

# Prologue

Between the Horizon and Burning Seas, there sat a peninsula. Windswept deserts of Vex-Tol-Rak in the south, renowned for the harsh beauty of their dunes. The rolling barren plains of the Hinterlands far to the northwest which embraced the Burning Sea along its southern shores and the great Spine-Ridge Mountains to the east. Almach to the north, with the great cliffs overlooking the rushing waters of the Tsere River amongst the sparse woodlands.

In the ancient days, Almach had held sway as the only true united power on the continent of Oria, through the strength of their blades and the wisdom of the great mages who commanded such powers as never before seen or since. Their armies flowed without hindrance through furrows and fields, subjugating the smaller city-states in the central portion of the continent. One by one, they fell to the might of the great armies from the north. Those who dared resist found their fields salted and their people enslaved, taken to the far corners of the world never to reclaim their homes.

In a small corner of the central peninsula, a small city stood as a beacon of hope and refuge against the tide of war. The city of Maroth flowed with silver and steel thanks to their trade and connections amongst their neighbors as well as their pursuit of ancient knowledge. As more of the northern lands fell into the clutches of Almach, Maroth drew those who remained closer together to form an alliance against them.

Atop the stones of Hammerpeak to the east, the united forces stood against the approaching ranks from the north. For three days they held their ground, withstanding arrows and stones meant to dislodge their forces from the foothold up in the mountains. On the fourth day, with the breaking of the dawn, King Maroth Un-Merrick charged down the mountainside atop his great steed Thunderhoof wielding his great hammer and crying out his challenge to the foe.

With a great cry, they had followed him, every man and woman ready to die on the field to take down as many of their enemies as they may. The soldiers of Almach were taken by surprise, most still asleep in their tents. The united armies of the central lands showed as much mercy as their foe had to their people, slaughtering them as they lay.

Driving the armies of Almach back across the northern rivers and fjords, the central lands united through oath and crowned Maroth Un-Merrick as their rightful liege. Through blood and pain, the kingdom of Maroth was born, and still they marched ever forward. Across the new nation, the call went up for any and all who were able to join in common cause against the invaders, to cement their place amongst the view of the gods that none may ever place their necks beneath the boot of conquest. After many more months, the tide had seemed to turn. Until a horrible mage by the name of Hecktat drew upon the old ways to call upon a power never seen by mortal eyes. Death once more swept unhindered across the entirety of Oria, from the Hinterlands to the great central plains death flowed in the streets and fields of the new nation. Only through great sacrifice and perseverance did the powerful magician finally withdraw in defeat.

Almost two hundred years later, with tension on both sides, finally, peace seemed to come between Almach and Maroth with the joining of King Merrick the Third, King of Maroth, and the second daughter of King Sigur of Almach, Eliza Sigursdottir. The wedding feast lasted three nights and four days, some from Almach had taken as a slight as it seemed to reference the battle of Hammerpeak, which had been the turning point of the distant war. But from that time peace had come to Oria.

- Excerpt from The Histories of Maroth, On the Founding of the Kingdom and Histories of the Nations of Oria. By Brother Simon, Scribe, Brother in service to the Temple of the Sun.

*Chapter*

# ONE

# DAWN

The smell of iron hung densely above the rolling fields. The once chaotic scene in the fog-swept rolling hills and rocks had fallen to silence. A crow called out in triumphant glee at the bountiful feast these pathetic land-borne creatures had provided this morning. All around his feet and scattered amongst the debris of battle the bodies of men, elves, orcs, and goblins all clad in the varying colors of their respective houses and clans lay in their final rest. Soldiers of the renowned House Tollstead lay next to mercenaries of The Black Hoof Guild, spearmen of The Fallen Company crushed under the weight of the very steeds they slew, the crumpled bodies of the armored riders sometimes a dozen feet away. The lucky ones had died on impact with the brutal surface, never having to feel the sharp, thin blades that had snuffed out their final breaths of life. Those who had been conscious screamed horribly while they were dispatched like steel oysters; their armor pried open to reveal soft flesh. But there were no screams now, no matter how keenly he listened. The young squire, bloodied and covered in mud and other liquids, stumbled weakly from corpse to corpse searching for something, for someone.

Tears would have stung his young cheeks if there were any left to give. But the poor soul had grown numb from the fear. When the battle had started the first thing to leave his mouth had not been a cry of rage or valor like his fellows; "The Phoenix will Rise!" from the Phoenix

Company of Mounted Swords, "Palthanos Protects!" from the Holy Order clad in their silver and red armor, "Kill, Kill, Kill" from the countless hordes of footmen and men-at-arms. But from his mouth; only vomit and the accompanying whimper.

"Shameful, maybe I am just a coward after all." He had said to himself. "And after I had boasted to all my friends that Sir Callen had chosen me to squire for him over all the rest." Maybe 'friend' was a bit of a stretch, but nonetheless, he had boasted so proudly to them and reveled in their envy all the same. How he now wished that one of them had been chosen instead. Twin hells, he would much rather have stayed home with the women and babes than see this.

His foot bumped against a mud-covered form, a leg in plate armor, and attached was the one body that mattered to him; Sir Callen's eyes stared unseeing through the silted visor into the clouded gray sky. The sight was all the more horrifying since his chest lay completely open and caved in; the impression of an octagonal war hammer's face outlined in the hardened steel which had crumbled like tissue paper beneath the strength of the dead orc not more than ten feet away, riddled with arrows and spears.

Not quite sure why, Bart, a lad who had barely seen his fourteenth winter, shivered from an internal chill whilst he slowly lifted the visor and stared upon the face of the man who had been his liege his entire life but his master for barely a week. The knight had trained him from day one how to ride a horse, to care for armor and weapons, how to march, and even how to mend wounds. But no amount of bandages and herbs would bring back the dead.

Sir Callen's sword lay a few feet away, placing it in the knight's cold grasp over his shattered chest, the young boy spoke a silent prayer over his lord. The words were unfamiliar, and his voice trembled and stuttered as he stumbled through the recitation, words he had heard others say only a handful of times. Completing his task, Bart lifted his head in silence, just as the barbed arrow flew through his throat, blood filled his airways and mouth. Choking and gasping he collapsed to the ground feebly reaching for the feathered shaft which had released him from his shame, his grief. Heavy footsteps approached from up ahead as the giant, green-skinned orc smiled with contentment at his trophy like a hunter approaching a wounded deer. The curved blade at the archer's waist danced out with a flourish across his neck, a cold kiss of steel that seemed the most welcome embrace at that moment. And then, darkness.

Bart bolted up from the bed of straw and reached for his throat. The same dream, the dream that had haunted his thoughts and nights since that battle six years ago. His sleep-addled mind could hear the sounds of steel ringing like a cacophony of bells accompanied by a chorus of screams and curses. Slowly his senses regained themselves and the smell of blood which had wafted out of his nightmare began to dissipate. Bart rubbed his eyes and frustratingly kicked the heavy wool blanket away as he resolved sleep would not come for the time being. It never did, and even most nights he found it hard to rest without the aid of a stiff drink, much to the dismay of those who had known him these past few years.

As the blanket fell away, Lorena groaned quietly and pulled the newly freed folds closer around her pale skin contentedly. Her strawberry-red hair clung to her face in a tangled mess lifted slightly with each exhalation. The young magician kept it cropped at shoulder length, to keep it out of the way when casting spells, or so she claimed, although she would often lament not possessing the long flowing locks of most beauties. Bart would disagree, he found her most becoming when she was enthralled in the process of casting spells; no such grace had ever been witnessed, even amongst the swans that graced Lake Tovar in the spring. Her deft steps would have been the envy of any dancer who bore witness. A veritable ballet of death and furious power. He gazed at the still form beside him musing over the previous evening, her warm embrace, those soft lips, the memory calmed his troubled heart. She was a handful to be sure, he traced the scratches on his chest and arms she had left him with. Bart sighed contentedly at the memory of the previous night; grateful he had not drank so much as not to remember what had passed.

Moving to the table in the small room of the inn, Bart pulled on his linen breeches, heavy boots, and the patched gambeson, there was a new hole under the arm he would have to get mended soon, wonderful. The steel breastplate and pauldrons he left as they lay, but the sword he strapped to his belt with practiced ease and familiarity. How strange it would seem to that scared, weak, sobbing boy from so long ago that he would become so familiar with death and the dealing of it, for the proper amount of coin of course. It was strange how his dreams brought terror, but when engaged in matters of life and death he felt at ease.

Silently, Bart stepped out and he made his way to the communal area on the ground floor. Each step he took down the wooden stairs seemed to be greeted with a cry of protest from the timbers, as though they too had been awoken from much-needed rest. As he reached the stone-floored common area most of the tables and seats appeared to be empty, it was only two hours before sunrise, and yet the stragglers from the late shifts down in the mines or those who sought a warm breakfast on their way out had already congregated in the Red Mare Inn for refreshment. Who could blame them? Even if the stone and timber structure had not been the only inn in town everyone within their right mind would tell you that only the Red Mare could pour a proper pint and boasted the best fare within the region.

The familiar smell of roasted potatoes with spices and butter coupled with the sizzle of bacon cooking wafted over him as Bart made his way to one of the smaller tables at the center of the room. The torchlight coupled with the fireplace left little of the area in shadow much to his comfort. Better to have a full view of everything rather than run the risk of some unknown threat lurking beyond in some dark corner unseen. He settled in at the table and waved a hand to summon breakfast.

"Can't sleep either eh?" The voice behind him carried a raspy undertone; like stones rubbing against rough gravel. Glancing sideways, Bart acknowledged the third member of his group on this journey; the six-foot-tall, gray-skinned naga slithered forward and joined Bart at the table curling his serpentine lower half in a coil beneath the table. When Bart had first met the creature, he had been off put from the beginning by those haunting reptilian eyes coupled with the upper human torso covered in reptilian scales. A native to the sands of Vex-Tol-Rak far to the south, up here the creature was a foreign sight. Strapped across his back were the two scimitars that on many occasions Bart had seen put to effective use, coupled with the fact the naga's saliva was venomous only made it more fearsome.

"Morning, Thrax." The greeting came naturally to Bart now, "Just more of the same is all."

"At least this time there was no screaming, well, there was screaming but you know what I meant." The reptilian's orange eyes glinted, prodding his companion playfully with a long, clawed finger as he spoke. Thrax had joined up with him and the others almost two months prior back on the road from Parnathsis. The naga had mistakenly made the acquaintance of some rather murderous bandits at the time and had gotten themselves captured as a result. It was only by a stroke of luck that the same gang had become the subject of a bounty Bart, Lorena, and Della the elven tracker had decided to collect. For a mage, Lorena had been unusually enthusiastic to take such a job; most mages would deem such work beneath them preferring to delve into forgotten ruins or seek out lost knowledge. But the redheaded lass with a temper to match was no ordinary mage. She had always struck Bart as the sort of older sister who constantly dragged their siblings into the most precarious of schemes and ideas. But most of her schemes resulted in a cacophony of explosions and flames.

The ensuing battle had ended with Della smashing open the lock on the cage holding Thrax who then bolted out like a demon to wreak havoc on the scattering villains. Nobody was sure exactly how Thrax had dispatched the remaining foes in the woods, but their horrified screams made it certain it was not a quick death for them in the end. But since that evening the naga had become bonded to the three who had rescued him from a life in the fighting pits, and he had proven himself to be an excellent swordsman and tracker for the group. No bloodhound could compare to his sense of smell, and Thrax's vision in the darkness would have been the envy of most even amongst the elves. Bart's only complaint would have to be his apparent ignorance of just how terrifying he could be. But that too had proven useful on more than one occasion; it is rather hard to lose an argument when you are shadowed by a massive half-serpent, half-human monstrosity wielding two of the largest scimitars anyone had ever witnessed. Bart had tried to wield one of the blades himself and it took two hands just to hold it upright, let alone swing the damn thing. But Thrax wielded one in each hand as though they were two short swords. Taking a blow from one of these must have felt like getting cleaved with an axe.

"I swear by the gods, you are becoming more human by the day you scaly bastard." Thrax looked at the human perplexed, head cocked to one side.

"Perhaps you are mistaken, friend Bart, there are no bastards amongst the naga as we do not hold to your silly notions of 'coupling' and 'lineage' you all seem so keen on."

Bart just shook his head, sometimes he forgot just how differently some species viewed certain human terms and customs. Undoubtedly, to Thrax, it was the humans who were the odd sort. The platter of potatoes and thick-cut bacon with crusty bread materialized from the hand of one of the serving maids who made no effort to hide her intention to keep Bart between themselves and the half-serpent creature.

As she turned to retreat to the safety of the kitchen Thrax spoke softly, petrifying the poor girl mid-stride, "Eggs, please" and did his absolute best to smile, the corners of his near humanoid mouth spreading far more than would be natural on any other face. The poor girl almost fainted as all color left her cheeks, but with dogged determination, she held firm and simply nodded.

"We really need to work on that smile of yours," Bart mumbled through a mouthful of bread and bacon. He silently regretted ever suggesting Thrax should practice being more friendly. All it had resulted in was that the mercenary had yet one more weapon of intimidation at his disposal.

Before any protest could be made in his defense, a platter heaped with golden runny eggs topped with small green onions clattered before the ravenous eyes of Thrax who, summarily, put his jaws to work on more important matters. The rich texture coupled with the fragrant addition brought him to sweet bliss. There truly was no better way to enjoy eggs, whipped to perfection and gold like the morning sun over the sand-swept dunes he had called home. How silly he had been to eat eggs straight from the nest raw for all these years; that is why he loved humans, the perfect ingenuity they could find in all manner of cuisine. But eggs, eggs were the pinnacle of the culinary world in his opinion.

Whilst Thrax conquered his breakfast with unrivaled gusto they were finally joined by the rest of their party; Lorena holding her twisting oak staff topped with a red crystal, Della in simple breeches and linen tunic under leather armor with two daggers strapped to her belt. And lastly the half-awake stumbling form of Armen, a mountain of a man standing four hands greater than most dressed in brown trousers and tunic wearing a delicate silver chain which glinted in the torchlight same as his shaven head.

Lorena's singsong voice cut through the silence between bites, "I am really going to miss sleeping in an actual bed after this place, by the gods why is it that these jobs can't ever take place anywhere with a good inn?" The joke was met with silent chuckles all around.

"I'm not too sure how much sleeping the two of you even get whenever we do manage to find lodging." Della's matter-of-fact tone was betrayed by the mischievous glint in her hazel eyes. Bart choked on a mouthful of potatoes as Lorena's face blushed to match her fiery hair.

"It's nothing like that!" Protested the girl, "It is far cheaper to just share rooms, that is all! And I will have you know that one of us snores like a mountain wyvern and talks in his sleep. I just graciously accept these hardships for the benefit of everyone."

Della nodded empathetically, her face solemn, "Well, that is just horribly inconvenient. But if it is that bad, we could just have Armen trade places with you next time."

Armen, mid-bite of a fistful of bacon, glanced at Bart then shook his head dismissively, "Nah, he ain't my type, too scrawny."

Bart blew a kiss in return, "Aw, you don't know what you are missing out on."

The elf reached across the table, pouring herself a mug of water, "Oh I doubt that, I am pretty sure half the town knows what they are missing out on. I've heard cave trolls that were more discrete than the pair of you."

Laughing amongst themselves and enjoying what would most likely be the last home cooking they would enjoy in the next few days, the five eventually made their way back to the rooms to start packing and readying their respective gear. Each mulling over the details of this job in silence.

Two weeks prior a courier had shown up at the village of Timberview, far northwest of Lakeshore and the comfort of the tavern. The message had been simple enough; highwaymen operating along the northern roads had disrupted the routes normally taken by merchants and travelers. Not that uncommon of an occurrence in these times, but in the last few attacks things had taken a darker turn. Up until this point nobody had been seriously injured, the odd stabbing or a bruised face to be sure, but nothing fatal. But now reports of some victims being dragged into the darkness of the surrounding forest. They varied in age, race even sex. None could speak as to why this behavior had become so prevalent. The bag of silver talons dissuaded any further inquiry for more details. Mercenaries and sellswords had no need for more information.

Looking over the map he had acquired for the journey, Bart traced over the red markings indicating the locations of the last few attacks that witnesses could best remember. They were clustered, it appeared as though while the same road was their hunting grounds, the actual point of attack varied all along the road along the Timber Glenn through Kaelith's Pass to the southeast, about thirty miles of possible terrain they would have to search.

"Are you waiting for that scrap of paper to show more than is already there? I'm surprised you don't already have it cloistered to memory by now." Lorena's arms wrapped around his neck as she rested a delicate chin on his broad shoulder.

Bart turned and embraced the mage in return, the map falling to the tabletop temporarily forgotten. "I know I am missing something, Lorena. It just doesn't make sense, there is always a pattern to these kinds of people. But no, aside from a few clusters that appear closer together than others there doesn't seem to be a way to narrow this down. It's going to be a long while to find them if we even manage that."

Lorena's clear blue eyes glistened like sapphires, Bart always felt as though he could drown in those eyes and gladly never resurface for air. Nodding she spun around his frame and grabbed the map herself and ostentatiously perused the diagrams with the air of some haughty professor judging their least favorite student's work. "Well clearly this map shows that they are only attacking the road, not the many alcoves or hidden areas used mid-journey by anyone who knows the area. So that makes it simple; we just give them something to attack."

Bart began strapping on the assortment of armor he had acquired over his career; a pair of pauldrons made from cold hammered steel, a simple backless breastplate in the common style mostly seen by guardsmen from the town proper, studded greaves which he strapped over his boots and trousers, and finally he strapped the nasal helm to his belt by the chinstrap.

He glanced over at his companion arranging her belt of pouches and components along with a thick leather-bound spell book which she kept strapped to her waist with a brown leather harness, "It is a sound plan, no doubt, but you and I both know what risks run along with acting as our own bait. It wouldn't be the first time one of those hair-brained schemes blew up in our faces."

The mage smirked mischievously, "Oh I don't know, lover, wouldn't be the first time something blew up in my face." She laughed at Bart's flushed face, patting his chest as she leaned in, letting her lips grace his.

The next few hours on the trek from Lakeshore towards the deep woods that made up Timber Glenn passed without much incident. The addition of a simple uncovered cart pulled by what could only have been described as the oldest cart horse in known existence made travel much more bearable, especially for Thrax and Armen. The journey up to now had been harshest for them; Thrax was still recovering from the lesions caused by rough gravel and paved stone and had tried to shrug it off as 'early shedding' until Della had decided to invest in transportation. Armen, as strong as he was, had little in the way of endurance and stamina required for long journeys. Gratefully he had deposited himself amongst the baggage and doffed his steel cuirass and helm, leaving only his greaves and chain hauberk worn. Studiously, he honed the edge of a massive halberd across his lap; the shaft was as long as he was tall and capped with a wicked inward curved blade at one end topped with a broad spearhead.

The rocking motion over the uneven road made Della and Bart sway from side to side with the steady pace of the aged but sturdy horse as he held the reins loosely. Lorena sat with her feet dangling over the edge watching the small dust clouds form behind them as they passed over the winding path. All five sat in silence watching the horizon and the hidden alcoves around them, but concertedly to not appear to be too obvious that they were. From a distance they were just another wagon full of loot; the mostly empty barrels and sacks sat enticingly in the back with the three weary passengers. At least that was the plan. While it would be obvious to any who saw them the massive passenger was clearly not a farmer or merchant, Bart had donned a brown woolen cloak with a hood to cover his armor and weapons in the hopes he would appear more like a farmer or Wagoner. Della had opted to simply wear a simple bodice and skirt, secreting the bow and quiver under her seat, and hiding several small daggers on her person for easy access. The small frame of Lorena could easily have been mistaken for that of a girl of some relation or another to the pair driving the wagon onward, but for good measure, she too had taken the liberty of dressing the part and opinions swayed between 'country bumpkin' or 'tavern wench' regarding her appearance.

As they traversed northward on the trodden road, over the rolling plains that made up the area between Lakeshore and the village of harvest to the northeast, the rolling grasslands teamed with wild game. Hare and pheasant sprung out here and there whence they passed, filling the air with birdsong and the rustle of dense vegetation. The sun hung low on the horizon bathing the surrounding landscape in deep golden hues, darkening with passing clouds in the western sky. These were the most blissful moments for Bart, sitting at the front of their wagon holding the leather reins loosely in his controlled grasp alongside Della. How peaceful it would be to hang up his sword and armor, perhaps he could find a little spot of land in some far-flung village where he could raise crops and tend sheep or cattle. To leave his violent past and the nightmares of his past behind. He could build his own house, nothing fancy, just a quaint modest home with the necessities of a simpler life. He could have a bed he would not have to pay half a talon to rent for the night, prepare meals in his own kitchen to his liking, and work the land to sustain himself in blissful monotony. Would Lorena and Della even consider joining him, he wondered. He glanced over at the blond elven warrior in consideration, she sat gazing over the countryside watching the countryside with calm serenity. Her green eyes shone brighter than the morning sun.

Thrax had drawn the worst of the lot; his voice traveled softly up from beneath the stuffed sacks on the floor, "I still don't see why I have to be the one hidden the entire time; you know it is rather hot under all this!"

Armen, still gazing at his handiwork replied matter-of-factually, "Oh sure, because if these bastards saw a twenty-foot-long half-snake demon riding in a wagon they would simply think it was just another family of farmers with their giant monster friend. I bet they have seen plenty of nagas in their time; nothing suspicious here."

The reptilian face peaked out from amongst the burlap, "You really think so? Because since I came to this rain-addled place I have yet to see even one of my own kind." The reptilian eyes stared at Armen with hope at the prospect.

"Well, I have heard rumors of a gigantic serpent that lives somewhere far east in the vicinity of the Dead Forest Bog..." chimed Bart. "But I doubt they hold any water."

Thrax pondered the idea for a moment. "How would a rumor hold water? Wouldn't it be better to use a bucket?"

Della stifled her laughter as best she could manage, trying her best not to fall from her seat in the swaying cart. The heads of swaying oak and birch in the approaching distance heralded their imminent arrival to the vicinity of where the attackers had been active in recent weeks. She gave a low whistle signaling the others who quietly returned to their watch in earnest. The soft clatter of hooves and creaking of timbers filled the air in oppressive silence, the pressure was palpable to the five travelers; it almost had a faint smell like wet fur the closer they approached the dark forest. Bart smoothly turned the cart along the northern fork keeping the trees on his left as they continued their steady pace through Kaelith's Pass. It was going to be a long thirty miles and the sun had maybe an hour left at best.

"We should make camp soon and start again in the morning." Bart's suggestion was met with approving grunts and nods from the others. There would be little point in traveling further that night if they could help it. If they illuminated the path, it would only serve to herald their presence as a target in addition to blinding their vision to the darkened terrain at the same time. It was a tactic they had used themselves on many occasions; wait until your enemy's sight had adjusted to the illumination and strike from beyond the shadows. Better still to eliminate the source and completely disorient their night vision while you slipped in and cut them down like helpless lambs.

As the amethyst sky retreated into the darkness they made camp a few measures into the woods; there would be no fires, and no tents. Light would travel further than one may expect, and the sound of tent flaps would be heard should anyone pass within the vicinity. Quietly Armen and Thrax covered the wagon with dead branches to break up the silhouette as best they could while Della secured their horse amongst some large shrubs nearby.

Dinner was thick-cut bacon with some bread from the tavern which still carried the welcome smell of earlier that morning. Paired with hard cheese and cool spring water they settled into the familiar routine practiced a hundred times prior. Two on watch with one replacing half of the pair at intervals every few hours. No movement, no sound, they would have to be like ghosts for the time being.

It was well past midnight when Bart awoke to his shoulder gently rocking him to consciousness. Lorena's red hair tickled his nose as he turned skyward. "We have a problem." She whispered, her tone leaving no doubt this was no time for conversation, only action. Thrax had already woken the others, the faint glow in his eyes reminiscent of two fireflies as his serpentine form skulked amongst the forest canopies.

That was when Bart heard it; the clatter of steel-rimmed wheels and the clatter of hooves along the road beyond the border of the tree line. Their camp was slightly uphill from the road which provided the benefit of a somewhat better view outward, three maybe four carriages were moving along the same route they had taken before. Each was illuminated by a swaying lantern next to the shadowy cloaked forms of a coachman. Even in the dark at this distance, he could tell they were clearly not merchants or farmers.

Armen lent voice to Bart's thoughts in hushed tones, "Damn nobles, not a care in the world no matter the danger."

Thrax's eyes turned suddenly, a finger pointing further up the hill whence they sat and further east, darting shadowy shapes could be seen darting from tree to tree crouched low and silent like a pack of wolves on the hunt. The others followed suit, spreading themselves along a skirmish line north and south to flank the would-be assailants.

"What are we dealing with, Thrax?" whispered Bart, his sword slowly drawing out with only a slight rasp like a breath heralding its awakening.

"Humans, I think," affirmed the coiled naga, his scimitars still fastened tightly across his back.

"You think!?" Bart's question was involuntary, cursing himself he hoped his voice had not carried as far as he felt it had in the darkness.

The serpent could only look on and watch in hesitation, "They aren't moving right."

Just as Lorena turned to press the question further, a scream ripped through the silence. Not of terror, but rage, even hunger, it was soon joined by others answering the call as the voices of men in panic-stricken terror and horses dying accompanied the animalistic chorus. The smell of blood filled the air with the sounds of slaughter, Bart knew that the time to act was now, the initiative was theirs and they must act.

"Now!"

*Chapter*

# TWO

# BLOODLINES

Snorri Hammerstone's hurried footsteps echoed down the marble floor as he marched past the lines of decorative statues, paintings, and suits of exquisite armor whose only battlefield had been the approach to the great hall of High Maroth. The seat of power held for generations by the Lords of Maroth stood as a looming sentinel with grace and oppressive military might over the city below. As any other dwarf would tell you, a castle was only as good as the foundation. The foundations of this kingdom were quickly becoming eroded despite the many warnings he had given his peers within the council of advisors and lords.

It had only been two weeks since their aged monarch had announced his decision to abdicate his throne, King Merrick III had reigned with a just and steady hand for almost thirty years. Victorious in war and politics, he had built this kingdom to the greatness it was today. He had expanded his kingdom from the Red Horse and Tsere Rivers along the Giant's Spine to the north, to the shores of the Burning and Horizon Seas, forged relations with the peoples of the Southern Sands, expanded trade within his borders, crushed the armies of Almach to the far north, and kept the hordes of the Hinterlands at bay. None could match his domain in military or economic might in the entirety of the continent of Oria, hordes of immigrants flocked to their doorstep to reap the benefits of the lands and the peace he had forged for his people. With a single missive and stroke of his pen, he had threatened to destroy the very jewel of his creation. Now the lines had been drawn, factions decided, and political intrigue and espionage were the course of the day.

"Good to see you haven't any of that fire in you, old friend." The voice behind Snorri caught him unawares. Turning, he saw the lanky form approaching from one of the side corridors to fall into step beside him. The dark red robes accentuated with black and silver embroidery tracing out serpentine patterns along the sleeves, hem, and hood denoted Sylvanus Chrystalan as an arch-mage of the highest order. Not only was his magic impressive enough to capture the attention of the royal court, but his invaluable wisdom and insight had swayed many changes in the past, including the foundation of a formalized education system and improved water distribution via interconnected aqueducts and pipes throughout most of the city.

"Well, well, well, this is an unexpected surprise. I thought you were so busy with your machinations and tinkering in that laboratory of yours to even grace us with your presence. What was that thing you showed me before? The device with the bells and the pearls."

"Ah, you mean the Vibabacus? Still, a work in progress to be sure, have to work on the sensitivity a bit as it will activate at its leisure with no reason at all." The item in question had originally been devised by the thin elf as a method to detect vibrations at great distances. He had surmised that by sensing the tempo of an army marching the device would release a marble which would, in turn, strike a series of bells arranged in an orbit around the perimeter showing the direction from whence they approached.

As the two approached the guards posted before the council chambers, the doors swung inward to grant passage within. The clamor of shouting and fists banging on wood greeted them as they joined the skirmish unfolding on either side of a long oak table in the center of the room, chairs on either side filled with counselors, advisors, provincial lords, and their aids.

"It is the order of the King, and that should be the end of it!" Cried one.

"And without him, then who is to take his place? You answer that, my lord" responded another.

"Surely you don't expect us to simply stand by and let some pup run this country into the ground?" growled an armor-clad representative of the knighthood, his breastplate adorned with the heavy calvary's insignia of twin swords etched in silver.

"Are you suggesting that you would risk war to sustain your claim?" accused the first.

With the mention of war, the room erupted into chaos. Chairs flew back, glasses smashed upon the stone floor spilling wine across the fine rugs nestled beneath. One counselor cocked back his arm to launch a partially full crystal goblet at the face of the man opposite, just as he was about to launch the projectile all came to a stand-still.

"Enough! All of you!" Snorri's harsh voice cut through the cacophony like a scythe through wheat. "Look at yourselves, are you lords and counselors of the realm or squabbling infants? By my beard, I ought to put one or two of you across my knee!"

Commander Zulla, the senior military advisor to the assembly and Commander of the famed Cloud Knights, rose and bowed courteously to the much older advisor. "To be fair, sir, your description of some of us as mere babes may be far too accurate considering some of us here were clinging to our mother's skirts when you first took your seat in the council."

"Oh, I remember that very well, good knight. I remember having to drag you by the ear to your father when someone had the bright idea to try and ride a yearling griffin through the kitchens!" Those who had heard of the youthful escapade could not help but chuckle. It was not completely young Zulla's fault, how was he supposed to know a horse saddle was no replacement for the sky saddles used on the beasts? But in the forty years since the boy had grown to be renowned as the greatest mounted knight in recent memory, and the troublesome black griffin had become his most faithful companion.

"Your continued advice and presence are invaluable, as always, good Snorri." A bespectacled, rotund man with wisps of grey hair protruding from his scalp stood as he spoke and turned to the gathered assembly. "No matter how much we debate on the issue, the crisis remains. We will be without a monarch come the beginning of the next harvest, meaning we have two months to decide on the rites of succession and declare our decision. To the North, many of our garrisons report the movement of troops and supplies along our border with Almach. Our spies have no word as to why, and the official statements via our ambassadors simply claim it to be a training exercise. And the Western Hill Tribes are now becoming bolder in their raids into the countryside. Then there is the matter of..."

Commander Zulla cut him off before the oaf went any further, "It is all for nothing unless we settle the succession as quickly as possible then! So, who is it going to be? Our king had no heir; no sons, no daughters, by law, the crown must pass to his nearest living relative. Which only leaves his cousin, Duke Rolfe of Heathridge. Or his other cousin of the same degree, Duke Timmon Firbank."

"That would be true in other circumstances," Snorri nodded, "however the king has brought this to my attention just hours ago." The collected assembly stared in shock as the dwarf produced a thick scroll sealed with red wax and stamped with the official seals and declaration of authenticity only available to the king himself. Passing the scroll over to Commander Zulla, the renowned commander inspected the unbroken seals intently. Nodding with satisfaction he broke the wax disk and opened the document to read aloud the contents in the booming voice of an experienced commander.

<u>Let it be known that I,</u>
<u>King Merrick the Third</u>
<u>Son of Wulf, Grandson of Merrick, Twenty-Sixth Lord of Maroth,</u>
<u>Under the eyes of Palthanos the Father, Friga the Mother,</u>
<u>Provicos the Warrior and all the gods do make it known that</u>
<u>I, Merrick III do hereby declare my son as the true heir to</u>
<u>my kingdom. And I charge my council to find him with all</u>
<u>haste before my abdication which shall be announced the</u>
<u>day of the Festival of the Fields in two months' time.</u>
<u>Should he not be found by the appointed date my kingdom</u>
<u>shall be entrusted to my cousin, Duke Timmon Firbank,</u>
<u>Lord of Twin Rivers, guardian of the Hinterlands.</u>
<u>May the wisdom of the gods be ever present</u>
<u>with this kingdom and this council.</u>

"A son! Since when has this been known? And why did his grace not reveal this sooner?" The voice belonged to Duke Rolfe, who with a single document had watched his candidacy devolve from being the first, to no mention at all. "He will not even give us his age, his name, nothing! This smells of a plot against my house, dwarf!"

"Calm yourself, my lord." Sylvanus, both hands raised before him in peace. "This is no plot I assure you. As to why this information has been secret until now, I can explain."

The suspicious, glaring eyes of Duke Rolfe danced between the dwarf and elf respectively as Sylvanus continued; his voice reminiscent of a professor regaling his captive pupils. "I am sure you all remember the night our late queen, Eliza, was taken from us by sudden illness twenty years past. Her funeral had been one of the grandest in memory. Her loss had scared not only the heart of our liege but also the people. All had mourned her passing. However, there is one critical detail that has been kept a closely guarded secret since that fateful evening."

"Pregnant." Whispered Duke Rolfe, disbelief etched into his features as he slunk back into his cushioned seat. "This changes everything, then according to the laws of our land, all claims and titles which would be bestowed upon the passing or absence of the king would pass to them." He waved his hand forward, summoning one of his aids aside. After a whispered exchange the man bowed and departed in haste via one of the many side doors which led to a series of antechambers around the halls.

"Indeed." Replied the Arch-Mage, "It would seem the assassin failed to recognize that detail."

"Assassin?!" the word echoed from nearly every tongue present.

"Now you expect us to believe that someone ordered the murder of our queen in addition to her producing an heir?" The portly little man rubbed vigorously on his glasses, sweat forming on his brow as he did.

Having composed himself, Duke Rolf turned to the gathered assembly. "Word will need to be sent to all corners. Perhaps even to our neighbors to the north in Almach, as it was one of their daughters whom our king took as his bride in order to keep the peace we now hold, it is only just that we inform them of these findings. If Queen Eliza was murdered and they find wind of this before we tell them it could mean war. I will also send word to my cousin, Lord Firbank of Twin Rivers of the news. Perhaps he can help with searching the northern lands for this missing scion."

Murmurs of agreement and approval responded in turn with the motion. But doubt still lingered, who was responsible? What had happened to the child? Who gave the order to keep this hidden? Who else knew more than they claimed? Had this threat come from without or within? The bombardment of questions, accusations, and general chaos filled the hall. Tempers flared and accusations flew from one side to the other fighting to be heard over the commotion. The Commander rose from his set and nodded his head towards Sylvanus and Snorri as he made their way to the door, the pair joined him in his departure, walking through the large oaken doors which hammered home with a thud as they passed.

"We won't be getting any further use from them today, let them brawl on their own." The armored knight's derisive tone was far too evident for polite company. "I will have my best scouts out looking within the hour. This is a time for action, not words. And we are to presume their resemblance is what would be expected? Near twenty years old with blond hair and such? But do we have any leads on where he would have been taken?"

The elf leaned in conspiratorially, "We cannot say for certain. After all the last anyone would have seen of the child would have been in their infancy. But there would have been one whom we could speak with as to the last known whereabouts of the child, you would recall our late queen had in her service a young woman with raven hair, the daughter of one of the minor lords of The Reach?"

Zulla knew the description all too well, "My wife?!" Ennell had been close to the former queen. He recalled how grief-stricken the poor girl had been. No one should ever have to experience such horror, years later they had married and had children of their own, including his eldest daughter, Eliza, named after the former regent.

Sylvanus nodded, "That evening, when the queen was discovered in her chambers, I made the decision to extract the child myself and entrust it to the one person who would never betray her trust. Ennell took the babe far from the royal palace under cover of darkness to a location known only to her. Upon completing her task, we insisted that no one other than the three of us; Ennell, Snorri, and myself would know of the child's existence or his location. And soon after the child had been deposited with their new family, we ensured that no one would know of our plot."

"But why hide the child?! Why deny them their birthright? And you kept this from our king, that is treason!" The commander had some inclination as to what the answer may be. However, it is one thing to surmise the answer and a whole other thing to hear it directly.

Snorri sighed, "If the assassin or whoever employed their services learned of the survival of the child, they would attempt to neutralize him again. As for King Merrick, do you honestly believe he would have sat idly by without expending every resource to find them? It was for the safety of the child and the realm!"

"Meaning it was the child, not our beloved queen who was the intended target. Or both it would seem." Zulla's mind organized the facts laid out before him, formulating the strategy of this as-of-yet-unknown adversary. "But if the queen's condition was a state secret, it only raises the concern that someone leaked this information. Spies? A traitor in the royal circle?"

The two advisors could only shake their heads in response. Whoever had wished the child and his mother dead, had left no evidence or intent to be found. The assassin was highly skilled as well, no trace had been discovered before or after the queen's demise, and while the signs pointed to poison there had been no signs or evidence of what substance may have been used.

Dismissing himself, Commander Zulla made his way down the hall, past the multiple reception chambers and galleries to the Crimson Tower, his personal headquarters. Upon entering, two of his staff jumped to attention from amongst the piles of dispatches, maps, letters, personnel reports, and requests upon their desks. He had chosen the twins personally as his aids and personal staff due to their keen intellect and organizational skills. Two for the price of one as it would seem.

"Gilder, Gallen, send word to the Captains of the Second and Third Cohorts along with the Sergeant-of-Arms; the Second and Third are to make ready for departure with all haste, and have the Sergeant-of-Arms report to me at once."

As the two aids departed, he made his way into the War Chamber. A large continental map had been skillfully painted on a large wooden table in the center showing the entirety of Oria. There was just too much territory to cover, and time was running out; he would have to cast the net now to find what he sought. As for his wife's involvement, it was all too much for even his mind to bear, he would need to speak with her in due time of all this.

—∭—

Down in the training grounds beneath the watchful eye of Captain Eliza, Commander of the Second Cohort known as the Emerald Dragons, two combatants with wooden sparring swords circled Vice-Captain Walter Hyde of the First Cohort. His twin-handed sparring sword had the advantage in range by at least two paces compared to the one-handed arming swords held by his opponents. However, they had the numbers, and each sported a kite shield which protected a good portion of their legs as well as their torso.

The first opponent lunged from Walter's right, a feint, as their compatriot swung in at the backs of his knees hoping to catch the Vice-Captain off his guard. Deftly the swordsman stepped into his opponent's attack and hammered the pommel of his blade into their gut, doubling the unfortunate man over just as he swung the hilt up and out catching them in the side of their head in two rapid strikes. Had they not been wearing the open-faced bassinet helm the damage would have been far more severe than a concussion and a pounding headache. In one fluid motion, he raised the blade up as if to strike down on the back of their exposed neck, baiting the remaining opponent to charge in. With a cry, the remaining fighter took the bait immediately; swinging a backhanded slash up from knee to shoulder to try and intercept the blow. Instead, the man was shocked to see the Vice-captain had dropped the large sword and grappled their arm from outside the blow which passed harmlessly by. Pining his next victim hip-to-hip, he shot his gloved left fist out across the exposed jaw with a crack, then, wrapping their neck under his arm Walter twisted backward, dragging his opponent to the ground as they gasped and choked for air.

"Yield, I yield" the man sputtered, gasping to catch his breath as the victorious Vice-Captain Walter, known as 'The Angel of Death', to those who faced him, released his strangle-hold and helped the man up. The second opponent lay unconscious as a few of the surrounding knights moved in to assist.

"Never announce your attacks, take the initiative and act when they least expect it. Tell your friend the same once he wakes up." Walter unfastened his helm and released the flowing blond hair from their steel prison. Even amongst the knighthood, he was rather handsome, his chiseled features reminiscent of some ancient statue in a forgotten temple. Strong shoulders honed and defined from long hours of physical and aerobic training. Bad enough that the man would be blessed with such beauty and additionally be one of the deadliest warriors the knighthood had ever seen. And although you might have been jealous of the adonis clad in steel, one could not help but admire or even love the man. He never let himself abuse his good fortune, much the opposite; the knight would most often be found amongst the conscripts and recruits training them personally. He showed no greater joy than when he witnessed the success of others after all their hard work and dedication. And in no small part due to his own actions, the Oder of Cloud Knights had drastically improved in their overall martial prowess. Just their very presence over or on the field of battle was enough to break the enemy's resolve or drive them to retreat.

Making her way down the wooden stairs, Captain Eliza joined Captain Berton Pike of the Third Cohort. His stark-white hair had been cropped short in contrast to the bushy beard which spouted from his jaw like an unkempt shrub. And despite his age, the man still possessed the prowess and strength of a man half his age, more than a few times he had been offered retirement from the Order of Cloud Knights, to live out his days in comfort and peace. He had always refused.

"I see your old student is still as full of fire and vinegar as his tutor." confided Eliza, patting her senior captain on the shoulder.

The oldest serving Captain in the order smiled with pride. "He hasn't been my pupil for many years now, everything he has accomplished is completely due to his own efforts, I hold only a small role in his greatness. He will make a fine commander when the day comes." Walter had joined as a squire five years prior, a strapping young lad, and the son of the Marquis of Hills Reach, a smaller vassal in the northern provinces. And while his family did not boast the riches of most high houses, they were fervently loyal in their martial service to the crown. Even from an early age, the lad had proven his status as one of the best fighters seen from his lineage. And while it was said he took after his mother in looks, he certainly had inherited his martial skills from his father.

Captain Eliza rolled her eyes, "Hah! Only if that weasel, Holew, lets him leave the First to take your place."

"And what would you say if I refused?" Holew's jovial tone called out from their flank, "I would be a fool to let my best blade leave the jewel of our Order, He makes a fine Vice-Captain of the Risen Phoenix, would you clip his wings just as he has taken flight?"

The Emerald Dragon, The Risen Phoenix, and The Silver Hawk were the First three Cohorts of the Order of Cloud Knights. Each held a place of pride that none could argue. These were the elite, the greatest knights in known history, their skill only matched by their ferocity and fearlessness. It took vast amounts of each to ride the large griffins which served as mounts to their order.

As the three laughed amongst themselves, Corporal Gallen hurriedly approached the gathered officers and saluted, palm over heart, and snapped to attention. "Captains Eliza and Berton of the Second and Third Cohorts, The Commander wishes to see you immediately regarding a matter of the utmost urgency. He is in the Marshall Chambers as we speak awaiting your presence."

The three officers looked at each other with grim faces. Captain Holew Longstride bowed curtly to his fellow officers, dismissing himself from further conversation, and made his way over to the side of his junior officer who stood looking on at the events unfolding while wiping off his face with a wool towel that had been provided.

"What is this about?" demanded Captain Pike, "Did the Commander give any details?"

The aide shook his head, "None. But he also requested that the Second and Third make ready to depart with all due haste."

The two captains regarded each other curiously, if the Commander was issuing these orders with this level of secrecy, then there was little room to argue. "Tell Commander Zulla we will be there shortly" ordered Captain Eliza as she departed to make her preparations and issue the command to make ready her troops. It would take at least an hour to have all her knights armed and kitted out in their gear, not including the baggage, supplies, gear inspections, and saddling the griffins which would make the journey, she was looking at two hours at least. But she, along with every other Captain, knew that their troops were up to the task. They were the Cloud Knights, the pride of Maroth, and they would not fail in their charge.

On the northern side of the castle lay the royal gardens, its winding paths lined with knee-high hedges of rhododendrons still in bloom with their delicate white flowers. Alder and rowan trees provided shade for the weary and homes for the nesting of thrush, robin, and all other birds which filled the air with song. At the center, an ornate fountain carved from marble with carved figures of animals around the trim. Atop the structure, a leaping trout spat water from its mouth into the reservoir below. Friedrich stared into the rippling water, watching the water lilies dance upon the clear surface in some coordination only nature could hear the rhythm of.

"It's not often one sees you enjoying the gardens, old friend." The dwarf turned and knelt at the approach of the familiar voice. King Merrick approached with the usual sage-like demeanor and bade the counselor rise. "I am glad you could make it; I am sure there is much you wish to discuss."

"There is little to discuss, your grace. I am bound to honor your command and serve the realm as you see fit." The dwarf bowed his head in respect for his old, friend, if a dwarf could even call a human old.

"Oh, come now, it is only us here. I wish you would just speak plainly with me without all the..." he waved his hand in search of the word "...formalities." Merrick embraced the shoulders of his old friend since his youth.

For a moment, as Hammerstone looked upon their face, he no longer saw the grey-bearded king, but the youthful face of a young prince who would disguise himself and sneak out of the palace to roam about the countryside and converse with peasants, the decrepit and other youth near his age. When Friedrich had discovered his excursions, the boy had insisted he had a good reason for it. How was he supposed to rule a people he knew nothing about? And so, the dwarf had relented to the experiment on the condition that he would be watched as he did so. It was not long before the disguised guards were bringing him reports of the young prince working the fields, loading crates down at the docks, and cavorting with village youth throughout the town.

In the end, the young prince had proven his point; unlike most of the nobility, he knew just how much effort went into sowing a field, harvesting crops, and the worry of drought or poor harvest. He knew the feeling of calluses from long hours hauling ropes to lift crates and barrels from ships docked at port or plowing a field by hand and having to pick out the stones left behind. The soreness one feels after a long day's work, followed by a tall mug of ale at your favorite tavern with your friends. The fear of being conscripted to go off and fight in a war or skirmish, and uncertainty of life. He looked upon the kingdom and saw, not the generalized diaspora of wealth and growth, but fathers, mothers, and children each with their own cares and worries. It would have been of little surprise to the old dwarf if King Merrick still had some friends or connections with those whom he had met all those years ago.

"You never asked why I wished to step down from the throne and relinquish my crown." The old king gazed upon the fields of flowers and lush greenery surrounding them, his hands clasped behind his back as they slowly trekked along the winding paths.

"It has never been my prerogative to question the minds of kings, I can merely hope that you have a good reason." Snorri fell into step alongside. "But as for your cousin, Duke Rolfe, to strip him of the inheritance so suddenly and in public might have been too much for his ego."

The old monarch nodded solemnly, "Indeed, but this was news that must be heard by a gathered assembly so as to dissuade any misinterpretation. And I believe you underestimate my cousin, Snorri, he has served this kingdom with honor and valor both on the field of battle and off. He has turned the Northern Reaches, a once desolate and barren place, into a fruitful bounty. He has governed strongly and well in my name all these years and has never failed me. We are bound by blood and by oath. Also, may I remind you; it was Rolfe who petitioned the Kingdom of Almach for my marriage to my beloved in order to make peace."

—⁓—

Duke Rolfe paced on the embroidered rug inside his quarters, furrowing the fabric with a defined tread with his continuing steps. His mind raced to process everything he had just heard; the queen, the heir, the sudden show of favor to his distant cousin who did nothing more than sit in his gods-forsaken fortress in the middle of nowhere. In a fit of rage, he grabbed the wine jug off a table and hurtled the clay vessel blindly. Clay fragments shattered against the stone doorway spilling wine across the sodden face of Counselor Griswald, his remaining grey hair dripping from the unexpected bath. Regaining his composure the portly man approached cautiously, devoutly wiping his spectacles, and inspecting them to see if they had sustained any further damage.

"And just when were you and your spies going to tell me about this?!" The enraged Duke's face darkened with visceral contempt as he turned to acknowledge his freshly showered guest. "You are always boasting to us how you have all these resources peppered across this continent; 'from beyond the River's Fork to the Sunrise Cliffs' as you love to put it!"

"Spies can only report what they have seen or heard, my lord. But I assure you, my eyes and ears have been appraised of the situation and will exhaust all sources to find the truth of these claims. If there is even a whisper of someone who may have been the heir my spies will make quick work of finding them."

The duke turned to face the stained-glass windows at the back of the solar, "You better pray to the gods they do. This is twice you have failed me, Griswald, do not even think to forget that it was I who pulled you from that gutter you called home and raised you to the station you so thoroughly enjoy." His eyes traced the rotund gut of the shorter man with disgust.

"If it would please you, my Duke, I do have some information which will aid in our success." He produced two scrolls and a map from beneath his cloak as he spoke. "We know that the child would be near twenty years of age now, is a male with blond hair, either green or brown eyes, and if he takes after his father in any other way; should be broad and as strong as an ox. Such a child would have been entrusted to a family with some means of protecting the infant through childhood. He would have been educated and taught the skill of arms under the pretense of joining the knighthood or perhaps in some mercantile capacity. The family would have needed to provide an identity for the child, so they would have been anointed in a sanctuary by his third spring to declare his name to the records of the gods. All this points to only two such cases; the records of which I hold a copy of here."

Duke Rolfe snatched the outstretched offerings and unrolled the parchment, burning the names of his two potential rivals to memory. Having done so he tossed the scrolls onto the smoldering coals of a nearby brazier. His face glowed amber as the flames licked hungrily at the parchment, erasing any trace of what had been written upon them.

"They both die. Do it quickly and do it quietly. Or next time..." he turned upon his confidant like a wolf towering over a wounded hare, "I'll be tossing you onto the flames."

# *Chapter*

# THREE

# SHADOWS

Della's bow arched back as the elf nocked an eagle-fletched arrow and took aim from her position above the mele. Three of the shapes had converged upon one of the guards beside the rear carriage, he swung wildly in abject terror at the dark figures, his futile efforts were of little use against their overwhelming strength and numbers. A dark hand reached out for his shield-bearing hand and tugged viciously, ripping the poor man's arm as though it had been paper. Blood poured from the wound, painting the side of the white carriage crimson as he screamed and collapsed from the shock. The other two quickly pounced upon their prey and tore into his body like a pack of wolves on a wounded deer. Pieces of armor and flesh scattered around as the ghoulish attackers feasted ravenously. Two more arrows in rapid succession plunged between the shoulder blades of their targets, as the third looked up just in time to meet the steel edge of Armen's Halberd. The lower jaw remained twitching in a grotesque smile as the remaining portions of its skull smashed against the carriage shattering bone, teeth, and gore across the pure rich surface.

"What the twin hells are these things!?" cried Bart, his sword dripping from viscera as he readied himself. Two of the figures sprawled at his feet; limbs outstretched with yellowed claws from hands that were human, yet not. With a flourish, he turned again to parry the lunge of another of the creatures as it hurtled towards his throat with glowing white eyes and needle-like teeth. Catching hold of the hooded cloak as it passed, Bart tugged back on the woolen garment and thrust his blade deep into its spine. Feeling vertebrae and ribs crack as the point drove out the chest of the creature from the force. Bart kicked the creature away, freeing his blade from the slumping corpse just as he felt a cold grasp reach around his throat from behind.

"Keraunós!" Lorena's voice rang out from above the fray as a blue bolt of lightning erupted the would-be assailant's form into chunks of flesh and bloody mist. Drenching Bart and Armen in the resultant cloud.

"Agh! It got in my damn mouth!" Armen spat wildly and tried not to heave. Two more of the creatures lifted their heads from the corpse of the coachman still seated upon the second carriage. They snarled in a challenge at the two men below. The reptilian form of Thrax materialized from behind the pair, scimitars raised to strike. Both heads flew skyward as the deadly blades swung inward like a pair of sheers. One of the bodies stood and turned reaching outward in its death throes before collapsing to the muddy, blood-strewn path below. A crossbow bolt flew past the serpent's skull by more than an arm's length, turning Thrax saw the shaking, crossbowman hiding behind the upturned carriage which had been first in line. Blood coated his torn face, and he had clearly lost an eye to one of the creatures. As he bent down to re-arm the weapon and ready another bolt Thrax lunged at the guard and wrapped his coils around his body holding him in place. Wiping the blood away as best he could manage, Thrax smiled gently into their eyes.

"Have no fear, we are friends." The guard paused, entranced by the glowing hunter's eyes, the smell of urine filled the air as he slipped into fear-ridden unconsciousness.

"If looks could kill." Laughed Bart, plunging his sword into the throat of one of the more fatally wounded beings lying prostrate before his feet. As the head lurched from the killing blow its hood fell back revealing a face not quite human. The features were sharp, angular with sunken cheeks and green-blue skin. Bart had seen starvation before; refugees, and the poor, but this was different. Its eyes now clouding over in death were pale white without any sign of a pupil. The ears were stubby with slight points at the tips almost like a goblin or an orc. He kicked the head over to the side, just to make sure there were not going to be any further surprises. A sudden gust of wind bellowed from behind him as his ears perked up at the sound of Lorena's flowing chant. As he turned, he could see her standing, arms raised holding her gnarled wooden staff above her head. Two of the creatures had been caught in a wind spell she had cast, they twisted and turned high above the ground.

"Anemos, kratito, schismar!" Lorena cried, the two snarling, flailing creatures contorted and ripped apart, sending limbs and guts flying in a myriad of gore and blood. Armen tried to place the side of a carriage between himself and the downpour, but it was too late. A second downpour of limbs, blood, and viscera shot skyward filling the air with the horrific results of the mage's spell. No matter how many times he had seen the red-headed mage use her talents, it seemed to shake him to his core. While magic users were rare, those who could use such intense levels of power were even more so.

Wiping away the gore from his eyes Armen blinked trying to regain his bearings, just as another of the feral monsters charged him from around the carriage, teeth bared and crouched low as though trying to tackle the much larger warrior. Armen kicked out with his foot, smashing into the snapping jaws of the beast. He could feel the jaw shatter and drive back into their howling throat as his boot hammered into the creature. It fell backwards, gurgling and sputtering as it clutched at its now useless maw. He stood over the flailing being and drove the steel spiked end of his weapon deep into their chest, twisting as he did. The creature jerked and reached wildly, blood pouring from its heart and mouth as it finally ceased.

"Any others?" Bart called out, sword at the ready in a low guard. The sound of Della's surprised yelp from behind made him turn on instinct just in time to see two of the creatures dragging his companion from behind into the dark woods beyond. With a cry of rage, he charged the pair of shadows with reckless fury. Dropping his sword into a low thrust he lunged into the first, driving his blade hilt-deep into the creature's belly with a wet squelch and the pop of escaping air. Driving his leg and hip forward, Bart twisted the blade viciously as he jammed his armored shoulder into its ribs and pulled the blade in a wide arc, catching the second across the lower jaw. The beast screamed in pain and anger, dropping the thrashing form of Della as it pounced on Bart with blood gushing from its shattered face. Blood, teeth, and broken flesh splattered across his eyes as he fell back, his sword useless as he used every ounce of strength to fend off the remaining jaw which snapped at his throat and face with razor-sharp teeth. The tip of a silver steel blade suddenly grew out from the creature's neck, stopping inches away from his own. Heavily, the monster slumped over and collapsed to the ground with a wet gurgle escaping the disfigured mouth.

Finding no other enemies to fight, the companions turned their efforts to sorting through the dead and wounded, mostly the dead. Three of the coachmen had been slain outright, the fourth sustained a gruesome wound across his face and chest, which he would never see again most likely. Seven of the guards were torn to pieces, and four were wounded in various ways but nothing too fatal. Their leader had not been so lucky; he sat propped against one of the steel-rimmed wheels, his legs mangled and bleeding profusely. The dying man reached out to his would-be saviors in desperation. Della knelt by him and took his hand, healing was of little use, but comfort for the dying could ease his passing. Weakly the man whispered something in her ear, blood speckling her cheek as he coughed from the exhortation.

"He must make it to Twin Rivers, he must...you must" his hand collapsed limply across the mangled form. A silver ring adorned with a pair of towers engraved around a single round ruby. The elf silently took the ring, offering a prayer over his soul and the souls of his men she turned grasping the cold metal pressing into her palm. The sound of a door slowly swinging out caught their attention as a young man clad in richly adorned traveling clothes holding a fine sword cautiously stepped out to observe his surroundings. Behind him sat the huddled forms of an elderly woman dressed in a deep blue dress and a girl a few years younger than him wearing a yellow gown with lace trim.

"I would have no further quarrel with you, take what you want and leave, but leave the good woman and my sister be!" His voice shook slightly, Bart could tell from the wavering tone that this man had most likely only ever seen a training field and battle itself had been a distant thought until that point. However, he seemed to have been well-trained;

the stance, posture, and position of his guard all spoke to years of dedicated training in the art of a blade. An artist who had never painted with crimson paint.

"Stay your hand, my Lord, we come only to assist, we are here on contract to rid this road of the... fiends...you see here before you." The scattered corpses, disfigured and grotesque, lay all around like fallen leaves in autumn.

"My name is Lawrence Firbank of Twin Rivers, Son of Timmon Firbank the Lord of Twin Rivers. This is my sister, Annalise, and her maid Erna. We are in your debt, good knight." Armen guffawed obscenely upon hearing the address.

"Well, how do you like that!? Congratulations on the promotion, Sir Bart, Slayer of...whatever the twin hells these things are." The tall lanceman held up half of a bloody corpse inspecting the features before him, through the ribbons of torn fabric he could see ribs protruding out from beneath mottled blue-grey skin. The creature's remaining arm dangled loosely in its socket terminating in vicious long claws attached to fingers that seemed just barely too long for its hand. Tossing the corpse away in disgust, Armen approached Bart wiping his hands across the hem of his Hauberk to rid himself of the thick black blood.

"Well, they certainly are not vampires or thralls," said Lorena, examining one of the severed heads. "The teeth are all wrong, and they normally don't behave this feral. The things moved almost as though they were crazed with hunger, or some sort of wild beast. But if they are completely mindless then why are they clothed?"

Lorena, using the butt of her staff, prodded under the woolen hems of one of the earth-tone cloaks and lifted it to pull away the blood-sodden fabric. It was of mediocre quality and roughly spun leaving holes and worn tears all over. "Well one thing is certain; some of these were female."

"Are you suggesting that these bastards can breed?!" Bart's soul shivered at the thought of a nest of these hideous things; with tiny squirming, squealing, blood-crazed infants packed together in some putrid hidden corner of an unknown place.

Young Firbank knelt beside the slouched form of the guard's officer who had been last to fall, grasping the blood-stained hands that now lay lifeless which had fought desperately to protect him and his companions. "If they do, then surely, we are all in deeper trouble than we could have possibly imagined. I should have never urged for us to carry on, I did this, I killed them." Tears ran freely down dropping silently on the blood-stained mail and leather.

"Why did you travel here through the dark? If you had known about the danger, then why the risk?" Armen stood behind the young lord, hand on hip as he did. "Even if they had been bandits and not these things it seems like quite the risk, if you don't mind me saying so."

All five turned to hear the response, the heir to Firbank and the Twin Rivers stood and slowly turned to face his benefactors. "Matters which would affect the entirety of this kingdom, and the good of the realm. I was returning, along with my sister and her maid, from the Hillpeak estate to meet with my father, Lord Timmon. But I cannot divulge any further, I beg your most gracious pardons on that."

"Hillpeak?" exclaimed Lorena, "That is almost two days from here, three times that from Hillpeak to Twin Rivers."

The younger woman from the carriage spoke, having finally regained her voice from the terror they had just been through. "We were visiting my uncle, the Lord of Hillpeak when we received word and needed to return to the castle. You must understand, this was all so sudden that we had no choice but to press on."

Armen stared at Annalise, she was exceptionally beautiful, and although she had just been through such an ordeal she carried herself as one would expect of a lady of stature. Her golden hair appeared almost ghostly white in the moonlight, like a solitary cloud that could be whisked away by the slightest breeze. He felt his face flush crimson as she gazed up at him in curiosity, that doe-like gaze drinking in every feature of his face, studying him intently.

"I must thank you, my rescuers, would you honor me with your names?" Even her voice rang like temple bells, no angel could match her melodic tone. Bart stepped forward, saving his armored friend from her inquisition.

"My name is Bart, leader of this company. These two are Della of the Elderglenn and Lorena of the Central College, the tall creature behind you is our companion Thrax of the Southern Sands." He pointed to each in turn as he spoke, each bowing courteously as he did.

"And you, good sir, might you be of the Holy Order? I see your head is shaven as is the custom I am told." The woman nodded at Armen.

"A-Armen, my lady." Stammered the awestruck lancer, dropping to his knee "And I am not from the order, I merely shave my hair for it was the custom in my family that all men shave their heads. I apologize if there has been any confusion."

"Ah, then you would be of House Bardiche, so named for their prowess with pike and lance. That would make us cousins!" Lawrence exclaimed, grabbing hold of the large warrior's shoulders, and embracing him without any regard for the circumstances. He acted now as though they were all attending some sort of summer banquet, heedless of the destruction amongst their surroundings. His eyes shone with a realization known only to himself. "This must be fate! The gods smile upon us even now as we fall into despair."

Della cut through the unexpected reunion, "That is all very good and all, however, there is still the more immediate problem of these things. And need I remind everyone that we are completely exposed here on this road at the moment!" She gestured at the surrounding woods, arrow at the ready.

"I do not believe there is any immediate threat, elf-friend," said the approaching form of Thrax, the unconscious crossbowman slung over his shoulders like a sack of last month's harvest. "I neither smell nor see anything for miles, so it should be safe for now."

"You don't sense anything?" inquired Bart. The group paused, listening to the forest for any trace, any sound, there was none. Not even the night song of birds, the hooting of owls, or the call of foxes. The silence consumed them, driving terror into their hearts.

"We have to move," whispered Bart in hushed tones, just loud enough for everyone to hear without letting his voice carry further. "Armen, Lorena, get the wagon and all our gear, we will load the dead on it once you return. Any wounded we will load onto the carriages. It is going to be close, but we should be able to get at least three of the carriages back if they are road-worthy."

The companions snapped into action, silently but with purpose. Della and Bart examined the wagons, all of which had sustained damage of one sort or another during the mele. One had been completely toppled over and both horses had been slain leaving it completely out of commission, another had broken the front axle leaving it teetering like a wounded animal. The last two were in fairly good condition, having only broken doors or torn roofs. The ride would not be as comfortable, but they could move. That was all that mattered at the moment. Bart thanked his stars that the beasts had not bolted in the chaos as he checked the harnesses and fittings to ensure there were no other surprises in store. Both were made of exceptional quality with embroidered collars emblazoned in gold with the twin watchtowers crest of House Firbank. The horses were spooked, who could blame them? He stroked their muzzles, calming the beasts as they dug steel-shod hooves into the blood-soaked earth.

Thrax approached cautiously, "It seems there are no other survivors, that one fellow I have placed with the young lord and his companions. It seems the old woman has some knowledge of the healing arts, and she insisted I place him in her care before I 'ate the poor soul' as she said" he explained, a wounded expression on his reptilian features. "I would never."

"You very well could, I've seen you consume larger prey." Chuckled Bart, his hands stroking one of the large horse's shoulders.

"Yes, but those had not screamed and pissed themselves! It ruins the flavor."

As the serpentine form slunk off to collect more of the dead, Della approached leading two of the wounded beasts which had survived. "These two are most likely not going to be strong enough to draw any carriage, but I will harness them all the same, we can't just leave them here for the wolves or more of those things."

Bart grunted in agreement, there was enough cruelty in the world, and there was no need to bring harm to innocent creatures. "I don't know what to think of this, Della. Nobody has even whispered about creatures like this," he kicked one of the mangled corpses at their feet, "but somebody has to know something! Don't you think?"

Della nodded, "I think we should bring one of them back and see if someone at the Twin Rivers, or maybe the college might have some clue as to what is going on."

Armen and Lorena returned with their small wagon and cart-horse, the five set about collecting the dead and placing them as respectfully as they could amongst the wooden crates and barrels. Covering the bodies with a large canvas, they began readying the caravan to move. Bart took his seat in the first carriage, followed by Della with the wagon and Thrax sitting in the back. Armen assumed the last carriage with Lorena, their passengers, and the wounded inside. Bart had studied the map as best he could and figured they could potentially reach the base of the Spinefoot Mountains by daybreak. The plan was that once they made it there the group could find shelter, tend the wounded, and examine the carriages in a better light after morning.

"And let this be the end of it," prayed Bart.

As the ramshackle convoy limped north to escape the danger of Timber Glenn, a pair of round orange eyes peered down on them from atop the branches of a large pine. With a silent flutter of wings, the owl soared upward and circled briefly before turning south, soaring over the sea of leaves and branches. Turning and twisting in the wind with ease, the silent hunter soared unrivaled over the landscape until it reached the shores of Arrow Lake, plunging downward to skim the crystal-clear surface of the water. Silent ripples passed in a trail behind the bird as it deftly maneuvered inches away from the cresting waves he produced.

Turning westward, the powerful brown wings effortlessly carried them towards the rising buttresses and towers of a stone fortress that jutted out from the rolling hills like a splinter against the starlight horizon. A break of deep amber and gold slashed across the sky heralding the imminent arrival of a new dawn. The grey stone walls of the garrison were splashed with hues and tones of morning light, the square white-faced banners emblazoned with a black fist fluttered lazily in the slight breeze that arose from the west as intricate stained-glass windows welcomed the arrival of the sun, filling the interior halls with dizzying color.

From overhead, one would see that the Garrison of the Order was oriented into three rings of octagonal walls accentuated with towers that rose higher in elevation the further it went. At the center stood the imposing main garrison itself, round towers on each of the four corners reached like fingers desperate to grasp heaven. Circling the western tower, the owl slowed its descent and landed gracefully on a wooden perch just inside the uppermost open window, hooting and bobbing to announce his arrival.

The slumbering figure rolled over, a grey beard jutting out from beneath an oversized nightcap that shielded the wearer's eyes from the morning rays, snoring loudly without any regard for his newly arrived guest. Frustrated, the owl hopped from his perch at the windowsill and troddled across the floor with razor-sharp talons scratching at the oaken floorboards. The large brown owl hopped deftly up onto the foot of the bed, bending low and bobbing the round-faced head tipped with his deadly curved beak like a snake, slowly the raptor stalked his slumbering prey, beak clacking open and closed slowly as his wings rose back, ready to pounce.

"And what do you think you are doing, Kukova?" the thin man's eyes peered out from beneath the folds of his cap. I may be old, but I am not that old.

Halting, the brown owl stood slowly up, puffing out his feathers and preening intently behind his shoulder. "Well one of these mornings, you are not going to wake up. And those days are soon approaching. I just wanted to make sure my favorite source of food was not joining the worms just yet."

Solon rose softly, stroking the soft brown and white plumage of his familiar. The old wizard had been the 'guest' of The Order for several decades. Presumably under the pretext that the holy knighthood had dire need of his services. And while the monk warriors could not pay him, they had provided him with ample food and safety, a place to study magic both known and unknown, along with access to the greatest collection of grimoires, texts, and ancient scrolls in the whole of the continent of Oria. All they had asked was that he would divulge all of his findings on a regular basis before the clerical assembly. In truth, Solon knew the true reason he had been 'invited' was due to some of the more reckless experiments he had pursued in his youth. But all-in-all the arrangement was not particularly bad, he even got to go outside when he wished, so long as three of the hulking, humorless, bald-headed, stone-faced knights accompanied him as he did.

The round room that he had been given had three windows facing the eastern horizon and several glass-paned sunroofs which provided ample light for most of the day without the need for candles or lamps, a benefit considering the risk of open flames around the piles of books and scrolls organized in a method only he could discern. A fire would be most terrible, considering the circumstances. On the western side, a thick oak door shielded him from the monastical world, through which the long spiraling staircase could be found. The bed was simple, yet comfortable, the few chairs and stools which filled the space amongst the bookshelves and desks were occupied by yet more books, scrolls, stone tablets, trinkets, half-finished experiments, or liquids in vials of unknown origin or purpose. The old man slowly stood and walked towards the open window clad in his nightshirt and having donned a pair of thick fur slippers, peering out the window at the morning sun he lazily poured a pitcher of water into a small kettle close at hand and set it on a small stone circle engraved with runic symbols and intricate geometric patterns. At the center of which was embedded a small red opal, waving his hand the patterns glowed softly with a strange red hue.

"So how was your nightly flight then? Anything of interest you wish to disclose?" Solon asked as he began measuring an assortment of tea leaves into a, mostly clean, glass beaker. Kukova fluttered silently across the room, landing back on his perch by the window.

"Salbek's mayor is celebrating the birth of yet another grandchild, while the town of Goldgrow is expecting an exceptional harvest as they do every year. There was a tavern brawl in Crossings involving a troupe of troubadours and the town watch which left most of the guards in the local infirmary, a pack of waheela is roaming the plains west of Hammerpeak and north of Kaelith's Pass," the owl paused, choosing his words carefully, "there has been an attack on the road by some strange beasts."

The wizard turned slowly, "What kind of beast?" The owl regaled his companion on everything he had witnessed; the sudden attack on a line of carriages, the howling of the strange beings as they tore upon flesh like a pack of wild dogs, how all had seemed lost until five persons of unknown origin had joined in the fight and defeated them after a pitched-battle. Solon drank it all in silently, mulling over the details over and over again.

There could be little doubt, he was sure of it. Solon dove into a nearby pile of tomes and scrolls, tossing the rejects aside with reckless abandon. "Where is it? I know I have it here, 'Lobek's Guide to the Care of Wyverns' no, 'Treatise of the Al-Sahib', no, no, no! Aha!" Holding aloft a leather-bound tome with black covers and pages, Solon turned victorious towards his friend and companion seated by the window.

Kukova stared, aghast, "That book!? How do you even have that thing, you know what would happen to you if they-"

"Oh yes, yes, another trial before a tribunal to explain why forbidden texts are in the possession of someone so clearly predisposed to violating the most sacred laws of the College and the Clergy." Solon paused, grinning mischievously. "If I have this book, just imagine how many others I have hidden around here."

The horror on Kukova's flat, round face was evident even to those who were not in ornithological circles. The tome in question; The Rites of Hecktat, High Sorcerer of the Golden Age, should not even exist by any right. His eyes widened as Solon cracked open the dark tome, turning page after page as he searched the contents within.

"You see, old friend, knowledge itself is not an evil thing. It is those who walk on the paths of mortals who dictate that which is evil, and which is holy. But when one steps back and observes, without prejudice, you will find the contents of any text are nothing more than words. While words do hold power, it is the speaker of those words, not the words themselves, who determines if they are used in malice or mercy. Who are we, these pathetic beings, to dictate the allegiances of gods? Who are we to decide if this god is evil or that god is good? Are we to place ourselves in the judgment of those who reign over the mortal realm? I say no, and I will always say no!" Solon's voice rose in fervent resolve, it was a speech he might have given many times over, and for all Kukova knew, he had.

Placing the dark tome open upon an open space amongst the collective disarray, the old wizard tapped the pages scrawled in thick serpentine script with a bony finger. Hopping from his perch, the shaken and disturbed owl cautiously glanced upon the image scratched upon the page in rough charcoal. His orange eyes widened in recognition of the grotesque, monstrous form crouched and snarling amongst the vellum.

Kukova hopped up and down, his beak clattering as he anxiously flapped his powerful wings, "That's it! That is what I saw! The thin body, the claws, the teeth!"

Solon nodded knowingly, "Then that means we are truly on the brink of a terrible age." The shrill shriek from the boiling kettle by the sill caused both to jump from shock, "Tea is ready, but that will have to wait for now." The old wizard pulled on his flowing green robes, unadorned and cut in simple fashion. It would seem that his quiet days of solitary study had at last come to a close. If the threat was any less, he could simply summon a messenger and dispatch a missive detailing what had transpired, but with a foe such as this he could not risk any delay or failure. His old bones creaked and groaned at the thought, it was truly unfair that such times should come when he had long passed the prime of his youth, why was it that fate always decided to turn her head when we were old and grey?

*Chapter*

# FOUR

# WARLORD

In the Northern Plains of Korb, amongst the sparse woodlands and marshes north of the Burning Sea known as the Hinterlands, the sprawling camps and burning fires of the various tribes of orcs, ogres, goblins and their retinue stood out in the sprawling hills and grasslands like a scar upon the earth. At the center of the camp stood a jagged wooden structure in pyramidal form. On the northern horizon, the peaks of Mount Knash jutted ominously against the star-filled horizon. The howls and barks of crocotta, hyena-like beasts larger than most hounds, echoed through the night mingled with raucous laughter, singing, and the beating of drums. Children darted from tent to tent armed with sticks locked in fierce mock battles amongst themselves. The smell of roasted goat, cattle, and all manner of wild game wafted and mingled in a serenade of flavors. Dotted amongst the camps wrought iron cages and large carts of the same held a variety of deadly beasts; lions from the far-flung plains of Karash-Tor, Leopards from the jungles in the peninsula, crocotta cubs mewling for their mother's milk, and great eagles from the northern mountains. Others, still, held slaves; male and female of various races, prizes of plunder over the course of the past season. All would fetch a high price or bring unbridled entertainment to the tribes. Screams of protest from the unfortunate souls echoed with the jeers and laughter of the barbaric horde as they were pulled from their cages in chains and tossed to those who either paid or rented them for their own purposes. Naked and shaking with fear as, one by one, the cages emptied, and their occupants dissipated into the tents of the warriors. Elves, humans, dwarfs, beast-kin, and even other orcs or goblins from disgraced or decimated clans were all bound in chains. Those who were clothed bore only whatever shreds of fabric or remnants of clothing they had managed to retain.

Huddled in the corner of one such cage, Gamona Halfstalk shivered from the cold. The clothes she had worn on her seaborne journey had long since been torn from her, replaced with the rough burlap tunic that did little to shield her frame from the elements or the gaze of her captors. The dwarf longed for the wool robes and leather boots she had worn on her voyage across the Burning Sea, or even a blanket. Anything to stave off the cold would be a treasure to her now. Hot tears stung her eyes at the memory of her home, she had longed for adventure, to find some purpose in the world. Is this how it was going to end? Shipwrecked far from the comforts of civilization, chained and enslaved to these murderous barbarians? The iron collar set around her neck hung heavily, chafing her skin raw about her shoulders. At the opposite end of the cage, a petite elf woman who had arrived a few days ago sat sobbing. The two had not said a word to each other, each overwhelmed by their own troubles. But it seemed the elf's were only just beginning, as the door to the cage swung violently open, two orc warriors clad in rough furs and leather bands pulled the trembling elf from the cage. Their laughter boomed in contrast to her screams, Gamona could only look on in despair, before curling up once more trying to block out the world.

Marguk Longfang, Chieftain of the Wolf Clan tore ravenously into the hunk of meat, watching as two male orcs forcefully dragged the form of a young white-haired she-elf kicking and screaming towards the dark confines of the tents of their encampment. Her wailing cries of desperation echoed in his ears as he sat by the roaring fire at the center of camp. There would be no reprieve; if she was fortunate they would be pleased enough with her to keep her as a bed-slave instead of tossing her to the whole of the tribe, subject to their whims without even the minimal protection afforded to those who were exclusively owned. All of the great Hill Tribes had come together for the ceremony of Pax-Gog, something that only happened every third summer amongst their peoples. It was a sacred time, three days of feasting and gladiatorial battles all in the name of the great Gog Far-Seer, lord of the hunt and the cycle of seasons. The orc chief gazed into the evening sky, peppered with stars in the cloudless night as sparks crackled in the kindling and wafted skyward along the rising heat to join their cousins above. For it was known that the stars were created each night by the cooking fires bellow; an offering of smoke and roasted meats borne with each spark to the great Gog. He lifted his hunk of goat to the heavens, acknowledging that even now he shared a meal with his deity and every ancestor past who sat with him in the great void.

His hulking green frame was covered from head to toe in an intricate web of black and red tattoos, which commemorated his clan, his achievements, his rank, and even enemies he had slain in the intra-tribal skirmishes he and his own had bled in since his youth. And when the orc tribes were not fighting each other, they were raiding the ripe villages south of the Hinterlands. Those pathetic man-folk always screamed in terror and hid in their giant stone castles and towers leaving the weak and infirm as easy pickings for their clans. There would be blood, meat, slaves! The anticipation sent a shiver through the great chief's spine as he growled in prospect. The howling of their death cries as he slammed his massive club down on their heads, the screams of terror as they took the women and children as slaves. There was no greater pleasure, no grander offering to Gog!

Marguk saw another lone figure approaching from the edge of his encampment, "Hail, brother chieftain." he cried, lifting his quickly disappearing roast in greeting as Chief Horka of the Dead Crows approached the roaring fire. In both hands, the massive dark-skinned orc wielded a ram's horn filled with the putrid beverage known among the orcs as 'airag' a thick fermented beverage made from the milk of mares or other large beasts. Horka passed one of the large horns over and sat opposite as the two greedily guzzled down their drinks, racing to the bottom of the horn as fast as they could physically manage. Throats pulsing with each monstrous gulp.

"Phah! Looks like you beat me again, brother!" cried Horka with a satisfied sigh. His horn faintly dripping remnants from the lip. Airag was a strong, thick drink, it warmed the soul and filled one with a fire in their hearts and loins.

"And it won't be the last!" chortled the victorious Marguk. "The day you beat me in any drinking contest is the day I go blind and grey!" The two guffawed loudly, enjoying the warm feeling flowing through their bodies.

While the two might have referred to the other as 'brother', there were no familial ties between the pair. All chiefs referred to each other as such, in respect and recognition of the other's position within their respective clan or tribe. Under the laws of Gog, being a chieftain brought with it no greater honor and responsibility amongst the tribes. While most of the time each was autonomous and independent of the other, even waging war or raiding those whom they pleased, every three years under the eyes of Gog they came together as one tribe. Thus, the balance of power and the bonds of kinship could be mended or forged anew. More so, should one tribe declare war upon another, it was forbidden for someone who was not a chieftain to slay them. A chief deserves a chief, and each knew the names and faces of the others. However, within the clans, it was not forbidden for one to challenge their chieftain to the rites of Gog-Ru-Kesh; a ritual duel in which only one would walk away head attached. Whoever was victorious would lay claim to the title and become the new chief.

Six times, Marguk had been challenged for the position and six times he had cleaved his opponent in twain. Each victory had been recorded on his bulging chest within the intricate web of tattoos.

The younger chieftain leaned in closer to Marguk, lowering his tone, "I heard that not too long ago you had a bit of a rumble with those damned Red Fangs. Is it true that you raided their camps because of a dream?"

Marguk's eyes narrowed, "It was no dream, brother, it was a prophecy. A prophecy granted by the great Gog Far-Seer himself!" His voice resonated with fervent resolve, doubtless in the truth of the matter.

"Hah! Now I know the great fire will soon extinguish, no orc would ever dare to suppose the great Chief Marguk of the Wolf Clan, the Devourer, the Slayer of Turk One-Eye would put so much faith in prophecy!"

Horka's laughter fell on deaf ears, his companion sat still, his eyes fixed on the dancing flames. "You don't know how powerful that woman is, her connection to Gog is without question; she sees things before they happen, hears words not yet spoken, she speaks with the authority of the Far-Seer himself."

The younger chieftain knew all too well the rumors surrounding Marguk and his She-Human Sorceress; it was said the strange woman had simply walked into his encampment at nightfall, straight past the sentries and the crocotta they kept as attack hounds. The large near-canine-like beasts had impeccable senses of smell and sight but even they had not sensed her presence until she had reached the center of camp. Stranger still, she did not wear the usual garb common amongst the man-folk, instead she had adorned herself with a bears skinned hide and nothing more. Any who had witnessed the sight insisted that the carcass was fresh, as her bronzed skin was bathed in the fresh blood of this kill. She wore little else aside from a hemp necklace adorned with beads and bones. In the end, she had walked straight up to Marguk's tent at the center of the cam and sat on the ground until he appeared. Since that fateful evening, not only had the Wolf Clan grown to be one of the most powerful of the Hill Tribes, but her powers and mystical arts had become legends amongst allies and enemies alike. Together, they had become invincible, and until the Red Fangs, no other tribe dared to stand before them or raise a challenge so long as the she-witch stood by his side.

The moon continued its steady course across the great night sky as the two parted ways, each seeking the warm furs and comfort of sleep. Marguk approached the flap covering his grand tent, lifting it slowly as he was greeted by the smell of incense and the warm glow of a small brazier at the center of the space. The lithe form of his sorceress, wrapped with one of the many furs from his bed, stood basking in the warm light. Her raven hair flowed over exposed shoulders and supple breasts like a waterfall, graceful yet powerful. He gazed along the curves of her body, not in the usual ravenous lust he was accustomed to, but in pure rapture. He had never felt such passion when he looked upon the females of his own kind; orc women were not only fierce warriors but fierce lovers as well. When he had been with them it had been pleasurable enough;

the gnashing of teeth, both fighting for dominance over the other in unadulterated, near-violent throes of passion. Strength was everything to an orc, male or female it mattered not, but this girl, this she-human was so small and frail in comparison to even the smallest of the orc race. Yet the hulking Marguk saw only the hidden powers that lay behind those green eyes. Those twin emeralds shone with more fire and more ferocity than even the great dragons that nested atop the peaks of the Giant's Spine far to the east.

"Susalla, I thought you would be resting." Fighting to keep his tone even and unfaltering, the Greatest Chieftain in all the Hill Tribes fought to keep his composure in the presence of the one being in this world who could bend his will on a whim. She had never demanded anything of him, never exercised her power to kowtow the barbaric Marguk. However, he suspected she knew very well she could.

"How could I rest, Great Chieftain, War Master of the Hill Tribes, without my champion at my side?" the woman approached gracefully, like a serpent on a wounded bird fallen from its nest. "Or do you find my presence displeasing? If so, I can leave."

She made her way past him, Susalla passed so close Marguk could smell the incense in her hair, that intoxicating smell which boiled something up from deep inside, a primordial urge to take what he desired without question grappled with his desire to remain stoic. From his height, the great orc could see the curves of her bosom in full, like ripe fruit begging to be plucked. The touch of her delicate hand on his arm was a stark contrast to his rippling arms honed through a lifetime of war and training. Her fingers traced the intricate tattoos mingled with scars of wounds sustained throughout his rise to where he stood now. Marguk shivered at the sensation, her touch cut deeper than any foe's blade and reached his heart without obstacle.

"Stay" His voice was a low whisper as he turned to face her, gripping the soft chin as delicately as he could manage with his calloused fingers, tilting her face upwards to meet his. "You know your presence pleases me, yet you continue to tease me so."

Her eyes sparkled with mischievous intent, gazing deep into Marguk's deep, dark eyes, meeting his gaze with intense ferocity. "I would never tease you, great warrior, you are the one the Great Gog has declared to be his champion, I have seen it. And I would never mock the decisions of the gods." Her hands slipped effortlessly to caress his toned form, his statuesque form hard as granite and warmer than any fire. Her fingers danced across the broad leather waistband of his kilt, easing under the band to find soft purchase. "My purpose is to serve, to cast my powers into the void and seek the path best suited for you. Have I not served you well, Great Chieftain?"

The orc's mind was flooded with images of every possible desire he could fulfill right here, right now, how he longed to pluck this delicate flower and breathe deeply of her until he was satisfied. Images flashed behind his eyes of the two of them locked in passion amongst the furs, all cares cast to the four winds never to be seen again. He could feel his hands involuntarily reach for her round hips, desperate to grab hold and never let go. Suddenly he could feel her leg caressing inside his thigh, her warmth and softness enveloping him and rising to flood his senses. That was when he realized the fur had now draped around the temptress's petite ankles, forgotten amongst the two of them as they stood, like a great oak enveloped by a twisting vine. He could feel her breath on his chest as she whispered softly, seductively, embracing his ears with her voice.

"I have told you what is required for my most powerful magics, have I not? All you need do is take what is offered before you." Her hand slipped entirely within his waist, caressing the orc's bold prowess in her soft grasp, "See? Your boldness betrays your restraint, great one, plunge your ram against the city gates and conquer the city. Ravage the prize before you and all will be yours!"

Marguk could feel the blood rushing unabated, his heart pounding from his chest, each pulsating sensation filling him with a fire that could never be quenched. "I do not wish to harm you, sorceress, what you seek would break you."

Smiling, Susalla, with her flowing black hair as dark as a starless night, her firm buttocks swaying before his eyes like the flow of an endless sea, crawled onto the piles of furs and turned to kneel facing him, legs spread open and inviting with her hands caressing herself accentuating her curves in every detail before him. "You can try, my stallion."

Marguk could hold himself back no longer, the insolent challenge along with the effects of the airag he had consumed swelled him beyond control. He grasped the smooth-skinned shoulders of the human woman who stood defiantly before him in his grasp and lifted her eye level with his own as he forcefully locked his fanged lips with hers. He felt her body tremble, her lips greedily seeking his own. He carried his prize to the pile of furs and tossed her amongst the pelts of wolf and bear upon the raised frame of his tent. As he gazed down at her voluptuous form, his fingers grasped the leather belt that held his pleated kilt in place and tore away the impeding fabric.

Susalla bit her lip, her eyes locked into Marguk's as her hands slowly caressed her heaving breasts as she gazed upon his towering form which slowly lowered towards her own. The heat of Marguk's body mingled with her own, his rough green skin taught over rippling and powerful muscles honed through years of battles and raids. "Make me yours, my chieftain," she whispered, her hands clasping either side of Marguk's broad face, "conquer me."

Marguk's senses were filled with the sorceress's sweet scent like honey and spring flowers tinged with sweat and incense. He slipped his hand between her supple thighs and caressed the pale, smooth skin in his own rough and calloused fingers. She gasped, her legs shaking as he inched ever northward. He burned for her, the sounds she made, the heaving and desperate breaths with each passing as he toyed with her every sense. "I will make you mine, no need to be quiet, my pet," he whispered.

A few hundred yards away inside the sprawling wooden temple of Gog, the only permanent structure amongst the tents and yurts scattered around the plain, four goblins clad in the red robes and hoods of temple acolytes escorted a line of chained slaves toward a central brazier surrounded by fine rugs and carpets plundered from the multitude of raids which the tribes had conducted for eons. Surrounding the brazier amongst the finery lay piles of gold spilling from open chests, statues of inferior gods looted from their burned temples, silks, furs, and jewelry from the far-flung reaches beyond their borders. A dozen priests and priestesses looked upon the line of slaves dismissively, intent on the words spoken by the seated figure upon a dais at the rear of the chamber.

Borba Green-Eye, High Priestess of Gog, Matriarch of the Temple, and Great Mother of the Hill Tribes sat in contemplation observing the newcomers brought before her. She was clad in the sheer silk robes of her station, accentuated by a thick leather belt decorated with the bones of small creatures and beads. Her hair had been woven into tight dreads with the sides of her skull shaved to expose the intricate array of tattoos which graced her amazonian form from toe to temple. "I see that the pickings are as bountiful this year as the last." Waving her hand before her regally she commanded the four acolytes, "Bring them forward, let us begin."

A murmur of anticipation wove through the collection of priests and priestesses as the line of chained captives was paraded before them. All of the captives were strong, and robust specimens belonging to the varying races, the peak of physical prowess. Chained wrists and ankles clattered as the group slowly made their way before the dais, halting as they arrayed themselves before the imposing female orc. Borba's eyes paced across each in turn, judging with focused intensity on their gathered features.

"Let those who wish to submit for the Goa-Mak-Gog choose their offering," Borba commanded, hands spread wide toward the chain of slaves before the assembled hall. The captives looked about in confusion, unsure of what was awaiting them as six of the gathered robbed figures stepped forward, clawed hands prodding and squeezing the offered forms, assessing their physicality and potential as though they were livestock at auction. One by one each seemed to make a selection to their liking, those who seemed to have been chosen were forced to their knees before the dais as one of the robed priests stood behind them in satisfaction. Those who were not chosen were quickly whisked away down a darkened hall off to the side, their fates as unknown as their fellow slaves.

The applicants spoke in turn, declaring for whom they stood as representatives; "The Stained Ones choose this He-Man, to stand before you in Goa-Mak-Gog!" As each of the tribes who would submit an offering spoke, cheers resounded from their fellow priests and priestesses. Until the final representative raised her voice.

"Sula, Sister of Marguk, of the Wolf Clan chooses this She-Dwarf to stand before you victorious in Goa-Mak-Gog!" Jeers and howls of derision met her words as she boldly called out her challenge. While not necessarily an insult, it was in bad taste to presume the will of Gog.

Borba lifted her hand in silent command, hastening silence to follow in turn. "The offerings have been chosen, you may prepare them as you see fit, tomorrow we shall observe the rites and rituals in the eyes of Gog! May your champions die well!"

Cheers and growls of excitement echoed throughout the temple, as the shocked captives were unceremoniously dragged out of the halls and out into the surrounding camps to their respective clans' camps and tents. The only compensation would be their captivity would be brief, unlike their fellow slaves.

Sula dragged her prize by the short chain attached to the leather collar locked around the female dwarf's throat. She stumbled and nearly fell several times from the comparatively rapid pace of the much larger captor. Her feet became bruised and torn on the rough stones which his in the grass awaiting helpless flesh. Briers and thorns dug deeply into her soles, making each step that followed all that more difficult to bear. There was no conversation, no explanation as to what her fate would be, even if she had wanted to know. The dwarf cursed her ill luck and silently prayed to the gods for some sign of their presence, their mercy. There was none to be found, not since she had been taken captive two months ago after the ship she had been on crashed on the shores south of this cursed place.

After what seemed like hours, they approached a ring of yurts decorated with the wolf sculls and black banners affiliated with the clan who would now decide her fate. Stopping before the largest, Sula handed her charge over to one of the guards who sat at the entrance, his massive club resting against his lap ready for use.

Entering the tent, Sula called out, "Brother, I have acquired our..." The words caught in the priestess's throat, and the sight of her brother lying sprawled amongst his bedding furs surrounded by shattered pottery and spilled wine sent her mind racing.

"Welcome, priestess of Gog." Susalla's soft voice chirped from beside the washbasin over on one side. The female orc slowly reached for the hooked dagger tucked into her belt at the small of her back, her gaze never leaving the human sorceress for a moment. "There is no need for that, sister", soothed the dark-haired woman as she glided back over to Marguk's bedside, she was still naked from the events that had unfolded, and deep red marks scored her body from across her back to around her delicate neck.

"You presume too much, witch!" spat Sula, venom trickling with every word. "No human would ever–"

"Ah, but you see, this human has!" she chuckled. "For you see, sister, under the laws of Gog and the Great Clans, as of a few hours ago I became your sister," her fingers nestled in the sleeping Marguk's long braids, caressing him as though he were just a newborn fast asleep, "and I enjoyed every moment of it. There can be no question as to why he is the one blessed by Gog. Or would you dare question his wisdom, Priestess of Gog Far-Seer? Daughter of the Great Temple?"

Sula's hands twitched hesitantly, how dare this pathetic human do such a thing?! How dare her brother keep this wretched creature as though she were a guest?! This woman should have been killed from the first, as soon as she had walked into their camp so long ago. And if not that, she should have been put in chains and kept at their pleasure until she had run out of use.

"I can see you are troubled, conflicted. But I assure you, I have nothing but love and adoration for Marguk, I don't wish for us to be enemies. I would much rather we worked together, for him, for your brother. He is my whole world, I wish you could see that."

Marguk's eyes slowly blinked open, a deep sigh of satisfaction shaking loose from his fanged lips. His gaze rested on the grim face of his sister, still poised to draw the blade she carried. "Sister! I didn't hear you come in, what brings you here?" If the great chieftain was embarrassed or ashamed of his predicament, he showed no sign.

"I have brought our offering for the ritual tomorrow, Brother. Bring them in." The same guard from the entrance appeared, dragging the bedraggled, kicking, dwarf along with him. Tossing her to the floor, the guard quickly bowed and hurried back to resume his post.

Susalla stared at the piteous young girl, she had heard about this practice. It was a sort of fortune telling in a way; two combatants, slaves captured specifically for the role, would stand in representation of the clan as a whole. The two would fight to the death in gladiatorial combat, and whichever fighter walked away breathing would decide which clan had been chosen by Gog. This practice regulated the number of conflicts between tribes or clans to some part, but since it was only held every three years or so it did little to eliminate raids or skirmishes entirely.

The ritualistic combat could be called for to resolve land disputes, marriage negotiations, transference of prisoners, anything the two parties involved could decide to wager on a single bout between two beings locked in a struggle for life and death. In the Wolf Clan's case; the stakes could not be higher. And all of Marguk's aspirations would come down to a single, gasping, female dwarf from some far-flung land.

"What is your name, dwarf?" demanded the chief, still unclothed and seated upon his bed in full display of his superior build. Even unarmed, the green-skinned barbarian was an imposing sight.

"Gamona, I come from..." A solid kick from Sula's sandaled foot met her ribs and the captive doubled over, gasping for air.

"It does not matter where you are from, slave! You are before the great chieftain of the Wolf Clan, your new master, for now."

Marguk, still staring at the dwarf, slowly rose and approached the gasping figure before him until his shadow enveloped her like some great obelisk. "You have been chosen to represent my clan in one of the holiest rituals of my kind. As such, I will explain to you what the future holds." Marguk pointed at a large wooden chest in the corner, filled with an array of weapons and armor of various designs and origins.

"Tomorrow you will face the other offerings in one-on-one combat. You may arm yourself as you wish, and should you win, I will guarantee your safety."

Gamona, kneeling and gasping at his feet, looked up into the fanged visage sullenly. "If I win, you will let me go?"

Marguk walked over to the open chest, selecting a short sword with a broad blade and cup-shaped hilt carved of some sort of redwood, twirling the weapon, testing the weight as he did. "That is not what I said. I said I would guarantee your safety." He walked forward, holding the blade loosely in his firm hand, it could barely serve as a dagger for one his size. The blade rose slowly, creasing the thin burlap garment from navel to neck, resting beneath her soft chin.

"You will serve, or you will die. Fight with honor for my clan, bring me victory before the eyes of the gods, the tribes, and the temple, and I will keep you safe for as long as you please me. But betray me," the point stabbed gently into the dwarf's flesh, letting flow a small trickle of blood, "and your screams will echo from the northern mountains to the southern seas."

As the camp fell into slumber, Susalla crept between the assortment of tents and yurts past the scattering of roving guards and crocottas towards the outskirts of the encampment. With the campfires descending into the distance behind her, she climbed the hills north of the assembly, towards the high-reaching mountains capped by the glint of dancing stars. Finally, she found what she sought, the small stone platform surrounded by a ring of boulders that crowned one of the many hills in the Plains of Korb. Kneeling atop the cool stone surface, she pulled a small stone dagger from beneath her cloak and raised the weapon towards the shining light of the silver moon.

"See now, your servant, Great Gog Far-Seer. I come before you in the light of your evening eye, your servant has done as you have commanded. They have tamed the heart of the one you have chosen to lead this horde against your enemies! They have given their body and soul to the Kin-Slayer! They have praised your portents and passed on your wishes to the masses!" She pressed the dagger against the palm of her hand, slowly drawing out her crimson blood which dripped down her arm and onto the altar.

Taking the dagger in her other hand, she sliced her opposite palm in the same manner. Dropping the knife on the stone surface, she lifted her hands skyward, reaching for the great eye that gazed down upon her. "Give me that which was promised! I am your servant, your thrall, your will be done!"

# FIVE

# BLOOD

Lorena shivered in the drizzling rain and pulled the oil-lined cloak tighter around her sodden form to try and salvage what little warmth it could offer. Watching the wagon in front of her from her seat upon the last carriage, the canvas rolled and fluttered as small rivulets filled with water and drained slowly off. A boot had slipped out from under the edge, each bump and divot in the winding road causing it to lazily rock back and forth like a macabre pendulum. The dark leather was stained deep crimson. As the rain took purchase on the exposed foot, a thin stream of blood dripped down from the base of the heel and trickled into the cracks of the wooden cart's floor.

Seated alongside, Armen paid no mind, his thoughts lost in contemplation of the young noblewoman currently seated in the carriage he now drove. The image of her luxurious hair, those deep almond-colored eyes, the delicate curve of her supple lips. More than once his concentration had faltered such that he barely avoided the scattering of large stones or exposed roots which made the journey bumpier than it already had been.

The peaks of the Western Spine reached high towards the foggy horizon up ahead, they had been fortunate to cross the bridge behind them before the river flooded out, but now they were in the open hills and outcroppings which made up the domain of Twin Rivers. Thin, near-barren trees dotted the landscape amongst the grey stone outcroppings and remnants of landslides of bygone eras. It had been said that in ages past, some great hero had slain a giant shortly after the world had been formed. In the giant's throes, his fingers had carved out the earth that had once been flat and barren, and his spine had become the mountains that now stretched from north to south where they now trod. A silly story one would tell children, nothing more. No being would have a spine made of stone.

In the first carriage, Bart scanned the surrounding landscape. They would need to stop and water the horses soon, they had barely stopped at the shore to fill up their skins and rest the horses back at the river. Everyone was tired, himself included, the paranoia of another ambush from those creatures had kept the group on edge throughout the night and even into late morning. Now instead of the comfort found in the light of the sun, the thick mist and spray of rain clouded much of their vision. It was almost as if the powers of nature themselves were seeking their destruction as well. Off to the north side of the path, Bart could make out a small outcropping from the base of the mountains, jutting out like some stone awning. Waving his hand, Bart led the trio off the path and towards the potential shelter. They were still within sight of the road, and there was enough room for them to tuck all the wagons and their occupants beneath the stone outcropping to escape the downpour. As they collectively gathered around the small fire, drying themselves as best the soaked group could manage, Bart handed over a few field rations to the three passengers who had gladly escaped the confines of the carriage.

The surviving guardsman, Edmon, had finally regained his senses. But he still kept as much distance as he could from the slithering form of Thrax. The open socket where his left eye had once been was still swathed in bandages. Della leaned in close to inspect the bindings.

"Let's have another look at that eye of yours." Her graceful fingers unbound the strips of linen, each pass relieving some of the pressure on the man's skull. The closer Della got to the wad of linen packing that had been packed over the wound, the more bloodstained the strips were as they slowly gathered in her hand, alternating red, then white, then red again. It reminded Bart of a trick he had seen a traveling bard perform once, they had shoved a single handkerchief down their gullet, then by some unknown method or trickery, produced them from his open mouth tied to even more handkerchiefs of alternating colors and patterns. He wouldn't be able to see that trick the same after this. Lorena joined her friend, holding a lit crystal over their heads to afford a better view of his face.

"The packing has clotted into the eye, if we don't remove it then the wound will fester, and you will fall ill again." The two women could smell the beginnings of an infection already; like a cheese that had started to go bad mixed with a sweet sickly tang reminiscent of old wine that had turned sour. As the packing slowly came away, Bart could see the sickly white and yellow pus begin to seep from the guard's open eye and trickle down his trembling cheeks.

"It's already started. He's going to lose that eye, more if we don't do something about it." Armen's tone was flat, near-emotionless as he spoke. It was a wound they had seen far too often in their line of work. And there were only two ways to remedy it.

"Well, we are flat out of Eldarsbark root. So that just leaves the alternative." Della reached into the fire, prodding the embers and flames with a thick heft of kindling, forcing the heat to bellow and spread. "You hold him down, I'll get the iron ready."

Thrax slowly slipped in around their patient, wrapping his coils tightly around the trembling form as he cupped either side of Edmond's head and stared down into his remaining eye. "It may be best if you just look at me for now, friend. Don't you worry, it only hurts if you think about it."

"The only thing I am thinking about is how I would rather you just kill me and be done with it!" screamed Edmon, sobbing uncontrollably as he struggled helplessly in the bound coils. His voice was shortly cut off by the introduction of a thick leather strap wrapped tightly between his teeth.

"So, you don't lose your tongue as well as the eye," explained Armen.

Edmond's remaining eye bulged in fear, pleading with his lord nearby for relief, for some small act of mercy as the blazing iron bar slowly rose from the flames, sending sparks dancing around the embers, and advanced like some fire-breathing salamander. The smell of burning flesh and the pop of the remaining fluid from his eye, mingled with the screams of pain and fear, echoing off the stone walls of their camp. Until, mercifully, he passed once more into unconsciousness.

Bart leaned in, listening to the wounded man's shallow breaths. Nodding with satisfaction he turned to the assembly, "We should make camp here for the time being and let the rain pass, none of us have had a rest, and we don't know what is in store."

"I can take the first watch, friend." Hissed Thrax, adjusting the leather straps that held his twin blades, "I spent most of the journey cooped up, no need for me to rest first." He slithered off towards a cluster of bushes at the mouth of the outcropping and settled in, disappearing with an unnatural ease for one so large. The rest pulled blankets from their packs and settled in, falling into an uneasy sleep.

—m—

Above the green folds of the Timberglenn, two griffins circled the section of road north of Kaelith's Pass. Their strong, massive wings tipped with copper and hazel feathers pumped forcefully, keeping them and their riders afloat as the two knights peered down at the remnants of a horrific slaughter. Even from their great height, they could see the pools of blood, which flooded through crimson rivers carved out by the rain. The leader of the pair motioned with a thick, leather-gloved hand down towards an opening in the trees just beyond the road and the two glided down, landing a few yards away from the site. Iron-soled boots clanked onto the gravel-strewn surface as they dismounted, weapons drawn, and approached the scene, their visored helms swiveling to either side.

"What the hell happened here do you suppose?" asked one, his sword prodding the crumpled blue-grey headless corpse before him. The taller one shrugged, still scanning the surrounding woods intently, his blond hair peeking out from beneath his helmet in a braid that had fallen from beneath his coif during their flight.

Walter lifted his visor and took in the scene before him as though there was some message that only he could discern in this chaos. He had been approached by his Captain and the Sergeant of Arms back in Maroth before the main force had departed with this assignment. Of course, he had jumped at the chance for adventure, for glory, to serve as the sword of the realm. Six pairs of knights were assigned to scout the roads in all directions, along with acting as an expeditionary force for the two cohorts which would focus their efforts on the towns, cities, and keeps which populated the kingdom. The net had been cast, now they just needed the right fish.

"This is something we cannot just ignore, that is certain. I know what you are going to say, but this must be reported to the Commander. Besides," he pointed at the twin trails of carriage wheels headed north towards the north, "no harm in tracking down whoever survived this and finding out for ourselves. We should be the closest to Twin Rivers as well. We can make our inquiries to Lord Firbank once we are done."

His companion nodded, walking over to his mount he reached for a small wooden cage that held a pair of pigeons and withdrew one of the birds as Walter scrawled a message on a thin piece of parchment. Concluding his report, he deposited the scroll in a small tube tied to the pigeon's back, releasing their messenger skyward. It fluttered in a rush of wings, then instinctively turned south towards its destination. A jet-black hawk screamed downward on the creature like a thunderclap, in a flurry of feathers and blood the helpless pigeon plummeted down, clutched in the cruel talons of the predator.

Before either could fully comprehend what had just happened, the whistle of crossbow bolts from the thick undergrowth sent the pair scrambling for cover behind one of the upturned carriages at the side of the road. Steel-tipped shafts thwacked into the painted wood and the corpse of a slain horse which was still attached to its charge even in death.

"Walt..." The other knight's voice was muted and weak.

He turned, staring at the blood-stained shaft protruding from his companion's throat, how he was still alive was a miracle. But one that would be short-lived if their attackers had any say. Walter stabbed his sword into the mud and reached for a crossbow he could see tucked beneath one of the upturned carriage wheels, but he could not see any quarrels.

"Walt, I'm dying. You have to get out of here. Just go, finish the mission." His trembling hand reached up for the twin-feathered shaft protruding from his throat like a deadly flower. Plucking it from its purchase in a spurt of deep red blood, he weakly tossed it toward Walter. If there was any chance of his survival, it was now mute.

Walter loaded his crossbow, he would only have one shot. Judging the distance from himself to his steed, which had crouched low, wings tucked in as it hissed and screeched at the surrounding forest unable to find the enemy, it was a greater distance than he would have liked. Ten, maybe twelve paces. But the enemy knew where he was, and the second volley would cut him down as soon as he stepped out.

A voice broke out from the bushes beyond the road, "Go ahead and come out, knight! We got your friend, why don't you just make this easier on yourself and end this quickly?"

Walt peered out through a gap in the timbers. "Who are you? Why are you attacking us?"

"Just a couple of folks hired to do a job, nothing personal! Gotta say you have us impressed you could move like that! Haven't missed what I was aiming at in a long, long time." The man jeered, hidden beyond a screen of brush and trees.

Walter glanced over at his griffin, her eyes now peered south, towards a bend in the road. He could just faintly make out the rustle of leaves, presumably where the voice had come from. But he didn't know for certain. The knight turned toward his fallen companion's steed, an idea forming in his head.

"Fly, Comet!" Walter's hushed command brought the well-trained beast to flight without hesitation as it spread its wings and leaped skyward. A hooded head popped up from the pushes, right in his line of sight. Walter squeezed the trigger, letting fly his bolt at the hidden assailant who dropped like a stone. The quivering shaft protruded from their chest with a thud.

"Kill the bastard!" cried another from off to Walter's left, as he turned, the hooded and masked figure charged out from behind a fallen oak tree and leaped atop the carriage over him. They pounced, twin daggers bared and ready, aiming for his throat. Walter twisted out of the way, shoving the assassin past him against the fallen horse. Mid-turn, he drew his sword from where he had stabbed it and brought the shining blade down in an arc upon the back of their neck, sending blood, mud, and their hooded skull flying through the air.

Two more masked figures, a man and a woman, stepped out from the brush slowly. The male carried a thin, needle-pointed rapier with an intricate basket hilt, while she wielded a short sword. Both approached, widening the distance between themselves to flank their lone target in a pincer. These two knew what they were doing, that much was certain. Walter knew if he didn't act there would be no way out.

Letting loose a sharp whistle, Walter charged the woman holding the short sword, bringing his blade in a slash from right knee to left shoulder followed by a downward cut at her collarbone. Blades flashed as both vied to out-position the other exchanging blows as they circled. At the same time, his griffin tackled the other assassin with a speed and agility unexpected for a creature its size, pinning them to the ground and snapping viciously at the man's face with their hooked beak.

Seeing she was outnumbered and outmatched by the knight and his companion, the woman slowly backed away, sword outstretched in a low guard, hoping to keep the two at bay.

"Now, now, why the rush? I have some questions for you. Let's start with why did you try to kill me? Who is paying you?" Walter advanced, sword tapping on his shoulder as he did.

The woman laughed, "You really don't know, do you? No matter, you and that other bastard are going to be food for the worms soon enough." Her hand slipped down grabbing at a small vial attached to a necklace, popping the wax and cork seal she downed the contents in one swig.

Walter rushed forward, grabbing at the vial which could only hold one thing, but it was too late. Her lifeless form slumped to the ground in his arms. 'What the name of the twin hells was going on?' he wondered, staring at the lifeless woman clutched in his mailed arms. A trickle of blood mixed with a pungent black liquid dribbled from the corners of her lips, lifeless eyes staring blankly through him. His griffin trotted over with a look of pride, still holding an arm severed from the now masticated corpse which lay strewn across the road like a paper doll torn to shreds. The eagle-like head bobbed as it swallowed the remainder of the unexpected meal with pleasure.

Walter stood, stroking the blood-stained plumage and patting the lion-bodied, winged predator he had raised from when it had been no more than a fledgling. "Thanks, Ginger. You enjoy yourself." His attention then turned to his fallen brother-in-arms. Comet had returned, prodding the lifeless form with the tip of her curved beak, small rolling chirps echoing from her broad chest, the only way the creatures could grieve. Griffins were bonded to their riders, very rarely could another rider assume responsibility for another knight's mount. Making his way over, he heaved the limp form up across the leather saddle and tied them down as best he could with a rope he procured from the saddlebags fastened on either flank of the creature's flanks.

"Take him home, girl." As he watched the dead form of his companion embark on their final journey, Walter considered his options. As he rummaged through the pockets of the four assassins, looking for some clue as to who they were or who had hired them, each of them had been armed with a small powerful crossbow and a quiver of bolts. Among the assortment of knives, darts, hidden daggers, and other materials of death Walter found a small folded parchment written in a series of lines and dots.

"Some sort of cipher" mumbled Walter, rubbing the bridge of his nose. Of course, it wasn't going to be that simple. Nobody in their line of work would just carry around an order that anyone could read. But all the same, he tucked the letter into his saddlebags wrapped in some oilskin to try and preserve the missive as best he could. Having searched the bodies and the surrounding path as much as he could, Walter mounted his waiting steed, and with a click of his tongue, they were once again skyward. Rising ever higher they turned north, following the trail left in the sodden ground in his continuing search. Whoever was at the end of this path had to have some answers.

The wind embraced his body with an enveloping rush as his griffin's powerful wings accelerated them just beneath the thin clouds. Walter never felt more alive than when he was flying; the solitude, the feeling of his mount's powerful muscles working in concert with his direction from the twin reins grasped in his hands. The weightlessness calmed his soul like no other remedy, the tremor in his hands eased as he let himself become enfolded in the thrill of flight. From high above the rolling forests and hills, amongst the mountain peaks and angelic clouds, he felt as though he could conquer the world. This had been far different from the tourney, on the training grounds and on the lists there was always the risk of injury, but death was a distant thought. A real fight felt so different than he had imagined, he could still smell the blood. Walter heaved over, violently heaving the remnants of his morning meal into the open air. He would have justice for his fallen comrade, and he would honor his memory, Walter's only regret was that he had never asked their name.

Commander Zulla looked up from the pile of reports towards the hurried knocking coming from the door. Two days had passed since the operation had begun, with little in the way of new information or progress to show for it. He hadn't even left his offices since that first day, sleeping on a field cot he acquired from the storerooms, and taking his meals as he worked through the night. The Second Cohort had dispersed scouts around the area of Hammerpeak to the northeast in the center of the main peninsula which made up the kingdom of Maroth and the southern deserts of Vex-Tol-Rak. The Third had dispatched themselves ranging from Deepwood to the south along the coast westward to Oldetown and Mare's Rest, searching the towns and outlying villages systematically. Time and time again they hit dead end after dead end.

"Enter!" The command carried more of a demand than an invitation to the visitor. The black mustachioed and scarred face of Maxwell, his Sergeant of Arms, appeared in the open door. He was clad in the usual manner of the auxiliaries which supported the order directly, with his white tabard emblazoned with the sword and griffin stitched in red and black thread. In addition to the leather armor beneath, the Sergeant wore a round medallion steel chain indicating his position amongst his peers and superiors within and without the Cloud Knights.

"Commander, a griffin has returned from our scouts north of Goldgrow. It's Sir Rolfe and his mount Comet." The grizzled soldier paused before speaking further, his voice saddened at the news he must now convey, "I am afraid I must report that Young Sir Rolfe, has been slain." The words came slowly from the grizzled sergeant's lips.

Zulla dropped the collection of papers had been reading, leaning back into the high-backed wooden chair carved to resemble the twin raised wings of an eagle. His position and office brought with it great honor and responsibility. But no matter how many times he received the news of one under his command falling, whether on the field of battle, illness, or tragedy, it never got any easier. While he may only have one daughter by blood, these men and women were like his children. The Order was bound to one another through pain and comradery. For some this had been the closest thing to a family they had ever known, for others, this place was more valuable than their lofty houses and rich lineages. To wear the sword and griffin held no greater place of honor for those who surpassed the trials, and to lose a comrade was to lose a brother or a sister all the same.

The knight's commander folded his hands before him, resting his head heavily against them, "How?! Do we have any idea how this happened?"

The Sergeant twisted his mustache thoughtfully, "It would appear as though he and his partner, Sir Walter were ambushed. Young Rolfe took a crossbow to the throat, a fatal blow, but we can surmise that young Goldhair is still alive since Rolfe's body was bound to the saddle, and there was this," he produced a small scroll, "it details the attack, along with what Sir Walter plans to do on his search. There is no indication of his need for reinforcement. Along with the letter was a small vial, presumably from one of their attackers. From the smell of it; there had been poison inside of it."

The Commander took both items, reading over the hasty message and examining the vial curiously. "I assume you also recognize this vial, Sergeant?"

His companion nodded, "The Shadow Guild, Sir. There can be no doubt."

Commander Zulla's eyes darkened, his premonition had just been proven in one fell swoop. There was a traitor amongst them, The Shadow Guild consisted of the finest spies and mercenaries within Maroth. Their reputation for secrecy and discretion was rivaled by none in the entirety of the continent and beyond. That group of assassins was as notorious as they were renowned. Few could say they had escaped the blades wielded in their service, but the hallmark of the guild was that should one of their members be captured they always ensured they took their secrets with them. The fact they had been hired meant two things; whoever hired them deemed their need necessary instead of some hired blade or poisoner from the seedy bars and taverns in the criminal underworld. And secondly, they had the money to pay for them. Commander Zulla had paid for their services and expertise in gathering information on more than one occasion, their skills were beyond question regardless of their lack of political loyalty. It was rumored they would even take jobs from opposing clients without question and had burned the candle at both ends as it were.

"I shall inform his father personally, thank you, Sergeant." Zulla watched as the man bowed, then turned to exit his office, closing the door behind him as he departed.

The Duke of Heathridge would not take the loss of his eldest son quietly. What's worse, the man had already returned to his far-flung domain on the borders of the rival territories of Almach where his keep watched over the region spanning from the Horizon Sea to the Tsere River in the north denoting the furthest reaches of the kingdom.

Solon's breath came in labored gasps as he leaned against the cool stone walls of the winding staircase leading from his domicile in the massive tower. What was it with castle architects and their obsession with gigantic towers? What sort of sadist would design a structure and method of travel to and from a given location that would torture mortals so? Was it some sort of sick obsession with inflicting physical and psychological torture? Or were they not familiar with having to traverse their own creations? How he wished for younger days long passed; to not feel every creak and pop of his joints from the exertion.

Continuing his arduous journey, the grey-bearded scholar finally reached the door which led out to the antechamber located on the upper floor of the main keep and slumped onto a small wooden bench.

Massaging his joints and legs that cried out in protest, his attention turned to the young man quickly approaching his seat. The lad could have only been into his thirteenth, maybe twelfth, year. Thin framed, yet from his face and shoulders he could tell the boy was much stronger than his appearance would suggest, the boy was clad in the black robe denoting their affiliation with The Order as a novice. They were serving as a squire to one of the Holy Knights, his smile of excitement and recognition betrayed the usual somber, humorless demeanor of these religious fanatics.

"Master Solon, it is wonderful to see you again! What brings you from your tower? I know you despise leaving without cause." The novice's eyes glistened with curiosity.

Solon had met the young lad on several occasions, usually when the boy would climb the damned stairs to bring him meals or supplies for his experiments. But over time, the young novice had begun extending those brief visits to learn about the world of magic and Solon's own theories on the subject. He was hungry for knowledge and reminded the old mage of himself in his youth. He had developed a liking for the boy as a sort of unofficial pupil. Of course, The Order would never approve of a member of their brotherhood, let alone a novice who had yet to earn the white robes of a Sworn Sword. So, the lessons had been kept secret, under the pretense that their conversations were more akin to Solon passing on news from the outside, which was not necessarily a lie.

"Ah, young Matthias, have you happened to see the Grand Master today? I must speak with him." Solon leaned his back against the smooth oak backrest and stretched his legs to ease the pain.

"He is still at his chambers for his morning meditations." Matthias frowned, watching the wizard struggle to rise from where he sat, "If you would use the walking staff I brought you it would ease your burden, sir."

"I am not so old as I need a stick to move about just yet, young buck!" But Solon did secretly regret his own pride, a part of him had considered using the staff on more than one occasion. But then he would appear as the stereotypical old man with a grey beard and staff. What was next; a giant floppy hat and long-stemmed pipe? Then his appearance really would scream 'Look- It's an old mystical and wise wizard! Let's go bother him with some sort of useless drivel and occupy his precious time!' No, thank you. He waived his hand toward the eager novice and leaned on his strong shoulders, supporting his aged frame as they walked.

"If you are coming to see the Grand Master yourself instead of sending a message, then things must be really important. Isn't that right, Master?" Matthias inquired, slowing his pace to better accommodate his companion.

"I have told you on more than one occasion to stop calling me that, I am no Master. Simply a guest of your lovely castle. But yes, Novice Matthias. And we must inform him with all haste." Solon's feet shuffled in concert with the younger novice's strong pace. Taking care not to tangle his sandaled feet in the long black hem.

Making their way past the libraries, armories, and dormitories, the pair approached a large wooden door banded with iron. Two armed Senior Novices, clad in black robes with the addition of a steel cuirass and bucket helms, each wielded a pike and carried a short sword at their side. Even though they recognized the approaching pair, both swiftly stepped forward and crossed the shafts of their polearms, barring the way in challenge. Both spoke in rehearsed unison, a script that had been drilled into them in the true fashion of an organization built on ceremony.

"Who approaches the sacred center?" Both voices were grim and unfaltering, as though rehearsing one of the myriad of prayers they would chant. Solon considered firing off some sarcastic retort, but before he could, young Matthias spoke for the both of them.

"Sentinels of the Sacred Center, Novice Matthias, Third Rank, and Solon the Wizard of the Great Tower, seek audience with his holiness, Grand Master Bernard, Sword of Light, and Keeper of the Oath."

The ceremony completed, both passed through the door which now opened before them and entered the Grand Master's chambers. Solon reviled having to endure these tiresome ceremonies and protocols, but given that the world may soon be at an end, he would have to endure.

*Chapter*

# SIX

# WRONGED

From the center of the hill-strewn plains and fields in the northern reaches of Maroth, Heathridge Castle sprung up from the near-empty surroundings. The castle town bustled with activity and trade. Merchants cried out their wares; Fish and oysters from Krot, Jewels and Gold necklaces from the craftsmen of Emerils, Leather and Furs from the elves of Sylthius. Soldiers patrolled two and fro amongst the throng, their heavy boots clambering against the stone paths that wove between the clustered buildings that were laid out in grids surrounding the castle itself. The somber grey stone walls cast the surroundings in shadow and provided a sense of authority and protection for miles around. High above the ramparts and lining the main gate, the green and white striped banners centered with a double-headed axe fluttered in the breeze. These were the northernmost lands of Maroth, what had once been a barren and empty landscape dotted with sparse villages and open, unprotected borders with Almach had grown to be a powerful center of trade in the few years their lord had come to power. He had made sweeping reforms after being granted the titles and lands from Bayhome to the west, along the shores of the Horizon Sea to the forests of Sylthius and the rivers to the north. There had been murmurs and rumblings when he had raised taxation and implemented his new plans for the rebuilding of the northern lands, but he had crushed any thought of insurrection with efficiency and ruthlessness. Most felt it to be for the better.

Duke Rolfe stared blankly at the letter lying on the table, his wife and mother of their now slain heir had already been escorted to her chambers by the servants. He could still hear her wails echoing through the otherwise silent halls of Heathridge Castle. The details of how their son had died, the as-of-yet-unknown identity of the killers, and the evidence provided by his son's corpse. What had this all been for? How did his son fall prey to these assassins? This wasn't supposed to happen! He mulled over the losses in his vault-like memory. There had been bribes to the instructors at the finest schools of swordsmanship to guarantee high marks on the exams. There had been payouts to other hopefuls who would rather take a bag full of coins rather than risk humiliation in pursuit of glory. The cost of feeding and clothing his spawn through adolescence, not to mention having to pay for the armor and arms of his son along with a few well-placed officers within the knighthood. A waste of an investment. His eyes lifted from the paper before him and landed on the pathetic excuse of a man who sat sweating profusely before him.

"You said your people were professionals, Griswold." Rolf the Elder's tone raked through the stillness like a blade sharpening on a blacksmith's stone. Fists clenched atop the polished surface of the long table as he glared across the table at the trembling, thin-haired man whose face had turned ashen. "But it would seem that all of the money I have provided for these services has resulted in nothing more than excuses, dead-end leads, and now..." Duke Rolf's hand slammed against the letter, sending cutlery and glassware rattling, "The death of my heir! My heir! Not the heir, mine! What do you have to say about this failure?"

"My lord Duke," Griswold stammered, "these things do happen, it was simply misfortune that placed young Rolfe with the target."

The duke's eyes flashed, leaping from his seat, "Don't you dare speak that name!" The uneasy silence that followed reeked of malice and fear. Regaining his composure, the fuming Duke of Heathridge slowly eased himself back into the wooden chair backed with cushioned red leather studded with silver nails. His fingers tapped unconsciously on the polished armrests as he continued.

"Misfortune, eh? When a blight kills the wheat and barley before the harvest, that is misfortune. When my horse breaks its leg and I have to put the beast down, that is misfortune. When the rivers flood, when ships sink, when the gods shit on my ambitions, that is a misfortune! Twenty years ago, when the former queen learned of our plots with Almach and the Hill Tribes, forcing me into engage your services in ending her meddling, that was misfortune!" With a snap of his fingers, two cloaked figures emerged from some unknown recess behind Griswold, before he could say or do anything the blade flashed swiftly across his throat, releasing a crimson flood across the fine walnut surface. Duke Rolfe lifted his glass, swirling the contents as he examined the red hues and sniffed the floral tones, "And now yours have come to an end."

Duke Rolfe beckoned the two shadowy figures forward who, upon approach, knelt before him with their heads bowed. "I do hope you have some clue as to where that blond bastard has run off to."

One of the assassins nodded affirmatively, "Of course, he is flying northbound along the road to Twin Rivers. What is more, Lord Duke, they will soon join the other potential target in due time. If we wait until both are joined, we can dispatch them in one fell swoop."

Nodding along at the prospect, the Lord of Heathridge eyed the two assassins before him. They differed in both age and gender, separated by enough years to make him wonder if perhaps the young woman could even be the older one's daughter. "Use whatever means you see fit, so long as both feed the worms before the week is out, I do not care. And when you have succeeded, know that your guild will have no want of coin once my plans come to fruition."

The stamping of feet and the raised voices of the gathered throng around the dirt pit lined with ropes tied to stakes echoed through the chests of the gathered warriors. Clubs, spears, and axes pounded in rhythm as the pair of slaves circled each other, weapons ready, bleeding from a myriad of wounds they had suffered from each other's hand. Both fighters were human males, one with the lighter tones common from the central plains, the other displayed the darkened tones and black hair found in the sea-faring peoples from west of the Scorched Isles. They were clad in assortments of leather armor and bindings which left the majority of their chests exposed, with simple grieves and sandals stained with the dark blood of themselves and their opponent. One wielded a pair of daggers, carved from obsidian with bone handles, the other hefted a large club studded with iron nails.

The club-wielding, light-skinned male charged, his weapon arching through the air in a heavy downward strike aimed at their foe's skull. His opponent tucked and rolled out of the way, leaping to his feet, daggers raised to counterattack. Only to be met by the swift sidekick from the aggressor, driving the air from his body as he stumbled back, trying to regain his position. The fighter with the club leaped forward, his weapon following from behind in both hands as he swung mightily like a lumberjack cleaving an ash tree. Again, the man with twin daggers rolled. This time, towards his opponent, driving his shoulders into their hips as he tackled the man to the ground in a cloud of dust and flailing limbs. Twisting behind the now unarmed man's back, he pinned their arm behind his back and brought one of the daggers down again and again into his victim's chest. The hiss of escaping air from their lungs followed by the growing pool of blood in the dirt beneath them signaled his hard-fought victory. A mixture of boos and cheers welcomed the victor's ears as he sprawled on his back, gasping for air, both daggers still clutched tightly in his trembling hands. Tears filled his eyes, whether from the exaltation of victory or regret from what he had done, none could say.

"The Northern Crows' offering is dead! Therefore, the Red Fang's Tribe shall hold claim to the hunting grounds of Shum-Ta Forest. Let it be decided!" The priestess' voice rose over the din, bringing further cheers and some grumblings from those gathered. At the edge of the fighting pit, Marguk and Sula stood at either side of their own offering. She had outfitted herself in a set of tanned hides which offered some protection given her smaller frame, for a weapon she had taken a small buckler shield and the sword which had once been held at her throat.

She now wore the blade at her side, ready for use at her new master's command.

As two goblins dragged the lifeless corpse out of the way, one of the priests from the Temple of Gog who had been acting as officiant for the day's ritual stepped out into the center of the altar of death.

"Who now lays claim before the eyes of Gog Far-Seer? Let them step forward and present their offering!" Their arms spread wide, gesturing towards the gathered onlookers in anticipation. From the far side of where Gamona and her master stood, a giant hulking dark green orc wearing a tattered kilt of blue and yellow marched forward, dragging the chained form of another human male.

"I, Kor-Nash, Leader of the Long Fangs lay claim to the right of War Chief of the Tribes. I declare it is my right as the strongest, and boldest of orcs to lead this horde in war and rage against the pathetic soft-flesh of our enemies. To raid and conquer their lands, and to bring glory to the Far-Seer!" a myriad of cheers of support broke out from the surrounding throng. Kor-Nash was known amongst many of the tribes as a brave and powerful warrior, undefeated in battle and in glorious conquest. The past two years had seen him envelop many of the smaller western tribes and clans, he now boasted the largest clan in all of the hill tribes of the Hinterlands.

Marguk stepped forward alone, pointing at the challenger who stood taller than even he. "I challenge your claim, Kor-Nash Long Fang! You hold no such right! I will lead this horde in war across the eastern lands to the sea. I will burn and pillage their lands! I will tear down their temples, trample their villages, scorch their farms, and destroy all traces of their pathetic kingdom! I will make slaves of their high-born and their priests! I will drink wine from the skull of their wretched king! And take their lands as our own to rule!" As he raised his hand, beckoning towards where Sula and Gamona stood behind him, the dwarf girl from across the sea stepped forward as though compelled by some greater force.

Seeing this slave, this offering, step forward willing and of her own accord, the surrounding crowds murmured in shock at the sight. More commonly the slaves chosen would have to be dragged out as the others had before, crying and shaking as they endured the jeers of derision from the horde, but this girl, this woman came forward willingly, resolve in her eyes to fight and possibly die for her captor.

As Marguk turned to walk past the shorter warrior, he placed his massive hand upon her armored shoulder and gave her a firm pat. "Fight well." He handed Gamona a small dirk, the dagger had a blade only as long as her hand, with a leather woven grip. She took the dagger and nodded, tucking it into the belt around her leather pleated skirt as she moved towards the center of the pit to face her enemy.

Both fighters stood alone at the center of the pit, Gamona looked at her opponent, they were unarmed and trembling. Was it fear? Was this just an execution? She felt pity for the human, watching as he collapsed to the dirt, clawing at the earth with his hands. She watched in horror as ripples of dark black fur exploded across his exposed limbs and back. His frame twisted and contorted, she could hear his joints and bones snap as he morphed before the eyes of the crowd into something much more than human. His jaw jutted outward, exposing rows of razor-sharp canines, a tail, and two large muscular legs lunged out from behind him covered in the same jet-black fur that covered his ever-growing animalistic form. With a resounding howl, he lifted his head, arms spread with vicious claws to reveal the form of a fully-fledged werewolf.

The Dwarf crouched behind her shield, she had already been at a disadvantage against a human. But now this feral creature was easily six times her size and outmatched her in almost every possible way. Defense was going to be the only option, but that would not win this fight. Her mind racing as she desperately tried to formulate some strategy against this new opponent, he lunged, one of his paws raised to slash at her shield. She remembered the fight before, how the other fighter had rolled to evade.

Gamona tucked in and dove forward, rolling beneath the attack and slashed upward with the point of her sword at the inside of one of the canine legs on either side as she did. She felt steel meet flesh and bounce off the bone. The were-beast howled in pain and anger at the wound, but it wasn't fatal, merely a nuisance. She jumped to her feet, keeping her shield raised as she readied herself for another attack. This opponent may look like some beast out of nightmares, but it was intelligent, the same trick most likely would not work more than once or twice.

Slowly, the werewolf turned upon her, circling to her right as Gamona matched his rotation. Shield raised and her sword tucked low supporting her only source of worthwhile protection for their next attack. The beast's maw dripped and snarled, exposing line after line of sharp yellowed teeth and mottled gums. Whatever resemblance of the human that had entered the ring before was now gone, suddenly the beast lunged outside of Gamona's stride flanking her sword arm, swinging inward and catching the lip of her shield sending her left arm outward with a violent slash. She could feel her shoulder strain, then pop as the bone dislodged from place. Her stomach reeled from the pain, almost sending her into shock. Instinctively she leaped back, swinging her sword out in a slash to drive back her assailant and put some distance between them. Catching her footing she tried to once more raise her shield, but it was no use. Her left arm now hung limp by her side, numb from the pain and weighed down by the steel shield strapped around her forearm and wrist.

Before Gamona could make any move, the beast was once more upon her, driving her to the ground and pinning her on her back beneath his massive black frame with his clawed hands. The gaping jaws of the werewolf pulled back in a hideous grin, his breath reeked of rotten meat and burned against Gamona's cheek. Desperately the young dwarf struggled to escape, but the beast was too heavy. Somehow, she managed to get her right arm to move, and slide it towards her belt, fumbling with blood and dirt-encrusted fingers she desperately tried to grab the thin dirk that she had stashed away. The small bit of steel would be useless for a killing blow, but she could make this bastard earn his next meal. Pulling the knife free, she brought the point up to where she hoped his ribs would be, driving the blade again and again, stabbing as hard and as fast as she could into the large beast.

The jaws came down, snapping at her face. Gamona twisted her neck to the side trying to avoid having her skull crushed, she felt teeth sink into her shoulder and neck, the hot blood spurting from her wound as his teeth sunk greedily into her flesh. With a cry of rage and fear, she twisted her face inward towards the werewolf's muzzle and bit him back with all her might. Her mouth filled with rough fur and blood, almost choking her from the taste as she clamped down desperately, she could feel her right arm suddenly become free. Without any thought or hesitation, she brought the blade up under the jaw of the creature and stabbed with the last bit of strength that remained into the beast's throat. The creature finally released her, clutching at the blade lodged in its windpipe with flailing claws.

The she-dwarf saw her sword only a few inches away, she lunged for the blade and crouched, her arm still hanging limply by her side. The pain in her shoulder throbbed with a dizzying heat, she could feel the blood pumping out and flowing down her breast with every fatal pulse. If she were to die, she would die well. Gamona steadied her blade, watching as the werewolf reeled and snapped before her, oblivious to his newly re-armed prey. Gamona sprinted towards the creature and dove between his legs once more, hacking at the insides of his tendons as she passed. The beast gurgled in a raspy howl, the blade still lodged in his throat as they collapsed, losing their balance and falling to the blood and dust. Gamona scrambled atop his back, sword raised, and with one final push she drove the sword through the black-furred skull.

As Gamona slowly regained her senses, she could hear cheers of approval rising from around her, not at the prospect of seeing blood spilled by a pair of slaves. They cheered for her, cries of "She-Dwarf! She-Dwarf!" resounded around her, filling her soul with a fire she had never felt once in her young life. Lifting her bloodied sword and raising it above her head, she let loose a resounding cry which the horde took up with her in a resounding crescendo. This was the taste of victory? Who could have ever described such a thrill? Her pain was a distant memory, she had never felt so alive! All eyes were on her, a young dwarf from across the seas, lost in the wilds and enslaved and now she stood as champion of the Wolf Clan! Never in her young life had she felt more at home than now. Her body may be owned and chained, but now her soul flew high and free, unbound by the restraints of this mortal world.

The priest stepped forward, his robes brushing against the blood-stained arena floor, "The Wolf Clan stands victorious! Marguk shall hold claim to the title of War Chief, let it be decided!"

The horde cheered with a resounding cry, bashing spears and axes on their shields and the dust-strewn ground. As the chant of 'Marguk! Marguk!' echoed through the camp, one could hardly catch a glimpse of the few solitary dissidents slowly making their way out of the crowd. Marguk did see them, however. He had expected there to be some division if his claim was upheld. This would have to be dealt with before his ambitions could be fulfilled.

—⟋w⟍—

Sylvanus Chrystalan sipped delicately at the glass of fine Falmat red, the fruity and earthy tones wafting over his senses and enveloping his mind with the memories of seasons long past. The hint of mushroom and moss, the scent of spring cherries caressed by a shower of rose petals and morning dew. The flavors coated his mouth, caressing his tongue before finishing in a rich, fruity after-tone.

Zulla smiled as he watched his companion enjoy what had been his third glass, "You have always had a finer pallet for wine than I ever had, dear friend. I purchased this on your recommendation in celebration of my installment as the Military Counsel some time ago, even I must say it has aged quite well in the cellars."

The elf, nodded appreciatively at the compliment, "A pity they do not sell this by the barrel, gods know I would willingly spend a small ransom for such a find. But you did not invite me here just to sample your wine, have you?"

Commander Zulla shrugged, he had forgone his usual military appearance in lieu of a fine wool tunic with frilled cuffs and silver buttons paired with black breeches and high-topped boots reminiscent of his calvary days. His villa on the outskirts of Maroth along the southern road provided an excellent view from where the pair sat on the open balcony. The far-reaching city proper sprawled out over the northern horizon, while the rolling hills met their view from the west. Zulla contemplated the open landscape, swirling the remnants of his glass as he spoke.

"The heir is out there, all this time and I never even knew they existed. I have lived these last few months in abject terror of the thought that some idiot would don the crown and drive this country into ruin. But now, it is almost reprehensible of me to even ask this, how do we know the true heir is even fit to wear the crown? What sort of life has the boy led? What lessons of leadership have they learned? It almost makes me question whether the true heir would be the right heir. But I keep telling myself that under the sight of the gods, this boy no matter his upbringing, is the lawful heir and must be crowned." Zulla's eyes reached out, searching, almost as if with enough focus his gaze would find the heir even from this distance.

The elven mage, finishing his glass, leaned back with his hands folded. "We are all forged by our surroundings. You, Commander, were forged on the training fields, the list, and the field of battle on foot and mount. You rose through the ranks, not because it was handed to you, but because you were recognized by your peers for your wisdom and courage in the face of adversity. You have seen death as a soldier, life as a father, and now as the military counsel I must urge you to see one last thing; hope. Indeed, we may not know what sort of upbringing the boy has had, or what trials and obstacles have been placed before him. But I would surmise he has been raised amongst the people, he has survived, he has thrived, and now he must come into his own. An heir who has never been tarnished by the spoils of power, fed on the glories of his predecessors, coddled in the warm silks of privilege. Wherever the heir is at this moment, that is who they are."

A polite cough from the doorway turned their attention away from the sprawling view, Zulla beheld his wife. She was dressed in a flowing gown the color of lavender blossoms in full bloom, accentuating her fair complexion and flowing dark hair which at the moment had been done up in the latest fashion of the ladies of the court under a crespine of silver and small pearls. She moved with all the grace and elegance of a woman far beyond Zulla's humble origins, if he could return to the days of his youth and tell that small boy from the outskirts of Mare's Rest that one day his bride would be paramount to a princess he would no doubt have been laughed out of the room. Every moment he looked upon her elegant neck, those rosy cheeks and emerald eyes he found his heart racing faster than if he were in the midst of battle. She had wounded his heart with Cupid's arrow, and by the gods, he prayed he never recovered from this injury.

"I must apologize, Sylvanus, for my husband's fumbling attempts at discretion. Subtlety has been one talent he has yet to attain. He is far too honest of a man to knowingly deceive someone he cares for or respects. But the truth is it was I who wished to speak with you, with both of you." Ella spoke as she made her way to one of the vacant chairs lining the veranda. Making herself comfortable she continued, "Dear husband, while it is true that the three of us; Sylvanus, Snorri, and I were involved in hiding the heir all those years ago, there is more to this story than even they knew."

Sylvanus cocked his head, "I am aware that only you know the location where the infant was taken or who it had been put in the care of if that is what you are suggesting. But how are we to know that the child remained where you placed them?"

Zulla waved off the interjection, "Even so, knowing where to begin the search would drastically improve our chances of finding the heir today; every trail has a beginning, one must simply follow where it leads."

Ennel nodded, "That would be true if that were all I had to disclose to the pair of you, a shame Snorri could not join us, we must use discretion to bring him into the fold." She pulled a small bundle of letters from beneath the folds of her gown, some yellowed with age and all bound with simple twine. "Twenty years ago, on the night my dear friend was murdered, it is true that it was I who escaped with the child. Any who asked me who the child was were simply led to believe it was one of the maid's children whom I was looking after for the moment. Once I escaped the castle and made my way to the livery stable in town, I hired a cart to take us to an acquaintance of mine from my childhood. She had married into a fairly well-off family and had yet to conceive a child at the time, so I knew she and her husband required an heir. Her husband, I knew, was a noble and loyal subject to the crown, but even still it was a gamble. Once I arrived that stormy night, the child swaddled in blankets from the livery, I explained the circumstances of the child and the dire need for their secrecy. Due to the urgency, I had only them to whom I could turn. Thankfully my friend took to the child instantly, and her husband was overjoyed to have a son by any means. When I offered to pay them to take the child, they refused, claiming that the gift of a child was all they had prayed to Friga the Mother for.

And that to serve the crown, even in secret, was more of an honor than they deserved."

Zulla shook his head, "So even the adoptive parents have known of the child these past twenty years as well. The more I learn the more I feel I must have been the only man not brought in on this conspiracy. I never expected that my wife would be so skilled in the art of deception, but I must say; your cunning and wit are just one more thing about you to admire. If you had not married me, you would have made a wonderful spy."

Sylvanus could not share the sentiment, his eyes widened with concern, "This is the first I have heard that the family has known who he was this whole time. What if your judgment had been flawed? What if they had decided to betray you, or worse, kill the child themselves?"

"There was no doubt in my mind as to their honor, that would have never happened." The noblewoman sighed, her breath shaking as she reached for her husband's rough hands. Those hands that had clasped hers for the first time on the day of their wedding as they danced, that had held her close that night in the tender embrace of passion so long ago. His gentle eyes which she had never seen in anger even once, the voice that had soothed their child, Eryth, to sleep. "Dear husband," Ennel's voice caught in her throat as she spoke, "I have wanted to tell you so many times, from the day I met you I have known you to be a just and honorable man. But the danger I would have placed you and our family in had I told you would have been too much to bear. I only hope that once all of this is over you can find it in your heart to forgive me."

The military commander's head reeled, stepping back from his wife, still clasping her hands as he stared down into the face of the woman with whom he had shared his life these past nineteen years, "It is as though I hardly knew you, both of you." His gaze turned accusingly at Sylvanus. "Am I so untrustworthy, so inept in your eyes that the two of you, no, Hammerstone too, felt that I had to be kept in the dark? I am not some lackey to be so easily turned against the good of the realm or of my king!" His eyes turned lovingly back to the teary face of his wife, "I am not angry that you kept me in the dark, that you conspired to hide the truth from the realm, I am saddened that even after all these years you didn't think I was trustworthy."

Sylvanus reached out, "It was not that you cannot be trusted, it was simply too dangerous to broach the subject until now. What would you have done if we had told you all those years ago that the heir still lived, hmm? You would have marshaled your forces and set out to find the child yourself and bring them home to the fold. You cannot deny it, you are an honest and noble man, driven by a black-and-white sense of justice. But these dealings are set in a world of grey, one that you are ill-suited for."

Ennel pulled her hand away, raising the bundle of letters from her lap. "But I knew that the day would come when you would need to know, that is why I kept correspondence with my friend who took the child all these years. Look…" she opened the letters, arraying them before the group, "it is all here, when he was ill with the fever, his sixth birthday when his father gave him a hand-carved sword, and when he learned to ride, his first fistfight with older boys, his first love, all of his experiences and history is here."

Zulla took a few of the letters, sifting through them until he found the most recent correspondence. His eyes sorted through the details, formulating a picture of just who and where this man would be today. The last letter was from two years ago, his face darkened as he read the words scrawled upon the page. His eyes turned to Sylvanus, disappointment dripping from his lips, "Raised by your environment, eh? I will be damned if a bloody mercenary is going to wear the crown!"

*Chapter*

# SEVEN

# SCARS

It was Della's turn to take watch from the bushes, as she sat in the concealment a rustle of footsteps and crunching gravel compelled her to draw one of the daggers strapped from her thigh as she lifted the blade, ready for whatever was trying to sneak up on her. The whispered voice halted her hand.

"Della? Della, are you in there?" Young Firbank whispered, crouched behind the bushes. "I think there is something wrong with your friend, the swordsman."

The elf peaked out cautiously, glancing at Lawrence and then past his frame towards the huddled and shaking form of Bart. The swordsman had opted to sleep in full armor, using his pack as a pillow huddled in his wool cloak. She could hear the moans her ears had grown all too accustomed to drifting from his lips.

"Is it a fever?" asked the young lord, looking on anxiously. "We must have been too long in the cold and rain."

Della shook her head, "Sadly no, it is not that sort of fever." As she looked on, Lorena sat up from near the mumbling form of Bart, the mage looked over at Della. She waved her hand slowly over Bart's face, her lips moving in a silent incantation as a faint blue light pulsed from her palm and shone over the swordsman's cringed features. Shaking her head, the mage made her way over and crouched near the two. Della understood without a word between them. Lorena smiled in defeat as she watched the elven huntress stalk over to the fitful form, she sat near her companion's huddled body and began to stroke his hair, soothing Bart's torment with a gentle practiced touch.

"What is wrong with him?" Lawrence's voice was hushed as he asked the mage.

Lorena glared at the incredulous lord beside her. "Absolutely nothing! Bart is the best swordsman on this side of the Giant's Spine, you don't get a reputation like that without seeing a few things that give you nightmares. But he is still strong, he is no weaker than you or I, my lord." The last bit dripped with just a hint of malice as she spoke. She bit her lip, embarrassed at the tone she had let slip, "I apologize, lord, I mean no disrespect. It's just," the mage paused, looking shamefully over at her lover's huddled form, "even with all this power, my ability to use the arcane at my discretion, there are some things even magic cannot solve." She gazed down at her hands, her eyes saddened and tear-filled. It was the only spell she had come to learn which could bring any sort of comfort to her love when they were caught in their internal torment. But she was uncertain if it was Bart who was brought relief through her aid, or herself by not having to witness the extremes his dreams could drive him to.

Della gazed down at the face nestled against her lap, thinking back to those far-gone summer days when she and a much younger Bart would meet in the fields north of Troutsmouth. That young boy had laughed and boasted about how he would, one day, become a great knight. He would have grand adventures, slay dragons and other foul beasts, and then come to her as a great warrior. Those memories of teaching him to shoot a bow and using sticks in mock duels brought warmth to her heart. She remembered the morning he had come running to meet her in the fields of spring flowers wearing the heraldry of Sir Callen, beaming as he showed her the tabard with pride. Days later she had looked on from the far-off hills as the army marched off to war, all those men and boys marching and riding into the horizon in pursuit of glory. She had kept watch for months, seeking the western horizon for any sign of return, the painful course of time passed before any word had reached the eastern reaches of the kingdom, victory! But it had come at such a heavy toll, the grief which had filled her bosom from the thought of that young boy lying dead in some muddy field far from home. As an elf she was used to seeing those of the shorter-lived races age and pass before her eyes, to see them cut short before they could blossom to their full potential. Humans were such delicate things, but the thought of Bart, this one human this boy dying before she could see him grow into the man she knew he could be had torn her soul.

She remembered the cart which had brought him and the other wounded back to Troutsmouth, her joy at him being alive at all had brought with it a rush of euphoria and relief. But his eyes were never the same after that, gone was the youthful joy and hope he had overflown with. He hardly spoke, rarely ate, and would often be found gazing over the waters north of town or into the rushing rapids lost in some unknown memory. That was when she had decided she would never leave his side, she would never lose the boy she had practically become a second mother to.

As the rain began to clear, Bart and the others loaded up their camp and once more made their way north along the puddle-strewn road. The iron-rimmed wheels made short work of the obstacles and mud, but the wagon at the center of their line creaked and groaned from the strain of the heavy load it carried. The only fortune they could bless themselves with was that the smell had yet to become too unbearable. Lorena had passed over each with her hands, imbuing their corpses with a spell of purification she normally used to keep their food from going stale too quickly. But bodies of full-grown men and women were harder to preserve than loafs of bread and cuts of pork. It had drained her almost completely of any strength she could muster each time she cast the spell, but the benefit of returning them as intact as possible could not be denied.

Finally, the road turned southward, keeping the Spinefoot mountains on their left which ran their course from Twin Rivers northward. To the right, they could see the rushing current of the wide Red Horse River which separated Maroth from the Hinterlands and marked the kingdom's border. The rolling dirt and stone path darkened with the passing shadows of clouds overhead, a welcome respite from the sun. As Bart steered the carriage onward, the sound of rushing wings from the eastern sky met his ear, soon joined by the sight of an armored rider astride a bronze-brown griffin. The beast reeled and screeched, circling the caravan, causing the horses to panic wildly and champ at their bits. Bart and the others fought desperately to keep the beasts under control, lest they destroy the bridling and overturn their loads. The sellsword cursed as he pulled on the reins, yanking back the pair of horses' heads to try and regain some semblance of control.

He could hear the desperate yells and commands from behind him as his fellow drivers did the same, the cry of horses and the shrill scream of the winged griffin echoed against the rocky faces of the surrounding mountains. Finally, the mounted knight landed his charge, leaning over the saddle as he lifted the visor of his steel helm. Bart could see the glint of flowing blond hair peak out from beneath the helmet, but his eyes were more keenly interested in what weapons this new arrival had at their disposal. Aside from the sword at his hip, the griffin itself would most certainly be a weapon as well. He saw no lance or heavy armor usually worn by mounted knights on a campaign, so this was likely a scout.

Scouts rarely flew alone, his eyes glanced skyward looking for any additional surprises. Seeing none, he called out to the knight, "What business have you with us, sir knight? Certainly, there are more pressing concerns in these troubled times than a few weary travelers longing for hearth and home?"

At the mention of 'hearth and home' Della and the others exchanged a subtle nod, the phrase was one of their special codes. In short, it meant 'If they make a move, put them down and ask questions later.' Slowly the others loosened their blades or readied bows and spells.

The knight raised a gloved hand, palm outward, the universal sign to show one was unarmed. "I see your carriages bear the mark of Lord Firbank, my partner and I had just come across a few such carriages further south. Tell me, sir, what do you know of this?" his eyes glanced over the motley assembly, assessing each in turn. Swinging his legs free of the stirrups, he dismounted and approached Bart sitting atop the lead carriage, palm raised.

"No need for alarm," assured Walter, "I am simply here seeking answers. Should they satisfy my needs, I will be on my way." His eyes slowly passed from one face to the next, taking each of them in turn.

Lawrence Firbank's head appeared from the carriage, his voice resonated with authority, "And what service can the Firbanks be to you, Sir Knight? I ask you to present yourself so that we may discuss this intrusion." Stepping from the carriage, the young lord walked steadily up to the front of the line, his hand resting on the pommel of the sword hanging from his waist. Having made his way to the front of the caravan, he stood resolutely before the knight and his ferocious steed.

Seeing the man before him, the knight bowed low, hand over his heart. "My Lord, I am Sir Walter of the Cloud Knights. Vice-Captain of the First Cohort known as the Rising Phoenix. I have been tasked with a matter most urgent which led me and my companion to search the northern reaches on the orders of Commander Zulla, Head of the Cloud Knights, and senior military counsel to the king."

Lawrence nodded, looking about and searching the sky, "And where, pray tell, is your companion? Unless you speak of the fine beast behind you?"

Sir Walter's face darkened, "He was slain in battle, my Lord, we were set upon the road by assassins when we were investigating the wreckage of the rest of your retinue. I come seeking answers as to what happened, perhaps there may be some connection to my charge."

"Well, this is no place to discuss such matters," replied Lawrence, "we are returning to my estate in Twin Rivers. If you would be so good as to accompany us, I am certain you will find the answers you seek, along with warm food and strong drink. Does this satisfy?"

The knight nodded, once again bowing low as he spoke, "It would be my honor, Lord Lawrence Firbank of Twin Rivers, I shall attend from the sky that I might not further impede your journey." He smartly turned and remounted the preening lion-bodied, eagle-headed steed. With a flutter of wings and dust, the armored rider was once again skyward, slowly circling the travelers below.

Lawrence joined Bart atop the first carriage smiling contently, "Well now, my good man, I do believe we have found ourselves a most useful addition to the final leg of our journey. Few would dare attack anyone protected by one of the famed Cloud Knights."

Bart nodded in agreement, flicking the reigns and clicking his tongue, once again the line moved forward. Overshadowed by their newly found guardian of the skies. The passing shadow of death shielding them from future harm, so he hoped.

This was the first opportunity Bart had to speak with the young lord in some sense of privacy, he glanced over at the young lord sitting beside him atop the swaying carriage. "With all respect, Lord Firbank, when you spoke with Armen you mentioned the two of you were cousins. I was not aware that he came from such stock."

Young Lawrence chuckled, "Oh I wouldn't be too hard on yourself, the Bardiche family is not one to flaunt their status. Even so, their family holds only a minor title due to their prowess in battle and service to the crown. We are cousins by blood, on my mother's side, but as my father has always reminded me; no bond demands more love and loyalty than blood, whether through marriage, birth, or oath. The Firbanks and the Bardiches have stood side-by-side on more than one occasion, that said, we are so separated by the geography of this land it is rare to see one another outside of certain occasions. But what about you, Bart? Where do you come from?"

Bart glanced uncomfortably at the young lord, who was leaning back against the seat. His feet propped up on the footboard as he lounged comfortably as though they were on summer holiday. "I come from a small town far to the east, Troutsmouth, my lord. I doubt you would know of it."

The young lord shook his head slowly, "Aside from the name, and that your town is known for leather-work and fishing, not much. But I believe the current lords of that province reside in Hills Reach, the Lady Callen is still well I trust?"

The mercenary shrugged, "I would not know, Lord, I am just the son of a bailiff. My father was more concerned about the running of the town, taxation, commerce, and the dispensation of law. What time he didn't spend governing the townsfolk he spent governing me. Lectures on allocating funds, taking me around to building and renovation projects to oversee the craftsmen, insisting that as his son I should know the faces and names of the most important craftsmen and traders in town."

The young lord's eyes opened wide, "That is a surprise to hear, I mean no offense, but I would have thought you came from more humble beginnings. Why would you leave all that behind? Surely you would have made a fine governor come the day you came into your own?"

Bart sighed, looking up at the clouds and the soaring griffin above before he spoke, "I didn't want to spend my life in the same bloody town, doing the same bloody job, every bloody day for the rest of my life. I wanted more, I wanted adventure, glory, and excitement. So, when the former Lord Callen, gods rest his soul, put the call out that he was looking to take on a new squire I jumped at the chance. I was barely past fourteen years of age when he took me on, and within the year I joined him on the campaign against the Hill Tribes who had raided the western reaches."

"I was twelve when they crossed the Red Horse," replied Lawrence, His gaze looking over the far horizon towards the rushing waters of mention, "They swarmed over these lands like locusts, burning anything in their path and killing that which remained. When they turned against our keep of Twin Rivers my Father kept the gates open as long as he could to get the people inside. But not everyone could make it, the old, the sick, and some who had decided to stand against the horde and delay their advance with futile effort. I remember standing atop the ramparts with my father as I watched the survivors flayed alive in full view of the garrison." His eyes closed as the young lord leaned back, remembering the horrors he described, "Sometimes, in the silence, I can still hear their screams. We couldn't do anything, for all our pride and resolve, we just stood there and watched as they were butchered like animals."

Bart gazed over at the young nobleman, they were of the same age and had seen similar horrors. He too could hear those cries as the man spoke, smell the blood seeping onto the earth turning the dirt black. "How do you deal with them, the memories?" The question escaped his lips before Bart could restrain his tongue.

Lawrence turned, a knowing gaze in his sad eyes, all thought of position between the two forgotten. For now, they were simply two men who had seen the horrors that could be dealt when blades were drawn and no mercy would be afforded, "I know each of us must cope with the things we have seen or done in our own way. I realized that in the greater scheme of what the gods have planned for us, there are those whom we can save and those we cannot. So long as we do not overstep our reach, then we can ensure that whatever course we take we have done everything we can to the best of our ability and influence. There are things in this life that we cannot change no matter how hard we try, we must accept that what has happened in the past has happened for reasons beyond our fault. To believe that one person could change the course the gods have determined is nothing short of hubris."

Bart gazed intently at the young lord as he spoke, "Sounds easy when you put it that way. But some of us are cursed to remember, to re-live those memories as intently as the days when they happened. I have prayed to the gods for relief, and I have sought the healers of the mind and soul, none has eased my suffering. The only solace I find is when I hold a sword in my hand and stand before my enemies, in my heart I hope secretly that one of these days I will face the one who will free me from my pain. I am too much of a coward to free myself."

"But have you forgiven yourself?" Asked Lawrence, his hands interlocked behind his head as he gazed over at the somber sellsword.

Bart bowed his head, struggling to fight the tears that welled up inside, and choked his voice, "I never could forgive myself, I failed my lord and master, I was a coward."

"You were a child!" spat Firbank, "And until you forgive that child for something that lay far beyond his control, you will never find peace. You must save yourself before you can ever hope to save others."

The chambers of the Grand Master of The Order were more akin to a temple or shrine than an office befitting the station of someone within a militant order. Along either side of the long room, tapestries hung from the high arched ceiling depicting the tenants of the faith. Holy knights, imbued with holy light and mystical power standing alone against the forces of darkness. Saints who had given their lives in the service of the gods looked on from their woven mantels with unseeing eyes. At the head of the room, a large round window embossed with stained glass forming an intricate mandala in the shape of a rose cast a rainbow of colors across the three statues of the primary gods of the faith; The Father, The Mother, and The Warrior. At their feet, a long granite altar sat, enveloped with a red shroud emblazoned with gold embroidered along the edges. And before the three gods knelt Grand Master Bernard, the pinnacle of power amongst the holy knights, and many would argue the temple itself.

Solon's footsteps echoed softly in the stillness of the stoic chamber as he spoke, "My deepest apologies for interrupting you at your prayers, Grand Master, but there is a matter most dire which we must discuss."

Grand Master Bernard's voice resounded through the stillness, his head still bowed, "I doubt that there is little you would regret, honored guest, and interrupting my prayers would be the least of these." Kissing the altar, he rose and turned to greet the newcomer, hands clasped before him, "Come, my son, tell me what ails you such."

The wizened old magician bristled at being called 'son' the Grand Master was hardly a few seasons older than he, it felt demeaning in a way. Bringing out a series of parchments, the wizard approached, "I have received word of many events which bode ill for the kingdom and this continent. As you know, Grand Master Bernard, the king shall soon abdicate his throne to make way for his lost heir. After I had received word of these developments, I reached out through my various informants ordering them to keep me appraised of any new developments."

"By informants, you mean the owl which has taken roost in the rafters of my tower, correct?" Accused Bernard, peering down his nose at the wizard with no small amount of judgment.

Solon nodded, "Amongst others, yes. I have found through the years that creatures are far more honest and perceptive than mortals supposedly graced with the blessings of the gods."

Bernard raised his hand, "I would take great care, if I were you, not to speak such heresy in this holy place, much less in my presence. If I did not know you any better, such talk could land you in the cells under the care of the Inquisitor. That said, what developments have you learned that would disturb you?"

Solon continued, reporting all that he had learned throughout the past few weeks. He spoke of the movements of members from the Guild of Shadows moving in concert throughout the kingdom, escalating their activities beyond what had been seen before at such a scale, how the Cloud Knights had been dispatched in force to find the missing heir and the attack on the northern roads involving creatures of the night. The latter brought a dark shadow to the monastic warrior's face, he gazed upon the tapestries in contemplation as he listened, in detail, to the nature of the beasts. How they had moved, their number, the seemingly frantic display of bloodlust. Of the survivors had made their way towards the Spinefoot Mountains along the road to Twin Rivers via the northern road.

The Grand Master turned, nodding at Solon, "What you are describing is indeed a greater threat than the political intrigues of the court. Kings come and go, but the faith remains. As you are well aware, wizard, The Order does not hold themselves accountable to any power other than the gods. If these creatures are, indeed, a threat to the mortal souls of the faithful then we will act accordingly."

"I believe I may know from whence these creatures have come, and I fear this may also mean your opinion of me may diminish if that is even possible." replied the old wizard. "You would recall the Sorcerer from ages past who had plunged the kingdoms of Almach into shadow; how he had used his mystical arts to forge a rift between our world and the realms of shadow beyond the pale. I fear that someone has rediscovered the process to perform the rites of binding and summoning he used to burn a swath of death across the mortal lands."

"The one of whom you speak has been dead almost two-hundred years!" growled Bernard, "And none could have performed such rituals had they not attained the tome necessary to perform the rites that demon performed in the service of their dark master."

Solon shook his head solemnly, "It is far more than that, Grand Master, for I can assure you that whoever is behind these creatures has succeeded. By what means, I cannot say. But the creatures themselves can be killed, this has been known since the dark days two centuries past. Had they not been susceptible to death, then none of us would be alive today. But what I find most troubling is that these creatures appeared in the reaches near the Hinterlands, where even now, the Hill Tribes and the scattered clans amongst them have gathered once more to worship their orc god. They may soon choose amongst themselves a new war master to lead a united front against our lands. I suspect, with little evidence mind you, that these two events are connected."

The Grand Master gazed up at the somber stone faces above him, "So as the enemies of the faith strike within to seed fear and disarray amongst the people, the foes of the crown make ready to once more sow death and flame upon the people." Bernard turned to face Solon, his head held high, with all the stoicism and authority of an experienced commander. "I would ask you to be of service, wise one. I do not ask for this lightly, I want you to depart hence and make your way to the Twin Rivers with all speed. If these events coincide, that is where the greatest threat will be. Lord Firbank has been a loyal supporter of the crown and the gods, he and his line have always been well respected by The Order as honorable. I would not see them fall due to our negligence to act. I will marshal our forces and embark within the week, will you do this?"

Over the next few hours, Solon found himself embroiled in the mind-numbing task of preparing for a long journey. He had good reason for only ever venturing into the neighboring towns for no more than a couple of days at most; trips longer than a quick jaunt involved packing supplies, getting luggage in order, and arranging for transportation and lodging, all of which were exasperated by the presence of the ever watchful holy knights.

The Grand Master was insistent he would be accompanied by a pair of the humorless neanderthals, for his own safety and protection he had been assured. Thumbing through the collection of scrolls and documents he selected a few which he placed into a round leather tube capped with wood stoppers. He would travel light, considering the distance they would need to travel. As he followed the pair of sentinels back down the staircase, the second time today he had been forced to endure the cursed stone steps, he was secretly grateful that the pair had taken his luggage for him.

The three walked through the great hall, built with fine smooth granite and accented with carved reliefs along the walls up to the long windows faceted along the east and west walls. The high ceiling echoed from the armored footsteps of knights and squires who passed along on their individual errands and duties, hardly passing a glance toward the wizard and his escort. The hurried rush of footsteps announced the arrival of novice Matthias who clasped in his hands an arm-sized bundle wrapped with twine.

"Master Solon, I have something for you!" panted the young acolyte. He held out the small bundle, a glint of joy evident on his features as he offered the parcel to Solon. "Don't open it just yet, but I wanted you to have this, I was going to give it to you on the day of our harvest feast, but I think you should have it now."

The wizard looked at the bundle curiously, "Alright, I will open it once I have left, and I am on the road then." He watched as Matthias smiled and departed to carry out whatever duties he had been tasked with for the day. If Solon had ever had a mind to take on an apprentice, he would hope they would be as studious and thoughtful as that young man, a shame he was embroiled in the holy order.

The three made their way to the stables, where a set of horses was bridled and ready. Two of the mounts were stout chargers preferred by the heavy mounted knights which served as the crushing force of The Order, one jet black with white socks on its forelegs and the other a chestnut. Both seemed indifferent to the third; a small grey and black spotted jennet saddled and ready for the long journey. The stable master waved at the approaching travelers and bowed as he greeted the trio.

"Good, sirs, I wish you safe passage on your journey. And Master Solon, I must say it is an honor to be in your presence."

Solon returned the bow in kind, "I am unworthy of such praise, good man, I am just a humble scholar and guest of these good monks while I study the mysteries. May I ask the creature's name?" His approached the speckled mare and stroked her muzzle softly. The long face leaned in and pressed against Solon's hand as he gazed at the beast.

"Her name is Juniper, when I was informed that you would be in need of a mount, Master, I felt that she would be best suited for your needs instead of one of the war mounts. She has a fine temper, although she can be a bit of a trickster when she puts her mind to it."

Solon felt the horse's teeth nibbling at the string parcel he held in his hands, loosening the string bindings. He pulled the package away to safety, which was now opened to reveal the contents. His eyes fell upon a grey woolen round-brimmed hat. Holding it in his hands as he examined the headwear, he could feel that the material had been embedded with oil and wax to waterproof the lining against the elements and a leather band had been strapped around the crown for added stability, all topped off with a floppy pointed tip. It was as though he was holding something ripped from the pages of a children's storybook. A snicker broke out from one of the armored knights now astride his warhorse.

"I don't believe I have ever heard one of you holy knights even let out so much as a chuckle." remarked Solon. As he took the wide-brimmed hat and seated it firmly on his head.

The knight leaned back, taking it all in, "Now you look like a real wizard, Master Solon."

*Chapter*

# EIGHT

# SINS

Marguk's eyes slowly peered open at the muffled sounds coming from the other side of the tent flaps. The voices were lowered, but he could tell from the tone that there were at least two orcs and maybe just as many goblins arguing softly in the early morning silence. The idiots were conspiring just on the other side of the cloth folds outside, but as for who there were the orc chieftain couldn't say. He didn't recognize the voices, but he listened intently. His hand slowly drew the hand axe by his bed closer, pulling the weapon within reach from instinct honed from years of war and paranoia.

"I'm tellin' ya, I saw the she-human coming back with blood all over her, I did." Whispered one of the voices, the accent and weasel-like voice common amongst the goblin races. "Wit' not a word you mind, she done walked on in from Gog-knows all covered in crimson and looking pale as the silver eye itself."

The chieftain looked about the tent, there was no sign of the sorceress within. But that was the norm, she had her own tent alongside where she usually spent her nights. As quietly as the large orc could manage, he lifted himself from his bed and made his way toward the door frame. The beginnings of dawn could be seen between the linen folds and the ground's surface. As he stepped out into the crisp morning air, Marguk breathed in the smell of smoldering fires and smoke. It intermingled with the sharp crispness of morning dew on the trodden grass which felt cool beneath the soles of his bare feet. His attention turned to the small tent that lay alongside, the darkness within contrasted with the early morning sun making it almost impossible to see if Susalla lay inside. He poked his head within, searching for any sign of her presence. The small wooden framed couch which he had gifted to the sorceress as a bed lay empty, the pillows and sheets unused.

"Do you require my presence, great chief?" Susalla's voice drifted from behind the warrior forcing an unexpected shudder to rock his spine as he turned. The woman had somehow managed to sneak up behind him. Marguk looked down at the pale hands barely protruding from her gown's flowing sleeves. There was no sign of any injury that he could perceive, and the gown itself seemed to be freshly cleaned.

He approached the woman standing before him, his voice lowered so as to not alert those who may be within earshot, "I understand you had yourself a bit of an eventful evening. Where were you?"

"I was offering my prayers to the gods, that is all." The sorceress' voice was calm and reassuring as she gazed into the dark eyes which stared down at her from their overbearing height.

"And these prayers, do they always use so much blood?" Marguk nodded at the hint of bandages which could barely now be seen from her robes.

Susalla glanced down at her scared palms, flexing her delicate fingers thoughtfully as she stood before the one to whom she had dedicated her services ever since that fateful night when she had walked into the clan's encampment. "The gods demand little in comparison to what they can offer, my chieftain. If they should require that I suffer such small an injury in return for their favor then I will gladly provide it."

"And just what, by Gog's eye, have the gods promised you?" spat Marguk, his eyes glowering down at the sorceress before looking about at the small crowd which was now slowly gathering about the pair in heated conversation. Their collective gazes were mixed between disdain for the presence of this human witch amongst their number and piqued interest in what may follow. His fellow orcs and a scattering of the goblin races formed a loose ring about their chieftain, all of whom had suffered through the cold winters with him, fought by his side against their enemies, and bore the scars of their shared comradery. Before he could turn back to continue questioning the human, a figure broke ranks and stepped forward toward the pair, their orcish face twisted in rage and grief.

"My chief, someone has murdered one of our number." Reported the orc warrior. Marguk shook his head, this was turning out to be one hell of a morning. As he watched, two more made their way through the throng of faces bearing the limp form of one of the sentinels that had stood the night prior. A jagged dagger protruding from their heart. As they laid the body before his feet, the chieftain of the Wolf Clan could see a scrap of parchment pinned to the corpse's chest, blood staining the fibrous surface. Slowly he reached down, pulling the dagger from the body along with the message. The words did not matter, the intent was clear enough. The Long Fangs were making their move, more sudden than he would have preferred, but this was expected after they failed in the fighting pit.

"The coward, Long Fang, has challenged me for my claim. I will answer in kind!" He waved the blood-soaked parchment before the gathered horde. There was a gnashing of jaws and growls of rage from those gathered in response. There had always been a rivalry between the Wolf Clan and the Long Fangs, on more than one occasion things had almost come to blows between the two.

Susalla reached out her hand, caressing the orc chief's rippling forearm. "You had asked what the gods promised in exchange, great chieftain, behold and you will see." She knelt beside the limp corpse at Marguk's feet, resting her bandaged palms on their forehead as she rocked from side to side, her lips silently chanting in a foreign tongue that Marguk could not place in origin, but seemed to resonate within his soul. A foul, purple mist seemed to emanate from the very air that surrounded them, encapsulating the body on the ground like a spider wrapping their silk around newly caught prey. The early rays of dawn seemed to dampen, a collective chill and the smell of death flowed over the crowd who watched on in horror as the body then twisted and turned beneath the sorceress' touch. The mist flowed over the green skin, leeching all color from their form as the once green flesh turned into a sickly dark blue hue. The fog rippled and collected, taking the shape of a serpent, and plunged into the fanged mouth, causing their chest to lurch upward in a hauntingly demonic inhalation.

Susalla lifted her hands from the body, rising to her feet as she spread her outstretched fingers over the shuddering being lying supine before the crowd. The onlookers gasped in awe as the once lifeless form slowly sat up, then rose to stand before the orc chieftain and the raven-haired sorceress. It turned to face Marguk, near lifeless pale eyes staring blankly without any comprehensible sign of life other than it appeared to now draw breath and move under its own strength.

The sorceress circled her creation, presenting the ghoulish orc hybrid which now stood at the center of the assembly. "Great Chieftain, warriors of the Wolf Clan, Gog has blessed us with his power and omnipotence! Through my hands he has worked wonders, he shows us all his power and his blessings! Even in death, there is a new beginning for those who have been chosen by the Far-Seer to serve in the coming struggles! Even the cold grasp of the eternal slumber cannot hold us back from victory! Know this, should you fall, you will rise again to serve in his grand design! He has chosen our great leader, Marguk, to lead his children against the realms to the east! He has assured your victory through blood and spirit! No blade can kill you, no axe can fall you! Through his power, you will rise again to slaughter your enemies and bring glory to your clan and the united tribes! This is the dawn of a new age! This is the age of Gog!"

A cacophonous roar broke out from the horde, spears stamped into the earth. Axes, clubs, and swords clamored against wood and steel shields. Feet pounded dirt, and fists hammered chests as the crowd roared in unison in exhilaration for the slaughter to come. Marguk looked on, the cold grasp of fear gripping his beating heart. The pressure within felt as though it would overtake him and subdue any will to resist. He gazed at the exhilarated face of his sorceress, her eyes blazing with a fire that threatened to consume anything that stood in her path. The fear of the mystical and the unknown compounded with the awe and reverence welling up inside as he gazed at her dancing and twirling form which hovered like a banshee over the mob. This power, this magic would cement his place in the annuls and sagas of the united tribes, he would use this army of the dead to wreak havoc on his enemies, he would burn the high cities and crush the skulls of the weak flesh to the east.

As for new recruits, well, he knew just the place to further grow this army of the dead and swell his ranks. And they had just given him due cause to put them in line, he gazed down at the scrawled challenge in his grasp. The parchment was still wet with the blood of the once-deceased warrior who silently stood before him, it now served as their death warrant, and it would be carried out at once.

"Bring me Long Fang!" He roared, holding the parchment aloft. The entirety of the assembly howled and rushed off toward the tents and campfires of their rivals, the great chieftain slowly followed the throng of howling warriors, a fanged grin plastered over his face. Today was looking better already.

The cloaked and hooded figure sat atop the buttresses of the northern watchtower which overlooked the borders of Maroth with the territories of Almach. While there had not been open conflict between the two nations, the decision had still been made for a garrison to remain and keep watch over their temperamental neighbors all the same. Three towers had been built for just such a purpose, eighty meters in height, with multiple vantage points for archers around the perimeter. A barracks built into the base of the structure provided living quarters, kitchens, store rooms, and offices for the thirty soldiers who were stationed for periods that varied per the availability of manpower. The man leaned heavily over the stone ledge, looking beyond the shores of the rushing river flowing westward, fed by the melting snows of the mountains further east and north. A gust of wind whipped the edge of his cloak to reveal a fine, silver-hilted sword hanging at his waist, accented by small opals in the pommel.

The chilling autumn wind drove him back inside the guardroom, it was nearly barren aside from a pair of wooden benches and a small table that hosted a single candle to provide some illumination to the room. On the far side of the wall near the stairwell, a wooden rack supported a pair of longbows and two quivers filled with arrows which stood ready for use should the need arise. He toyed with the fletchings of one of the latent shafts. The steady creak of footsteps upon the stairs announced the arrival of his guest. The sole reason the cloaked man had traveled to this gods-forsaken place on the edge of nowhere. As the footsteps came ever closer, he moved towards one of the benches and reposed himself as comfortably as one could, given the circumstances.

"Thank you for agreeing to meet with me on such short notice, my friend." Duke Rolfe pulled back his hood as he greeted the newcomer. The man now standing before him was broad-shouldered and sported a cropped rusty beard. He moved with all the confidence of a bear amongst sheep, raw physical power evident from his build.

The bearded man smirked from beneath his own hood, "You presume too much, Heathridge, our interests may be aligned for the time being but let us not forget the nature of our so-called alliance. I will say that it is strange that you insisted we meet here to discuss whatever matters you seemed so hesitant to put into writing."

Heathridge nodded, "All the same, I thank you for making the journey to speak with me. True, if these were any other times I would not bother with such measures, but it is imperative we decide here and now what to do to remedy the current issue. I presume your spies have told you of the current movements from the mounted knights? And their disposition away from the capitol?"

The bearded man nodded, "Aye, they are looking for this so-called lost heir there have been whispers of amongst the underbelly. And I understand that amongst them your son had been slain, an irony that the one whom you would have named your heir after the fruition of our plans should die in the search of the king's own. That said, you have my deepest condolences, I too know the pain of losing a son. It does not ease with time, all we can do is move forward for their sake."

Duke Rolfe bristled at the mention of his son, fighting to maintain his composure. "And what of your end of the bargain, has there been any progress with our friends?"

"Indeed," nodded the larger man, stepping out onto the rampart and gazing northward towards his homeland. "We have garrisoned additional troops along the outposts high in the mountains, as well as gathered enough food and provisions for the initial campaign. We should be ready to march within the next few days, well before the planned time. My mercenaries are more than capable of supporting your forces should the time come. As for the others, well, loyalty can be bought as you know."

"Loyalty?" Rolfe scoffed, "Let me tell you about loyalty. I showed loyalty to that fool of a king when he marched our armies against the green skins in defense of our borders with the hinterlands. I was loyal when he handed me the lands and peerage of the northern reaches, these lands were barren and fruitless before I came here. I was loyal when he increased my taxes, took my retainers and men-at-arms for his garrisons, and when he stole the richest of my lands and gifted them to another lord. I remained loyal still, even funding the construction of the towers which now stand along the borders with Almach, the quarrying of the stone, and financing the labor from my lands, quarrying the stones from my quarries. And what has my loyalty given me in return? Nothing. I have lost wealth, position, privilege, and even my own son! If that is the kind of loyalty which bears nothing in return, then I will turn against them and wear my own. So, when the time comes, those who have aided me and shown their loyalty will not have to suffer the same treatments I have had to endure."

The bearded man nodded, stroking his beard, "Well I, for one, look forward to a long and fruitful alliance. I cannot wait to see just what kind of king you will be. You will wear the crown well, and I do not say that just because you have promised to hand over the lands we discussed in compensation for our support."

Duke Rolfe looked southward towards the rolling hills surrounding the far-off towns of Bayhome and Krot. He had worked his fingers to the bone after being cast out here to this once fruitless and poor domain, turning it into the sprawling farmlands and trade routes that now flowed with commerce bringing gold into his coffers. Should his designs unfold as he desired, the duke would have little need for this corner of the kingdom, and he would be glad to be rid of it along with the memories of humiliation throughout.

Their business having been concluded, the visitor watched as Duke Rolfe rode south astride his black horse, swathed in the nondescript cloak that concealed his identity to any who would have seen him pass.

There was truly no better ally than a man who hungered for his personal brand of vengeance, mounting his horse, the cloaked figure rode east toward the sprawling woods that grew along the northern river. Under the cover of the high branches scattered with the colors of autumn, he slowly rode into the open clearing along the banks of the Tsere. He sat there, slowly watching around him for any sign of pursuit, the only sounds that could reach his ears were the babbling waters and the rustle of dying leaves as he waited. Satisfied he was alone, the rider spurred his steed onward, crossing the river and making his way north into the kingdom of Almach.

Not long after crossing, he turned westward along the foot of a long cliff-side that overlooked the southern borders of Almach, weaving his mount along the rocky crag until reaching a cut set into the face of the steep cliffs. He dismounted, leading his horse within the narrow passage until finding the small camp where the rest of his men awaited his return. They rose silently at the approach of their commander, some raising their fists over their hearts in salute as he passed. Soon he would return, he thought to himself, and behind him would follow such a force that none would dare challenge him. The delicate peace which had been paid for through blood and marriage had lasted long enough. The man's bearded face broke out in a wide grin, Maroth would fall, and with it, Almach would sweep across the land once more to regain their lost glory.

The dwarf gazed into the bulbous form of a strange glass decanter which was slowly filling with a viscous green liquid. Sylvanus' study was filled with such experiments, small arcane tablets heated bottles filled with liquids and minerals, capped with leathered tubes made from the intestines of sheep which through some unknown design or purpose, transferred, sorted, and mixed the various fumes into yet more receptacles. Small wooden models of devices and mechanizations cluttered what remaining space could be found amongst the scattered notes and drawings which anyone who didn't know the author would presume were but the ramblings of a madman. He picked up one such pamphlet, a massive drawing in charcoal of what could only be described as a wooden cart with griffin wings molded to the sides and peaked with twin sails such as those found in the smaller fishing vessels of the southern lands. The tail of a fish rested at the back, and within the round-bottom portion of the construction sat a row of crudely drawn figures.

"Griffin Cart? What the blazes would be the point of this, elf?" Hammerstone waved the parchment in the direction of his friend, who was currently occupied organizing small round weights at one end of a balancing scale while pouring small sand-like granules into the other bowl, seeking the correct proportions for whatever fever dream the elf had concocted.

"Why to move troops, supplies, goods, the miracle of flight should not be limited just to those who have tamed beasts with the appropriate temperament to take one or two riders at a time. If I am able to unlock the secret of how to propel oneself with the right force, while balancing the weight of those who must operate the device then it should work. The problem seems to be that the stronger one may be physically, the more they will weigh. It would work if that were not the case, so up to now I chase the balance of power to weight equivalence. Perhaps if I made it bigger, then I could fit more rowers for the wings?"

The dwarf stared at Sylvanus with concern in his eyes, asking the question he most likely did not want an answer to, "So you have built one of these before?"

"Oh yes, some years ago now I would suppose. Sadly, when we failed to achieve flight, we decided to push the cart off one of the high buttresses overlooking the outer walls, much like how a bird would leap from such a height to achieve motion. If the captain of the guard had not insisted we remove the machine from his walls, perhaps we could have succeeded."

Snorri shook his head, "And this?" He pointed at the vial that was now half full of the strange green liquid. The glass itself seemed to form a film on the inside as the levels rose ever upward from the slow drips filling the contents, holding his hand against the surface he could feel a strange warmth fill his fingertips from the green ooze.

"Ah, yes, that one has been most enjoyable. You are familiar with the common subterranean organism that most people refer to as 'slimes' correct?" The dwarf nodded skeptically in response as Sylvanus continued, "Well I have found, through research, that the reason these creatures seem to be able to pass through solid walls is due to their fantastic nature. You see, the creature doesn't simply pass through solid stone or rock, but reforms itself into smaller portions and passes between via cracks or openings! I have been experimenting with just how small of an opening one would need to traverse from one glass to another. The hard part was figuring out how to entice the creature to move from one vial to the other."

The dwarf shook his head, sighing in exasperation at the antics of his long-time compatriot and confidant. "I don't suppose you have had any progress on the task I asked of you myself, have you? Identifying the poison which had been used on our late queen, or how to trace the process of making such a concoction?"

Sylvanus' eyes narrowed, his face was grim as he regarded his shorter friend. "How long have we known each other, Snorri? Forty, fifty years? What is your opinion of me, my character?"

The question caught the dwarf off guard, his head cocked to the side as he tried to process the inquiry. "I would say about that long, yes, but I have come to find you as a worthy and trusted friend. Sure, you may be a little..." his hand waved about the room towards the assorted collections of vials, papers, and glass beakers, "...eccentric, maybe even a touch mad at times. But I do not doubt your intentions to be of service to the people, the realm, and our king. But I fail to see why that should matter as to your answer."

The tall elf took a slow breath, collecting himself as he pulled a collection of sheets from beneath the remnants of what Snorri could only assume had been their dinner some days ago.

"The poison, as you know, left no discernible trace on the late queen's body. She had shown no symptoms other than the fever which had left her confined to her chambers to rest, given her state. Unlike most poisons which would be administered and take effect within minutes or even hours, logic would force us to assume she had been poisoned over the course of a few days or longer perhaps. There was no discoloration of the gums or fingernails, no puncture wound could be found either. So, it would be unlikely that she ingested the substance or was stabbed with a poisoned needle or skewer as might be the usual method from skilled poisoners. More so, given the fact that any food or drink which would have been in her presence passes through such strict regimen, it would be difficult to poison her by those means."

Snorri Hammerstone nodded, "Yes, yes, all of this is similar to what we have discussed before, what is the point?"

The elf placed a small glass bottle with a glass stopper on the table beside him. It was beautifully crafted, molded to resemble a floral bulb with intricate inlays of small gold flakes in the shape of a twisting vine around the circumference of the bottle. The glass itself was also of remarkable quality, very few craftsmen could achieve such clarity and purity in their work. The vessel was filled with a faint, rosy liquid the color of dogwood blossoms.

"A perfume bottle?" asked Snorri, lifting the small object and examining the craftsmanship with interest. "I presume this would have once belonged to sweet Eliza."

Sylvanus nodded gravely, "Far more than that, I am afraid." He presented the documents and notes which he still held in his trembling grasp. "Years ago I had experimented with a substance derived from several plants in order to create a poison that could be absorbed through the skin unbeknown to the victim. Before you ask, I had no intention of it ever being used, it was a matter of curiosity. But your inquest reminded me of that particular time, so I sought out my old records."

The dwarf looked down at the pages he now held, examining the contents within as he shuffled them one after the other. He paused, flipping the pages back and forth, something didn't seem quite right. "Pages are missing, or do I fail to grasp what these mean?"

"No, you are quite correct." Admitted the forlorn elf. "Not only may I be responsible for providing the means to poison our beloved queen, but somehow someone has acquired my notes on how to produce even more of the substance."

Hammerstone looked up at his friend, the elf's eyes were filled with regret and fear at the prospect, "Now hold on just one moment, surely the skills required to make this would require a vast amount of knowledge to make this poison?"

"Sadly no," Sylvanus mumbled. His hand waved over the array of bottles and herbal collections before him. "So long as you had the process and ingredients, one would simply need to just follow the directions and details on the formulation in order to make such a toxin. After all, from what I remember, the herbs and plants that derived the key to making this poison could be found at any herbalist shop or even growing wild in the surrounding fields. But the key ingredient was the azalea flower and oleander root. I called it, 'mummer's kiss', for the floral scent and soft complexion. To any unknowing person who would find it, it would appear to be a simple perfume, I would be more proud of the accomplishment had it not fallen into the wrong hands." He walked over to a small wooden chest that rested on a shelf along the stone wall. Pulling out a small key, the elf twisted open a small lock which shuttered the lid and opened the chest to reveal a collection of small glass bottles stoppered with cork and sealed with colored waxes. Each bore a label at the base, detailing the contents in the scrawling elvish script of his homeland.

The elven alchemist presented the chest for full view as Hammerstone gazed at the collection of what he presumed to be poisons of various hues and colors. Some held powders, other liquids of various quantities. But what caught his gaze was the open space amongst the articles of death that started him in the face. His heart sank at the prospect of what this revelation meant. The elf nodded, his shoulders trembling as he held open the wooden chest.

"I am the only one who holds the key to this chest," proclaimed Sylvanus, "And there are none besides myself who even know what this chest would contain. Whoever did this clearly had the intention of taking me down should this ever see the light of day. I made the poison, I was the only one who had access, if anyone else ever finds out, I doubt we will ever find the truth of who is responsible."

Snorri's mind reeled from the revelation. Unconsciously the counselor paced amongst the tables and desks which surrounded the study of his old friend. He could feel the cold chill of sweat dotting his brow from the strain to calm himself. He had no doubt as to the innocence of his friend, the king and queen had both been kind to the elf for many years, and Sylvanus' loyalty was unmatched in that aspect. The culprit would have to be well informed, in addition to having the means to orchestrate such a plot as well as having the motivation to do so. Someone whom the queen had personally wronged? No name could come to mind, she had been loved by all, noble and commoner alike. She had advocated for lifting the taxation of smaller provinces and built schools and orphanages. Her devotion to the faith had also been in high regard, bringing the kingdom the allegiance and respect of the clergy. Could this have been a move by a foreign power? Or was there still a traitor amongst them? If the threat had come from within, then there was only one group that could have been paramount in the success of this scheme.

"The Shadow Guild, once again their hand in all of this is far too obvious for it to be a coincidence." Whispered the dwarf, his face darkened as he looked about the room. "Those bastards will work for anyone given the weight of the purse offered suffices their needs. They have no loyalty to the kingdom or the crown, only the glint of coin can unsheathe their blades and hasten their footsteps. But as for their patron, what client would have the means to buy their services with such loyalty?"

Sylvanus hesitated, the words caught on his lips, "I hate to admit, the only one whom I could even surmise as having the motivation to strike back at the crown would have to be the Duke of Heathridge, the king's own cousin. But even he would not have the funds necessary to buy such loyalty for so long. It is well known that the silence of the guild can be quite expensive, even for a lord, to deal with the Shadow Guild is paramount to accepting blackmail for the rest of your life should you wish to remain secret. I must admit I too have used their services before on behalf of the king as an intermediary when dealing with secrets and the collection of them. They are far more connected and influential than is proper for a mob of assassins and spies, but that is precisely why they are so effective."

Snorri nodded, mulling over the prospect in silence. But if Duke Rolfe was, indeed, the one who had orchestrated the act, where could he have possibly acquired the money? Unless there was another, some unknown power which had decided to bankroll his scheme? If that was the case, war would be the only logical outcome. Blood would be spilled on the lands of Maroth. And Duke Rolfe, cousin to the king, Lord of Heathridge and the northern provinces would hold the dagger which pierced their heart.

*Chapter*

# NINE

# ʜEIR

The Castle of Twin Rivers loomed above the open fields on the peninsula bordered by the bodies of water that bordered the region's namesake. To the north, the town of Spinefoot ran along the road that had provided the route Bart and his company had traversed, predominately a mining town with a collection of agricultural fields that stretched along the road south towards the castle town. Further south beyond the protection of high walls and towers, the villages of Rivers Pass and Pointe along with the scattering of small villages filled with hovels, fisherman's huts, and cabins completed the surrounding inhabitation which stood as a buffer between the Hinterlands to the west and the rest of the kingdom of Maroth. Bart gazed up at the blue-tiled conical towers inset around the defensive wall that surrounded the city. The last time had seen them was when he was a young squire in attendance with his former liege. That blistering summer had been the first campaign he would participate in, memories of his past flooded his mind. He could swear he saw the ghostly image of Sir Callen riding alongside as he gazed along the rolling farmlands still flush with golden wheat and the flowers of flax mid-harvest. The apparition's armor shone in the midday sun just as it had all those years ago.

As the carriages and wagon made their way past the fields, under the intermittent gaze of farmers and herdsmen, Della gazed with concern at the back of Bart's head which could barely be seen at the front of his carriage. Thrax sat curled amongst the corpses in the back of her wagon, gazing hungrily at a small herd of sheep that had wandered closer to the road. His hand reached out over the wooden planked side, his fingers brushing against the rough wool of one of the creatures.

"Don't even think about it, you glutton." chided Della, her focus never leaving the road.

With a sigh, the naga leaned back into the cart and retracted his hands from the tempting treat. "You and friend Bart both seem to be on edge since we came up this way, might I ask why?" His orange eyes remained fixated on the herd of mutton and chops sidling alongside.

"I am not on edge!" spat the elf, flicking the reigns and urging the wagon forward to try and put some distance between herself and the herd of sheep before their numbers became reduced due to her passenger. The clamor of wheels and horseshoes filled the awkward silence before she continued hesitantly, "You have been with Bart and myself long enough to know he has not had the most pleasant of lives, you never knew him as I did. How when he was younger, he would laugh and joke with the other children, what a prankster he could be."

Thrax was taken aback, "You are still talking about our Bart, correct? Not that I find his company unpleasant, elf-friend, but that sounds like a stranger to me." He glanced ahead toward the human who had saved him so long ago from those slavers and bandits in the forest. The serious and stern man who sat at the head of that carriage seemed to be a far cry from the person Della was describing. He had seen Bart smile on occasion, but there had always been a tint of sadness as if the man forced himself to smile when appropriate. It was a bit ironic how Bart claimed the reptilian fighter was the awkward one.

Della continued, nodding as she spoke. "When he was a child, the knight who held the lands where he was raised was called to war here in the lands bordering the Hinterlands. The Hill Tribes who roam the far reaches of the west had begun raiding as they often would into the borderlands, including the provinces where we now ride. I remember how proud he had been to be chosen to squire for that man, he had come to me days before they embarked to show me the new tabard and armor he had been given as part of his role to squire for Sir Callen. I have lived a long time, Thrax, I am used to the idea of the shorter-lived races passing long before any elf or dwarf would even grow grey. I lived with my people in the Elderglenn, north of Troutsmouth where I met Bart as a young boy. There had been something about him then, a glint in his eye that hinted he would be destined for great things. But what happened here during that battle stripped him of what joy and hope he seemed to have. I admit that boy is lost to me, he died on that field along with the others. But I was so grateful to the gods that the man was returned to me, sure he has never been the same, but that doesn't matter. He is alive, and I swore since the day his bandaged body was returned to his family, I would stay with him and protect him. Soon he had grown to such a man that my protection was not needed, but I chose to stay with him all the same. As the years passed, he seemed to come to terms with what had happened, and when he came of age, he left Troutsmouth to join up with the mercenary guilds. I joined him as well, promising his mother I would look out for him as if he were my own. In truth, I do care for the boy, and I have for a long while. When he met Lorena and their love blossomed, I hoped that perhaps her company would heal his wounds, those two deserve to be happy, and I must do everything I can to make it come to pass."

As Della spoke, Thrax looked outward towards the open field between the farmlands of Spinefoot and the stone walls of Twin Rivers, if there had been such a battle here, there was little sign. The rolling lush grass waved in the breeze amongst small pockets of wildflowers filling the land with rich color and life. A stark contrast to the described death and torment that had occurred so long ago.

"It would seem time heals most wounds, Della. But if that has not cured Bart, then what will?" Thrax's rough voice was tinged with concern. "Of course, In comparison to your relationship, I am but a stranger. I am not familiar with the Hill Tribes of these lands, and many of your customs are still foreign to me. But if there is something I can do for Bart, then I must."

"Just be there for him," responded the elf, her shoulders sagging in resignation. "That is all any of us can do for him now."

Growing closer to the northern gate which led into the city surrounding the castle proper, Walter began his descent and landed mid-stride alongside Bart and young Firbank, keeping as much distance as he could without further distressing the pair of horses which led the carriage onward under Bart's control.

"It would seem that there is a heightened sense of security, my lord, there is quite a bit of activity along the walls, archers and crossbowmen and the like. I also saw three platoons of spearmen forming up along what I presume to be the north garrison. I thought it best not to fly ahead, Comet might be a fast flier, but even she isn't immune to a sky full of arrows."

Upon reaching the open gates, one guardsman approached cautiously, keeping his eyes on the large griffin. In the shadows of the gatehouse stood a half dozen others, all were outfitted in simple steel armor with blue and white gambesons. Their shields which stood ready for use along the guard room were emblazoned with the grey tower of Firbank on a blue field. A small part of Bart was impressed, the logistics of outfitting a standard uniform for a standing force was no small matter, clearly the lords of the Twin Rivers had more wealth than would be supposed given their isolation. As they passed by the guards posted at the northern wall, they saluted the crest emblazoned upon the sides of the two carriages, Young Firbank nodded lifting his hand in return for the acknowledgment.

The roads had been paved with flat square stones along the main thoroughfares and were wide enough for two carts to pass along side by side with ease in most places. Houses and workshops constructed of wood and plaster reached up on either side painted in a variety of colors which brought the street to life. Everywhere Bart and the others looked, it was evident that these were people who had endured in the face of adversity and reached for the joys of life wherever they could. Blacksmiths hammered away at glowing bars of steel, sparks spraying like wild fireflies before being quenched in buckets of oil with a profound hiss and clouds of steam. Marketeers called out the prices of their wares for the day, eager to offload the last of the day's goods before closing up and heading off to unwind from a long day of selling and haggling. There were fruit, smoked meats, silk, and wool garments. Armorers polished their latest projects, rounded breastplates of steel with leather straps, brigandines inset with steel or iron bands, and bands of chain mail ready to be cut and woven together for shirts and coifs.

Weaving their way through the bustling streets, the party eventually made their way towards the castle gates, the large banners of Lord Firbank flying proudly over the buttresses. A bearded guardsman wearing an open-faced barbute helmet affixed with a white eagle feather approached stoically and saluted Lawrence Firbank who sat alongside Bart at the head of the carriage.

The old soldier's voice was gruff and worn, "Good evening, Young Lord. I trust there is a good reason why we find you in such company on this fine day?" He eyed Bart and the others with no lack of suspicion.

Lawrence nodded, his sad eyes lowered, "There is reason, Lieutenant, but I am saddened to say the circumstances of which are less than pleasant. Allow me to introduce Bart of Troutsmouth, he along with his compatriots happened upon us in dire need and lent us their aid. He has been kind enough to escort us along our way. We have one wounded who requires care and others who will need to be given the rites and their kin given notice." He gestured back towards the open-topped wagon, the ruffled tarp still covering their load.

The officer's beard furrowed hiding the frown on his face, "I understand, my lord, I shall see to it they are organized in all haste. Your father awaits your presence in his council chambers, might I suggest one of my men escort your companions to the guest house to be bathed and fed while they wait?"

Lawrence looked over at Bart seated alongside, who nodded, with the matter settled the two carriages were led up towards the entrance of the manor which sat opposite the main western gate separated by a parade field lined with round stones painted white. The estate was lined with stone walls reaching over twenty feet in height and almost half as thick, it surrounded the perimeter with a half dozen towers placed at intervals providing excellent coverage of the surrounding city. The wagon was taken over by a pair of soldiers who led the bedraggled horse and its load to the garrison housed along the northern wall. Bart and the others gathered their belongings and followed their escort to a smaller manor built along the main castle facing south, a two-story structure roofed with fired clay tiles and plastered in the style of the old days reminiscent of a lost age. Having found rooms, they stored their packs and sat at one of the long tables in the common area on the first floor near the entrance of the guest house. Della and Lorena had departed in search of the baths, leaving the other four to gather their thoughts.

Bart eyed the blond-haired knight as they settled into one of the high-backed wooden chairs set by the long table. Without the trappings and adornments of knighthood, he appeared fairly similar in stature and build to Armen who sat opposite, albeit Walter had not shaved his head since his youth as the tall spearman had. Thrax had deposited himself by the stone fireplace at the far side of the wall and was luxuriously reclined on the stone floor before the fire soaking up as much warmth as his scales would allow. His presence didn't even seem to fluster the mounted knight, most who would lay eyes on him would either shrink back in revulsion or draw their blades, Walter had done neither. The same could not be said for the guards who had witnessed his debarkation from the wagon, it was nothing short of a miracle that their party had not been reduced in number outright.

"I heard the young lord say you come from Troutsmouth, correct?" the blond knight asked, pouring himself a cup of mulled wine from a pitcher set at the center of the table.

Bart nodded, "True, although I have not been there in many years. Most of my time has been spent on the road or in the service of this lord or the other."

Armen laughed as he reached for the pitcher himself, "Aye, a much better use of his skills with a blade than gutting fish and cutting fishing lines. You won't find a better blade than him! Why, I once saw this man take on three swords in the service of the Grey Eagles and put them down like they were naught but amateur brawlers."

Walter looked impressed at the remark, "The Grey Eagles, you say? I've had the displeasure of dealing with them as both friend and foe, they are not to be trifled with by any means. What brought you to blows with them, might I ask?" Walter eyed the swordsman as he sipped at his cup.

Bart shrugged uncomfortably, "Nothing too serious, just a simple tavern brawl, I just happened to be more sober than they were, so I had the advantage that night. Had it been more than that, we would have all left with more than a few cuts and bruises."

"A tavern brawl, he says." chuckled Armen. "Those three were terrorizing the pretty young barmaids, carousing like a bunch of drunken goblins and groping at their skirts with greedy fingers before this fellow stands up, quick as you please, holding a half pint of foaming ale and declares that if they didn't lay off the lasses and remove their hands he would remove them himself. It was like a line from a bad play you might see strolling players put on for a Spring Festival."

"Ah yes, Bart the hero of the Dancing Bear Tavern." Chuckled Thrax from his place by the fire, "Tales of his great victory are still sung to this day all throughout the land how he bravely fought off the lecherous advances of those three hooligans. Women swoon at the mention of his name and faint as he passes by."

Bart flushed, "Oh shut up you two, you were both there and you know that isn't how it went!" He reached for the pitcher himself, suddenly in need of something stronger than water.

Walter chuckled, shaking his head as his shoulders rocked. "I do envy your comradery, as a knight I do enjoy fraternity but nothing like what you five seem to have." He gazed into the crimson contents in his grasp, "Sometimes I wonder what it would have been like if I had not joined the knighthood. Suppose I had joined up with a company for hire instead, I spent most of my days practicing or training with my brothers and sisters in the garrison. This is the first time I have ever been on a true mission myself, and the one person who I was responsible for looking out for died right in front of me because of a decision I made." The knight pulled out the oil-skin-wrapped letter he had taken off of the bodies along the northern road, "And the only answers I have so far as to why he died are written in a bloody code, of all things."

Bart and Armen looked at each other uncomfortably, unsure what to say. Armen hesitantly broke the silence, "Well, it might not be our place to say, Bart and I have worked together the better part of a few years now. We have lost friends and seen things that most people would rather not mention let alone witness, but my old man used to say that each of us needs to find peace in our own way. Some find religion, others drink, but you can drown in both. But someone else once told me that any mortal who would dare question the will and workings of the gods or believe that their actions alone could turn the course of time in their own image, is a fool of the highest order."

Bart looked quizzically at the large warrior, "That sounds far too intelligent for the usual company you keep! Are you keeping a secret philosophical side hidden from me, you lummox?"

Armen chuckled waving both hands before him, "No, no, it's just something an old man said to me once when I was a young boy on a journey with my father. He had taken me to visit the Garrison of The Order to pay our respects to the new Grand Master, and this old man was staying there as a guest. My father had me learn history and philosophy, or try to, during that summer. What I remember most was the little quips and phrases he would utter, and the tricks he could do with coins and butterflies."

Walter's eyes narrowed, rubbing the silver medallion under his thumb, "I was under the impression you were the son of a minor knight, Armen. What business would your father have in sending you off to The Order for an education? Some noblemen would pay a fortune for the privilege even to grace those sacred halls."

Armen shrugged, "My family has always had close ties with the holy knights. From what my father told me, it stems from an oath one of my far-flung ancestors made to Palthanos in exchange for victory in battle. The long and short of it was, even if we never joined The Order, we would honor their tenants and swear to aid them on the field should ever the need arise. And while our lands have never been the richest or the most abundant, we tithe what we can. In exchange, each Grand Master has forged a bond with the patriarch of the Bardiche House and provides education, training, and a place of refuge should it be needed. It has been that way for the better part of a century, or so I am told." The blond knight nodded, listening in silence to Armen's story.

Bart mulled over the revelation, swirling the contents of his cup as he gestured at Armen seated down from him, "And how much of this education took hold?"

"Not a damn bit of it!" Laughed the tall warrior.

Laughter filled the small chamber, a welcome sound for Bart who had still yet to believe he had returned to a place where the sound seemed almost foreign. As he sat by the table facing the low fire letting the warmth seep into the soles of his sore feet and tired bones, he leaned back reminiscing on memories long forgotten. The guest house was by far more comfortable than the burlap and linen tents they had stayed in during the late autumn campaign which had brought him north as a young boy in the service of Sir Callen and his retinue, there had been a more somber atmosphere at that time. As the swordsman gazed into the flickering flames dancing in the stone fireplace, he could almost see the waving banners of knights and lords who had been called to muster in those far-flung days to fight back the tide of death that had swept their shores. It was nothing short of a wonder that the city, which now seemed so full of life as they passed through earlier, had been on the brink of extermination five-some-odd years ago. Perhaps it was true that time was the healer of all wounds. Lost in his thoughts, Bart hardly heard the knock from the doorway as a steward announced his presence. The man was clean-shaven and dressed in fine green robes lined with mink fur topped with a soft red cap decorated with a broach at the center.

The man bowed politely as he addressed the group, "My lord, Timmon Firbank, master of the estate and castle of Twin Rivers begs you attend him in his council chambers within the hour, I shall send someone to escort you in due time, gentlemen." Having said his piece, the steward bowed once more and departed before anyone could say otherwise or impose any question.

Armen sighed, slapping both knees as he stood, "Well, I suppose I will just have to take that bath now."

"You are the most in need of one," chuckled Thrax, "I have been smelling those creature's guts on you since we left the pass."

There were fresh clothes and warm towels made available for everyone. Courtesy of the steward no doubt, thought Bart as he pulled on the blue tunic and fastened it with his sword belt. As he adjusted the sword at his hip, a slight cough caught his ear, he turned to see Lorena standing at the door to his chamber. She was wearing a flowing red dress embroidered with white floral patterns along her bosom and along the shoulders along the flowing sleeves which flared out like spring lilies following the curves of her waist and breast with flowing grace. He would have laughed at how uncomfortable the mage looked in such fashion had she not been absolutely stunning. It was as though she had stepped out of a portrait hanging in the halls of some nobleman's gallery.

Lorena's face blushed at his gaze, "I must look like a complete fool, don't I?"

Bart was almost lost for words, "No, it's just, I've never seen you dress quite like that before."

Lorena sidled up to him, looking up into his eyes with her hands clasped before her waist. "Well don't get used to it, I can't breathe in this damn thing. And if I even tried to cast a spell right now I couldn't because the handmaids took my spell component pouches and put them away."

The pair made their way to the foyer, the others had already dressed and were waiting along with a guard by the door when they approached. Della had also been forced into similar attire. The elf now wore a gown as green as spring leaves decorated with embroidered silver leaves that wove their way upward from the hem to her bodice. Della's gown had been low-cut at the shoulders in the style preferred by ladies in the eastern provinces with a pronounced décolletage that enhanced the elven warrior's bosom drastically. Much to the pleasure of Armen who stood next to her wearing red leggings and a yellow quilted pourpoint decorated with small bone buttons up the front. Thrax had forgone any garment offered to him, aside from a large woolen chaperon which had been dyed a light blue with white tassels along the brim and crown. The knight, Walter, now wore his full steel armor for the field campaign with the addition of a flowing grey cloak emblazoned with the sigil of the cloud knights; a griffin with claws raised to the heavens.

The group made their way along the stone path along the courtyard and through the halls of the castle proper, past rows of armor and trophies from hunts and military campaigns from lords both present and past. The decor was elegant, but there was also a note of frugality. There were no statues, very few paintings, and almost nothing on display had been inlaid with precious stones or metals aside from a few weapons that showed use in battle long passed. The doors to the council chambers stood open, and Bart could see the figure of young Firbank standing alongside a much older man dressed in fine blue robes. The two were in discourse with a pair of steel-armored knights with white cloaks, and seated to the side was an ancient figure with a flowing grey beard dressed in muted tones of brown and green, a large floppy hat clasped in his hands as he spoke in lowered tones amongst the assembly. On entry, the group awaited in silence, hearing the exchange as it passed.

The old man tapped his hand on his knee as he spoke, "It is only a matter of time, Lord Firbank, the signs are all here. The attacks along the northern roads, the sightings of hordes in the Hinterlands to the west, spies and assassins in our midst taking action on behalf of those unknown to us, silence from the Kingdoms of Almach, and now the declaration of the heir by the king. I urge you to reconsider your position, this is not a time to hole yourself away behind your high walls and wait out the storm, the storm is here!"

"I appreciate your council, master." The lord of Twin Rivers replied, "But all of this is merely conjecture. And as I have said before, I will say again, if the heir still lives then it is my solemn duty to swear fealty, but I will not risk my domain by sending my troops where they may or may not be needed. They are of better use here in the north to answer the coming threat, as you said, the storm is indeed here."

"The storm is not just in the north, great lord." Cried the wizard, "It is also in the halls of the King's council! It thunders through the halls of his palace and reaches far to the borders of Almach and the sand-swept plains of Vex-Tol-Rak. The threat from the Hinterlands is certain, yes, but it is the unseen threat from within that will tear down our foundations! That is why I must urge you to support The Order now!"

Lawrence Firbank stepped forward, his eyes narrowed, "I will respectfully ask you to keep a civil tongue in your head when speaking to the Lord of Twin Rivers, Master Wizard. You may be an honored guest while within these walls, but it would suit you best if you did not find your welcome short-lived." He looked up, finally noticing Bart and his companions. "But as for the matter of the threat along the northern roads, father, may I present to you Bart of Troutsmouth and his company along with Sir Walter of the Cloud Knights. I believe they might have better knowledge of what we are discussing first-hand." He waved at the group, ushering them forward to join them before his father.

Lord Firbank regarded the group with interest, "I understand that you are responsible for the safe return of my children, for that you have my utmost gratitude." His eyes lingered on the massive naga now coiled in his presence, "I will say, it is a rare sight to see a son of the Southern Sands this far north. But you are all most welcome, the hospitality of my house is yours. Forgive my bluntness, but the current state of affairs demands we dispense with further pleasantries. What can you tell us of what occurred?"

Bart detailed everything that had come to pass, how he and the others had been hired to dispel the attacks along the road, how the attack had unfolded, and the nature of the creatures that they had slain. How the creatures moved, fought, and died by their hands. Walter also filled in what had happened following their departure, the state of the road, the ambush by a group of cloaked assassins, and the death of his comrade. All the while, the golden-haired knight rubbed a small silver medallion between his fingers, passing sideways glances toward the others as he spoke.

"You mention that you desire to find the heir as well, Lord Firbank," said Walter, still clutching the medallion in his grasp, "if you would pardon my insolence, but do I have your word as a lord and noble, loyal to the crown and our kingdom that you desire their well-being? That no harm should come to them should you find him?"

The high lord was taken aback, an expression of shock passing over his features. "You have my word, good knight. There is nothing to forgive, if you have any word as to whence this man could be found then I urge you to speak."

The knight stepped forward presenting the medallion and letter to Lord Timmon, "This is medallion was presented to me at the tourney after my victory by King Merrick the Third himself. You will see that his image is upon the face. If you were to examine this, my lord, you may find that the heir might very well stand here amongst us in this very room." The knight placed the round silver object in the lord's hand, "And I suspect that this letter which I took from one of the assassins who set upon me and my companion along the road holds more proof to my suspicion should this not suffice, Lord."

Solon coughed slightly, looking quizzically at the blond knight as he retrieved the letter from his grasp. The wizard looked over the series of lines and dots with curious interest, "Surely you do not mean to suggest that you are the lost heir, young man? Such a claim is hardly in good taste, given the current state."

Walter shook his head, "I make no such claim, good sir, however I do have reason to believe that the man I was dispatched to find by my captain, under the orders of Commander Zulla, now stands before us." He walked back towards Bart and the others, standing in shock from the news. He stopped short of where they stood and turned to face the rest of the assembly, placing his hand on the man's shoulder. "This man bears, I believe, every resemblance of our good king. He is of the right age and comes from a family well connected to the kingdom, he has been educated in the arts of war and higher learning as well as governance. I present Armen, of house Bardiche."

Bart stared at the tall warrior open-mouthed along with the rest of his companions. The spearman could only stammer and stare back in return, the claim having rocked the five of them to their core.

Lord Firbank looked down at the medallion now in his grasp, walking over to Armen as his gaze passed from one to the other, comparing the visage against the warrior's own. "Turn your head, if you would my lad, I wish to see something." Armen obliged, turning his head to one side and then the other as Lord Firbank held up the silver medallion alongside. The nobleman turned to the others, who stood just as shocked as the rest at the potential revelation. "Tell me, Armen, did your father or mother ever give you something? A ring, perhaps?"

Armen shook his head vigorously, "No, my lord. They never..." he paused, a look of realization on his face. Armen slowly reached under his tunic for the small silver chain adorned with a silver charm ringed in gold. Emblazoned on it was a hawk, wings spread as if in flight. "My mother's friend did give me this when I came of age, she said it was for protection and to never take it off."

The old wizard coughed, waving the parchment held in his gnarled fingers. "As for this letter, Lord Timmon, it is a rudimentary code popular amongst spies and cutthroats. I have several examples of such messages myself, so reading such a thing is trivial for me." He handed off the letter to one of the Holy Knights nearby who, in turn, placed it in young Lawrence's hand. "It details two targets by name, one of whom is indeed the young man standing before you."

Lord Firbank's eyes locked on the small pendant, tears filling his eyes as he looked up into Armen's own. "I know that necklace, it belonged to our late Queen Eliza, gods keep her." He grasped the young man's shoulders, "Welcome, my prince," Lord Firbank then turned, beckoning his son forward, "Send word to Commander Zulla, tell him the heir is found and safe within the walls of our estate. Request his immediate support and any reinforcement he can muster for us to depart once we are able."

*Chapter*

# TEN

# HORDE

Amongst the tents and yurts on the far side of the encampment screams of the enraged and the dying filled the air along with the scent of fresh blood. Marguk raised his black-steel axe and brought it down on the skull of a shrieking goblin that lay at his feet with a vicious gash across its chest. The smaller creature's head split open like ripe fruit spilling matter and blood with fragmented segments of its skull across the churned earth. Around the great chieftain, his warriors were making quick work of their foe, limbs, blood, and severed heads lay strewn across the encampment. Some had wisely chosen to surrender, tossing down their weapons and groveling before the might of the Wolf Clan as they mowed down their comrades like chaff.

"Kor-Nash! Face me you coward!" The towering orc cried above the clash of arms and bodies, his axe still wet and dripping from the blood of those he had slain. From amongst the throng of warriors locked in battle, the Long Fang chief stalked forward wielding his iron club. He too was covered in the remnants of the slain, his eyes glowed with rage and battle-lust as he shoved his way through the crowd and approached Marguk in answer to the challenge.

The large orc raised his club, pointing it toward his adversary, "Come then, little wolf pup, the worms, and crows cry out for your flesh! I shall give them such a feast as there will never be a famine for the vultures again!"

Slowly the two circled each other, each appraising the other as they gradually closed the distance. Around the two hulking warriors, the mele had died down, Long Fang and Wolf Clan warriors turned their attention to the duel unfolding. Marguk eyed his opponent's iron club warily, it had been rough-forged, molded with round studs along the head. If he tried to block that thing with his wood-shafted steel axe it would certainly shatter his own weapon, and he had seen the Long Fang chieftain use that strategy many times over their past encounters. This fight, Marguk knew, had been long coming. Eventually one of them would need to die to end this feud. With a boisterous roar, Kor-Nash leaped towards the smaller warrior, his club swinging from over his head and down at Marguk's exposed skull. Despite his massive size, Marguk hopped nimbly back and brought his two-handed war axe in a wide swing from behind his right shoulder aimed at his opponent's thigh. The blow would have easily cut straight through the bone like a sapling had the large orc not deftly stepped aside, blocking the axe head with the solid mass of iron. Within the same motion, Kor-Nash leaped once more, propping his full weight atop the iron club which he used to lever himself into a flying double-legged kick into Marguk's chest. The Wolf Clan chief staggered back, catching his breath between coughs. Sensing the opportunity, the Long Fang warrior rushed in, swinging the iron club at their sputtering face. A cloud of sand and dirt shot out from Marguk's foot, blinding the massive orc. He clawed at his eyes, desperate to clear his vision. The chieftain charged in, swinging the black steel axe head up across his foe's chest. The blade cut deep, exposing flesh and layers of fat as blood-powered out from the gaping wound. Marguk spun, following the momentum of his strike and continuing the motion in a downward chop into their shoulder, just missing the arteries of the neck. He could feel bone shatter and break from the force as the dark steel caught in Kor-Nash's flesh. He lifted his foot, kicking the larger free from his weapon, the Long Fang chieftain collapsed back onto the blood-stained earth, his iron club lost and forgotten from his grasp.

Marguk towered over his bloodied opponent, axe raised over his head, "Looks like you will be feeding the worms, just as you promised!"

With that, the chieftain brought down his axe once more, cleaving the fallen orc's head clean from his shoulders.

Roars of victory filled the air around him as Marguk lifted the severed head up for all to see, Wolf Clan warriors stamped their feet and cheered mightily, hammering shields and chests as they cheered his name. The defeated now knelt in the blood and dust, their weapons cast aside as they awaited their fate. Under the laws of the hill tribes, they now sat at the mercy of Marguk and his tribe. The orc chief reveled in his victory, spinning slowly as he showcased his trophy before all who bore witness.

The victorious chief then addressed the crowd, "Long Fangs, you fought bravely. You are all fine warriors, but no longer will you have to wallow in the despair of following a weak chieftain, a foolish chieftain! Kor-Nash had his chance to make amends, instead, he dragged you and your kin into needless bloodshed! I will do no such thing! I take you as my warriors. I take your mates and offspring as our own! Your slaves, possessions, and weapons will remain in your hands. But the name 'Long Fang' I bury with your fallen chief, from this day until the last I name you wolves!"

Those who had knelt in defeat now leaped to their feet, weapons raised, and those who had once faced each other as foes now stood side-by-side as brothers and sisters. As he raised his blood-stained hands before the crowd, Marguk took mental stock of this conquest. Many were now wounded, and nearly the same number now lay dead from both sides. Even still, his tribe now potentially stood as the largest clan amongst the children of Gog. His gaze passed over the array of corpses strewn across the torn-up dirt. The image of Susalla raising the corpse from the dead earlier filled his mind. Even in death, they would serve him.

Sula approached her brother, her face twisted with worry and suspicion. She wore the regalia of the temple of Gog, the robes a stark contrast amongst the fur and leather-clad warriors in her midst. Those whom she passed bowed their heads in respect and reverence for her position, while their chieftains may stand as the embodiment of their god's strength the priesthood stood as his will. By her hand, she led on a long chain the collared form of Gamona. The dwarf still wore her blood-stained leather armor, but the sword had been confiscated.

As the enslaved dwarf was tugged lightly along, she caught a glimpse of the few curt nods of begrudging respect from the towering green-skinned warriors. This foreign land was filled with surprises, how was it that as a slave bound in service to the orcs, she had garnered more respect and acknowledgment for her accomplishments than she ever did as a free woman in her homeland? The contrast almost filled her with confusion and rage as she followed her captor along.

The Orc priestess bowed before her brother, her chief, before speaking. "My chieftain, I congratulate you on your great victory. As we discussed before, I have brought the slave as you wished, for you to do with as you please before all who stand here, and in the sight of the great night's eye of Gog in celebration."

Gamona looked up, shocked at what she had heard. Her mind raced as her eyes darted around, looking at the fanged smiles and expectant faces surrounding her as she stood bound before her master. Panic filled the dwarf's heart as she felt the massive green warrior approach and tower over her, she could feel her heart suddenly race as she felt his firm grasp take hold of the chain attached to her collar and pull her forward to stand before him. Wild thoughts filled her mind as flashes of what may happen to her filled her thoughts in an overwhelming torrent.

Marguk gazed down, smiling at the captured dwarf maiden bound before him then turned to face the gathered throng. "Brothers, sisters, warriors of the Wolf Clan, you all recognize the one here before you! This one has served me well, she has fought well for the clan, she has killed for the clan, and she has bled for the clan! Perhaps this slave deserves a reward for her service, what say you?" Roars of approval rang out, feet stamping in the dirt and dust as horns of ale and airag rose up, flinging their contents like a light rain. "It would seem you are in agreement then," Marguk looked back down at the dwarf, his fangs jutting out in a proud smile as he gazed down at his captive still held firm by the chain in his grasp.

Gamona yelped in surprise as she felt the clawed hands of Sula reach in from behind her, tearing open the fastenings of her leather armor leaving her exposed before her master and the now howling assembly.

Her hands quickly clasped over her exposed breasts, seeking some modicum of decency given her predicament. This was it; this was what she feared would happen, what else could she have expected from these barbarians? Tears welled in her eyes as she felt her master's firm hands reach out and lift her chin to face him. She gazed into the orc's dark eyes and was shocked to see there was no hint of malice or blood-fueled lust within them. Seemingly satisfied the orc chief nodded and turned to wave forward two others from the crowd, a pair of goblin females clad in furs. One carried a bowl made from the skull of presumingly a slain enemy filled with a dark blue liquid, the other held in her grasp a long thin blade, too delicate for even carving the roasting meat on the fires around her.

Marguk towered over the dwarf, his voice lifted for all to hear. "Gamona, I name you 'Beast Slayer' and you will be marked as befits your title. I claim you as a warrior of the Wolf Clan, and you will bear the mark as your brothers and sisters." The surrounding warriors lifted their fists, howling in approval of the words.

As the two goblins approached, Sula grabbed the dwarf's arms and forced them down to her sides, holding Gamona in place before the pair as she watched the thin blade dip into the thick liquid, coating the steel. She bit her lip, drawing a faint trickle of blood as the goblin's deft hands pressed the point into the flesh across her upper chest, rapidly pricking and drawing out the pigment beneath the dwarf's skin as the pattern emerged. Between the deft fingers of the goblin, the needle hammered home again and again, the pain slowly turned into a strange numbness for the young dwarf. She felt her mind swim lethargically, focusing on nothing but the steel blade and the firm grasp of the orc priestess on her small frame. Had she not been held up, Gamona may very well have passed out from the ordeal. After what seemed an eternity, the blade withdrew from her flesh and this time, it did not return to continue.

Gamona looked down at her chest, her breast heaving from the exertion, as the goblin reached out with a scrap of linen and wiped away the faint trickles of blood from across Gamona's skin to reveal the pattern which now stood proudly over her upper chest from one shoulder to the next. Below her neck, centered above her breasts now sat a bold wolf's paw flanked on either side by a series of rings which resembled a thick chained necklace. One of the rings had been filled in solid, the others stood empty and unfilled. Unsure of what to do or say, she stood as firmly as she could, fighting the urge to grasp at the wound inflicted on her before the horde.

Marguk reached out, clasping her shoulder with his massive green hand, "Gamona Beast Slayer, you have earned your first victory." His finger prodded lightly at the filled ring tattooed on her chest. "If you should fill every ring, then by the beard of Gog, and before all those here to witness, I will grant you your freedom. So once again I command you; fight well."

Raucous cheers of 'Beast Slayer, Beast Slayer!' filled the encampment, and roused within the reborn girl a fire which she had only felt on the sands of the fighting pits. Pride swelled in her chest as she gazed up at her master and smiled, "I will kill them all."

As the evening drew ever into the night, the clan laid out a feast, even those who had once born the title of 'Long Fang' now drank and sang alongside their new fellow clan members. There was roasted meat and plenty of wine, ale, and potent airag all around. After collecting the dead and the wounded, they had erected a larger open-sided canopy where the wounded now lay under the care of wise women, shamans, and what few slaves there were that possessed some manner of healing knowledge. The scent of herbs and incense along with the muttered prayers to the Far-Seer filled the space.

Those who had moved beyond their skills were soon moved over to the rows of corpses that lay outside the encampment. There the sorceress stood, basking in the evening light as she muttered silently to herself, lost in the performance of her strange foreign rituals. Gamona stood with her by command of her master, Marguk. The freshly branded warrior stood armed with her short sword and clad in her leathers which had been altered to display her new brand fully. The gentle breeze felt cool on her skin which still burned from the ordeal as her eyes passed over the strewn bodies, the dark-haired witch had insisted that the limbs of those that could be found be reunited with the deceased. The female dwarf had looked on in revulsion as Susalla had passed from one to the other, covering each in strange flowing script painted in blood across their foreheads, chests, and limbs. Between the rows of bodies, she had also drawn out the same language in the dust with the end of a long stick which she continuously dipped in a bucket filled with blood from several boars and chickens from the cooking tents.

"This is blood magic?" asked Gamona, her face twisted in disgust as she watched the witch continue her macabre work in silence, "I have my doubts that my master would approve."

Susalla laughed, still focused on her work, "Oh, young girl, what care do you have whether your master approves or disapproves of something not done by your hand? Surely just being chained to him in service for no more than a few days has not led you to believe you may know his heart? Or is it that in such short a time you have found a strange fondness for your master?"

The dwarf blushed, unsure how to respond. True, she might now be a slave to the Wolf Clan chieftain, but here she had discovered a side of herself she had never known. Here she had found the inner warrior, the champion, the victor. Marguk had chosen her! A silly young dwarf girl from beyond the Burning Sea. The fresh ink adorning her chest still burned as she gently caressed the strange patterns granted to her by her master. For the first time in her young life, she had discovered purpose, a goal that she could work towards with no thought of compromise. Somewhere deep within she felt a strange sense of pride from having been marked as one of them, the prospect of having something to earn and achieve fulfilled a longing the young dwarf girl from beyond the burning sea had never known needed fulfillment.

The sorceress straightened herself, satisfied in her preparations. Under Gamona's watchful vigil, Susalla lifted her hands over the collected bodies arrayed before her. A chill passed through the dwarf's body, causing her to shiver and clutch at the hilt of her blade involuntarily. It felt as though the very air was now so heavy that each breath came at greater effort. Her eyes stung from the wind that arose around the taller human female, her black hair wiping around from the unseen force that had answered her call. The same tendrils of dark smoke arose from amongst the corpses, tracing the intricate patterns drawn over dirt and flesh alike. Near Gamona's feet lay the corpse of a goblin that had lost an arm, to her horror she saw the smoke form thin threads and began sewing itself into the wound, drawing the severed limb ever closer to its needed place. The same thing was happening with other limbs and heads which slowly became whole under the power of the raven-haired sorceress. A faint glow filled the myriads of lifeless eyes, pockmarking the darkness with an eerie glow from the lifeless orbs.

From the perimeter of the tents, Marguk joined the two as he looked out over the mass of rising blue-grey corpses that stood silently before them. "I still have my doubts about just how well they can fight after you raise them from their rest. How do I know that they can even live up to the task?" The orc chieftain paused, "Maybe that was a poor choice of words, are they even alive?"

Susalla smiled gently, turning her back on her new creations. "They do live, great chief, but not in the way we mortals understand life. As for just how effective they can be in battle, I would ask if this answered your doubts." She pulled out a small white orb, no larger than both of her hands put together. As she presented the object to Marguk the sorceress waved her finger across the pale surface which mystically formed a haze-filled image deep within its face. The orc chieftain, along with an equally mystified Gamona, stared deep into the swirling orb as the scene unfolded before them. Shadowy, blue-skinned creatures lunged wildly at armored figures desperate to protect a line of white carriages on some far-off road amid a deep wood. There was no sound from the orb itself, but the two observers could hear their screams and cries within their minds. Bodies were rendered to shreds beyond recognition as the creatures tore into the fray like wild dogs.

The sorceress, pleased she had made her point, withdrew the orb once more amongst the folds of her robes. "This was but a few days ago, I acquired an array of slaves, and performed the ritual as you have seen. I sent them eastward to wreak havoc upon the lands of Maroth, even now our enemies whisper in fear, unsure of what plagues their land. If we send these servants before the horde, all you need do is clean up what survivors remain from their rampage. They do not sleep, never rest, and their hunger is never abated. They are like locusts who feed upon the flesh of those whom their master commands."

"Their master, meaning you." Accused Marguk, his mind still mulling over the prospect of the two score creatures now standing listless before him. All hints of what and who they had once been had been stripped away, replaced with the puppet-like lifeless gaze of the dead.

"I am no more their master than I am of the rising or setting of the sun, great chief. I am but a vessel for the will of the Far-Seer, and these creatures are tools of his will as are we all." Susalla's voice was level, without any hint of deception as she waved her hand across the undead throng. "I merely offer up their bodies as vessels to be filled. Once that has been done all that remains is to provide guidance."

Gamona's face twisted with skepticism, "With all respect, master, what more will forty or so of these things accomplish? They do not appear to be able to use weapons, and they are mindless in battle."

"Who said these were the only ones we had been granted?" The sorceress smiled softly, as she lifted her hand to the star-filled sky, a haunting cry could be heard from the surrounding mountains far to the northern horizon. It echoed boundless across the plains without measure, like a single voice carrying a thousand empty souls from graves torn asunder. "By your word, my chief, they will sweep across the lands before your tribesmen. You need only give the command."

Marguk stared, jaw agape as he listened to the faint cry. In his mind, he could see the mass of pale-eyed corpses writhing and standing en masse awaiting his word. "Send them, Susalla. Let them feast on the flesh of my enemies. Give me a war!"

The camp roused with motion in haste, tents were displaced and tied down to pack animals or carts and lined up along the train at the rear of the many columns which now began to form in the open Plains of Korb. A sense of anticipation ran through the many assorted tribes which now set aside their differences under the command of the new War Master. Marguk had moved swiftly, once those who had stood opposed to any move he could make had been disposed of, there had been little in the way of resistance amongst the other clans.

From atop the large wagon where he stood, the orc chief could see the myriads of once-opposed clans and tribes now unified with one common goal; conquest. No longer would his people have to scrape in the dirt or tear away at the scraps of what little they could scavenge from the poorer reaches of those too weak to resist the pitiful small-scale raids which they had subsisted on until now. He would lead his people east and conquer those lands in full! He would create a new home for his kind forged in the blood of his enemies.

A familiar voice reached Marguk's ear from above the scene, "Hail, brother!" Horka of the Dead Crows called out, his face and torso covered in dark ash in the custom of his clan. "It's about time someone got these snot-nosed babes working together."

The war chief smiled wide, bearing his yellowed fangs, "Well met, Horka. Careful that none suspects you and your clansmen for one of the walking corpses, you are ugly enough already. Have your scouts departed as I asked?"

The younger chief nodded. His wolf riders, goblins who raised the beasts themselves, had departed at first light shortly after he had received the command. From anyone's best reckoning, it would take them four days to reach the western banks of the Red Horse at the earliest, maybe five. What none had accounted for was the speed of the thralls which had been raised by Susalla. Their unnatural gait had shocked those who witnessed them in motion, they moved with a speed unnatural and unnerving. Lumbering, jerking limbs had carried the mass of unknown numbers far over the horizon without warning before any word could come from the guards who stood watch around their encampment. Dread had passed through their souls, for it was then that they knew that the witch had placed them in the mountains and foothills all this time, and none had known. How long would they have lasted against them had the witch decided to turn them upon the clans? If Marguk had fallen, how long until she had set them upon the tribes in revenge? The only consolation was that they were on their side.

But now the entirety of Gog's chosen children gathered and joined together as one people. Their feuds were forgotten for the time being as Marguk now stood at their head, uniting them in one cause with a single ambition. The old and those too young to fight would follow along in the wagon trains along with the slaves and supplies. None would remain in the Hinterlands after this was over, the time of the orc had come.

As the horde moved slowly eastward dust rose up from the mass of trampling feet, the earth shook from the sheer size of the force Marguk now led on his campaign, a swell of pride filled the great chief's chest, he had dreamed of this day since he was a young budding warrior. So many years ago, before he was even a chieftain, he had seen visions of his people crossing the great river and taking those green lush lands for their own. He would keep his promise to his people and to Gog Far-Seer, he would flay the pink skins and the weak humans and lesser races that lived beyond the Giant's Spine, he would crush their stone cities and burn their villages of wood. He would take their lands and riches for his own, make slaves of those who survived, and flay the hides of their lords and kings as an offering to the gods.

The golden light of morning shone on the smooth water's surface. Seated along the banks of the Red Horse, a young boy sat with his father. Fishing rods in hand, a basket of the morning's catch between them, it was as calm and peaceful as any other. As the fisherman lazily watched the painted knob of cork bobbing gently on the water at the end of his line, the sudden splashing of water upriver tore his attention from what had been a peaceful morning. To their horror, the father and son saw the mass of clawing, stuttering creatures lashing at the deep waters in an effort to cross. The father stood, grabbing his son by the arm he pulled the boy away from the riverbank and backed away from the commotion, his eyes fixed on the strange creatures that now streamed over the rolling foothills on the other side of the water headed straight for him. He crouched low into a thicket of rushes, pulling his son as close as he could and covering the boy's mouth with his hand. His palms could feel the hot tears flowing from his son's eyes, the poor boy was too scared even to make a whimper, thank the gods.

The line on his rod snapped taught, pulling the long pole out into the water with a sudden and violent splash. To the man's horror, the sudden noise drew the attention of a half dozen of the beings close to shore who jerked their heads with a motion unnatural amongst the living. Their haunting eyes pierced through the veil of morning mist which had clung so lightly over the morning dew. He prayed, wished with all his soul for that fog to thicken, to shield him and his offspring from the devils that now seemed to hunt him and his boy. They were almost halfway across the water by now, and more were slowly making their way down the banks from the western hills. The man risked lifting his head just a bit, to try and better take account of how many of them there may be. His blood ran cold as his eyes filled with the sight of the dark mass forming and flowing over the western horizon. The sun still lay low over the man's shoulder but not even the sun's warmth could give respite to his fears.

The scream of a woman ripped through the still morning air, pulling the creature's attention away from the area where the man hid in the tall rushes with his sun, they turned upstream and lunged wildly in the direction of the voice, their demonic howls and screams filling the air with a tumult of death and terror. The boy cringed at the sound, a soft sob escaping his muffled lips. As he peeked through a gap in the tall foliage, he could see the grey-skinned beings rushing away up the shoreline towards the collapsed figure of a woman from the village. Poor girl, she had brought her basket of washing for the morning. The garments now lay scattered in the grass and dirt near the shore soaking up the blood which now flowed from her ravaged body.

It had happened so suddenly that he had only heard the woman cry out briefly, but now there was nobody between these things and the rest of the village, he had to do something. The fisherman turned to his son, a boy of only eight years, there would only be one chance.

"Listen, boy, you need to get to the village and let the Ealdorman know to get everyone to the castle. Stay in the rushes and keep low, and no matter what you hear you don't turn back, and you keep going, can you do that, boy?" The father gripped his son's shoulder, gazing at the green eyes and straw-colored hair of his freckled son. Their tear-stained face red from fear, the boy nodded in silence. The man smiled softly, embracing the boy in his arms one last time. "Good lad, now go." The boy crouched low, keeping his small frame hidden in the flowing grass and reeds, swiftly making his way along the path toward the outskirts of the village.

The fisherman watched his son proudly, reaching for the small knife he normally used to whittle branches or cut lines from trout's mouths. It was no weapon, but it was all he had at the moment. He moved silently toward the bank, cutting a path opposite to where his son traveled. Satisfied in the distance he had made, the man stood and yelled out at the creatures in defiance, "Hey! You mottle-skinned roaches! I have something for you, you cowards!"

The huddled forms turned from the corpse at their feet, blood staining their fanged moths and clawed hands. The fisherman couldn't even react before they were upon him, he futilely tried to bring up the small blade, to take just one of the beasts with him, to buy some time for his son to make it to the village, to warn the others. Someone had to know, they had to do something! The last thing he heard in the world of the living was the sound of his son's dying screams as the creatures pounced upon him. Death had come for them, and there was no escape.

The small fishing village along the banks of the Red Horse fell into disarray, homes filled with pools of blood that ran like streams into the dirt paths flowing between the small huts and storage buildings. Screams of men, women, and children echoed into the stillness of morning before ending in silence. Only the crows would bear witness to the slaughter, their cries of hunger mingling with the snarls and howls of the ravenous beasts which tore through the small hovels with as much destruction as the fires which soon sprang up from overturned coals from the cooking fires. As the smoke rose into the clear morning, blocking off the light of the golden sun, the shadow of death hung briefly over the small village before moving slowly eastward towards the road.

# ELEVEN

# ʟOYALTY

Captain Eliza sat by the fire at the center of her encampment. In her hands, she read the collection of reports which had come by rider and raven from across the area of her search. Once she had received word from the garrison of the death of Rolfe the Younger, the Cloud Knight Officer had dispatched riders to round up the scattered remnants of her forces to consolidate her strength. Her Lieutenant, Theodoric, stood alongside checking off the names of those who had returned. Of the eighty riders assigned to the Second Cohort, forty-six had rejoined their ranks. The remaining riders and their mounts would join with the main body north of Arrow Lake which sat almost a full day's flight to the northwest of where she now camped.

"If you don't mind me asking, Ma'am, should we not continue the search here in the central regions before rushing off on the word of a rumor?" The dark-skinned Lieutenant asked, his skin glowing bronze in the light of the dancing flames, only his eyes seemed to hold any light. Had there been no fire, Eliza doubted she would even see him in the darkness of the surrounding copse of trees.

She proffered the unrolled parchment toward her attendant, "The lord of the Twin Rivers does not deal in rumors or gossip, nor does my father. So, if both are sending me messages detailing the same information, with minor differences of course, then I can only take it to be the truth. And if that is the case there is little use for us to remain here searching through the back alleys and stables of these far-flung towns and villages. What's more, we are the closest to the western lands, and I for one wish to hear from Goldhair himself just what happened to our brother-in-arms."

Come the break of dawn, the mass of griffins and their riders took to the skies in force. Soaring ever higher to the safety of the clouds so as to shield their path from prying eyes. They raced northward, over the rolling green hills and golden fields ripe with bounty. The scenery soared ever past them beneath their passing, all haste had been issued, no rest unless absolutely necessary, this was a forced flight. Only their success mattered.

Rolling in the sky-saddle of her griffin, Tempest, Captain Eliza, daughter of Commander Sulla, reminisced on the conversation she and her father had before her departure back in Maroth. He had sworn her to secrecy before revealing the hidden parts of her mission, while the other officers had been informed of the heir's existence, the nature of the former queen's demise had been left out. Assassins have killed the queen, and now shadowy figures have slain one of her men? Were they connected, had there been a mistake? Why had they attacked two riders on the road? There were too many unknown factors for the captain, her brow furrowed beneath her helm. There was no worse feeling in command than to have to take action without knowing the full picture of what you were leading your forces into. The only consolation she could find was that Lord Firbank had apparently kept this information from all save Commander Zulla, her father. It made sense, The Lord of Twin Rivers and the Commander of the Cloud Knights had forged a strong friendship over the years, even inviting each other to balls or feasts from time to time. Her thoughts turned to Lord Firbank's son, Lawrence, he was a sight to be sure. They had danced during a feast at Hammerpeak just a few years ago, Commander Zulla had insisted that she forgo the armor and regalia in favor of that flowing gown for the evening. She had felt so foolish, standing there in that flowing dress, her tanned and muscled arms a stark contrast to other girls her age. But the younger Firbank had not jested, inviting her to the floor with such grace that, just for the evening, Eliza had not been the muscle-bound warrior daughter of the knighthood but a lady of stature. A smile cracked across her wind-chapped lips, of course after they had danced the two had stolen off to practice at swordplay in the gardens, the mud stains had never gotten out of that dress.

As the sky darkened, the riders finally made their way to the northern shores of Arrow Lake, bordered by the beginnings of the northern forest known as the Timberglenn. Below her in a small clearing, Captain Eliza could make out the signs of other riders there before them, red and yellow strips of cloth had been tied in a perimeter around the small clearing in the trees, guiding the rest of the cohort to the rendezvous. In pairs, the riders made their way into the clearing and guided their mounts into the surrounding woods to clear the way for others to land. Captain Eliza and her lieutenant came last, landing graciously amongst the boughs. As her mount ruffled his aching wings and preened at the leather straps holding the harness in place, eager to be freed of the encumbrance after the journey, the officer slid down from her seat and patted the beast roughly on his strong flanks. Another rider, also bearing the rank of lieutenant, approached giving a swift salute to the two arrivals.

"Welcome, Captain, Lieutenant Theodoric, I trust your journey was safe and uneventful?" Lieutenant Frig smiled politely as she saluted her fellow officers, her short-cropped black hair and slim build were still covered in the dust from her journey.

Eliza smiled, the lieutenant's appearance had caused her to be mistaken for a boy on more than one occasion, her raucous behavior and penchant for fist-fighting and drinking didn't help matters. Other than that, she was an exemplary officer, which was why Eliza had hand-picked her as her second. Sometimes the men needed someone around to kick them in the ass from time to time and Frig had just the boot to do the job.

"Please tell me we have something to eat here," groaned Theodoric, his face twisted as he rubbed stiff legs and aching shoulders, "all I have had all day has been ration cake and a few stray bugs that slipped beneath my scarf."

Frig bowed, arms wide as she grinned from ear to ear, "A feast fit for a king! But yes, there were a few deer we fell, the men have eaten as well. Given the evening we should make good time if we leave at first light."

The captain's brow furrowed, gazing over her cohort which was engrossed with the raising of tents and feeding of their steeds after the long journey. "No. We leave tonight, tell the men to strike camp, we sleep open-air for now. And everyone is to don full battle plate for the final leg."

"Tonight!?" Lieutenant Theodoric gasped, "With all respect, Ma'am, the men are spent as are the griffins. If we push them too hard before they are ready..."

Capitan Eliza turned to face her subordinates, her eyes glinting like a hawk watching a hare in an open field, "Do you doubt the abilities of the men, or do you doubt my judgment, Lieutenant? Which is it to be?"

The officer froze, unable to tear away from the piercing gaze of his superior. Frig quickly stepped in, saving the poor man from further torment, "What I believe he means to ask, Captain, is you must have some reason as to why?"

The commander of the Second Cohort released her victim, relaxing her gaze as she spoke in hushed tones. "If we move in daylight, anyone with eyes and ears for miles will know that an entire body of knights is moving, in force, and where we are headed. Given the circumstances, we know that there are those who would see us fail in our task. I will not give our enemies the satisfaction or the advantage of knowing our every move. They may already know where we are now, but they must not know where we will be. I want every third man on watch, and once everyone has eaten all of these fires are to be snuffed out. I do not want our presence known any more than it already is. Once the moon has crested the treetops," Eliza pointed eastward into the deepening sky, "I want you, Lieutenant Theodoric, to take ten riders ahead of us towards Twin Rivers and inform Lord Firbank we are to be expected. The rest will follow within the hour."

Both saluted smartly, departing to prepare the men for the coming journey. Theodoric having made a quick detour to snatch a slab of roast from the spit could be seen passing among the men, passing along the word. Eliza beamed inwardly, her ears picked up no grumbles or groans, no sighs of derision or contempt. The atmosphere within the camp was as she had come to expect of her command. Her cohort, The Emerald Dragons, with their green Tabards and plumes were the elite of the knighthood in her eyes. No mission was beyond their skill, no sacrifice unworthy of their cause. As she cast her eyes towards the heavens, she gazed into the sky which quickly filled with pinpricks of light in the deepening sky. What would her father think of her decision? What would he do in this situation? She shook her head, chasing away the scattered doubts, no, this was her command. Her men, her mission. Her father's time had come and gone, she was the commander of the Second Cohort, not some sniveling babe clutching at her father's hand for need of approval at every step. To doubt oneself is to fall victim to the greatest enemy one can face, your own mind.

Her meditations were cut short by the return of the boyish Frig, water skin in one hand and slice of venison in the other. "You need to take a rest as well, Captain, everything is in hand for now. All that remains is to wait." As she handed over the offering the junior officer sat beneath the arms of a wide oak, leaning her back against the rough bark as she stared into the violet sky thin with clouds and shades of blue. "Care to explain what is really going on, Liz?"

Taking a draft of water, the knight captain sat alongside her companion, regarding the food still untouched in her hand. "There are just too many unknowns for my liking, Frig. Was it all a coincidence that Walter and Rolfe were set upon on the northern road? Or were they targeted? The message he sent led my father, the High Commander, to believe this was a calculated ambush. Then there are the carriages for Lord Firbank that were left in ruin on the scene upon the road, the blood and gore but no bodies to speak of aside from the strange beings. He described it as an animal attack of sorts yet calculated as though someone or something had driven them to that end. And all the while we are looking for the heir to our king who none had known of for these past twenty years. I don't know, there is far too much happening at once for me to wrap my head around it all."

Frig nodded along, her eyes watching all the while as her Captain, her friend, availed her troubled thoughts. Stretching her arms back behind her head, she reclined against the bulging trunk at her spine. "Well, you know what I always say when things are too chaotic to focus, just punch the bastard in front of you until they go down then move on to the next one. No point trying to tackle everything all at once, sometimes you have to ignore everything else until they take a swing at you. Once they do, hammer them into the ground until they can't get up again."

"You ought to be a scholar," laughed Eliza, "with wisdom like that you are going to find yourself on the high council before long."

The lieutenant peaked open one eye from where she lay, "Well, as your advisor then, I recommend you eat that before it gets cold and get some rest. It's going to be a hard ride to Twin Rivers through the night if we are to get there."

—◊◊◊—

In the great council chamber within Maroth Keep, Commander Zulla sat resigned in the stiff, wooden-backed chair set along the long oak table. As the droning voices of aldermen, counselors, advisors, and others mingled together with as much unity as could be found in a swarm of bees caught in a thunderstorm, his eyes lazily passed over the long wood timber. Here and there, he could still make out stains of wine and ale from past 'conversations' which the servants had valiantly tried to remove through every means availed to them. How he longed for the battlefield once more, at least there those wielding a blade were standing before you and not behind. The thought of his daughter now out at the head of her command filled him with both the pride of a commander and the worry of a father. Or could it be the other way around? Either way, his daughter had her battle ahead, and now he faced his own, these sniveling, pampered, whining men and women whose self-inflated worth and ego blinded them to anything beyond what would be of their own personal gain. Things had been different when the throne at the head of the long table had not sat vacant, his gaze rested on the long-empty chair, how long had it been since the king had sat in attendance? The ornate carvings on the back, once hidden by the figure of their monarch, had now been burned into memory. The ornate woven form of two serpents coiling about a tree in full plumage with the sun rising above. Or perhaps now that the sun was setting? And the serpents sought to consume those last vestiges of life? The old knight sighed silently to himself as he leaned back, closing his eyes in hopes of drowning out the ramblings of the fools around him.

"Don't tell me that the great Commander Zulla now sleeps while in attendance of the High Counsel, whatever would they say?" Chuckled the voice beside Zulla's ear.

The commander's lids remained closed, determined to shield his gaze as much as possible from the foolishness about him. "Sylvanus, the day I fall asleep in this chamber is the day you sprout wings and fly."

Snorri pulled up a chair beside Sylvanus, joining the two at the table, "I wouldn't mention anything too outlandish like that, Commander, gods know what sort of hair-brained ideas you would give this mad elf."

The elf chuckled dryly, "Funny you should mention that, recently I found a most interesting manuscript. It details a device which, when attached to one's arms, allows..."

"All rise and attend! The King approaches!" The cry from the door tore through the chamber, bringing a stillness none had witnessed since any day Zulla could account. As he and the others in attendance stood, the sound of marching footsteps could be heard echoing from the hall, the measured cadence announcing the approach of the King's Personal Guard, clad in steel plate and mail with barrel helms crested with the royal seal. Each bore a heavy shield across their back and wore a two-handed sword at their waist gilded in silver with red gems in the pommel. In their grasp they carried the royal banners; a sky-blue pennant bordered in gold with twin silver serpents entwined on a black tree with a golden crown above. Between the columns walked King Merrick himself, dressed in his regalia and as stoic and imposing as ever. As his steps breached the threshold, all who stood in attendance bowed low, their gaze transfixed upon the floor in silence.

The aged monarch strode past them all in silence, ascending the raised dais at the head of the table and seating himself upon the throne, he looked over his counsel with practiced authority before addressing them. "Gentlemen, you may be seated. We see our presence comes as no small surprise to most, and many of you might wonder as to why now of all times we must grace you with our presence." King Merrick's gaze passed over the room as those gathered took their seats or shuffled about in silence, vying for a position to better hear his words. "As you well know, we will abdicate our throne on the dawn of the harvest. As such, preparations were made to that end in order to ensure the safety of the heir to return them to the fold and the crown. Commander Zulla dispatched his knights and scouts to the reaches of our lands to that end, and missives to the local gentries were sent on our behalf. We can now confirm, thanks to these efforts, that our heir still lives."

Silent murmurs rippled through the chamber as those gathered took the news in turn, some seemed to find it too astounding to be believed while others sighed in relief at the prospect of royal stability well within their grasp. Commander Zulla's eyes narrowed; jaw locked as he listened intently.

The elven sorcerer leaned over, whispering in his grim neighbor's ear, "Did you inform the king already? Even I had not heard that you had found the heir."

Commander Zulla shook his head, producing a scroll from under the table furtively. "I only got word myself, I had not yet sent word to him as yet for I wished to confirm further details before speaking with him."

Alongside Sylvanus, Snorri shook his head with worry. Leaning over his elven neighbor he hissed at Zulla as loudly as the dwarf dared, "Then where, by the twin hells, did word of this reach the king?" The three looked at each other, eyes widening at the silent realization. "Gods, our goal was for the safety of the heir and the return of them alive to the kingdom and the crown. But that is not the only reason to locate them, there is one other faction that would have the means and resources to find them and learn of their location. Sylvanus," the dwarf grabbed his friend's arm, "you need to leave, now!"

As the elf slowly slid back his chair, the king raised his hand ushering silence to the cacophony which echoed amongst the assembly. "I have also been informed, in addition to these most fortuitous tidings, that for the past two decades, a heinous viper has made their home amongst us. A traitor who, through their actions, facilitated the assassination of our dear Queen Eliza and risked our peace with Almach." The king waved forward one of his guards, the man approached carrying a small cloth bundle wrapped in twine. Along with the reports we have received, evidence has come to light of this treachery from within these very walls! He took the small bundle and, unwinding the bound twine to unfold the cloth parcel, he produced a small vial. Holding it up he displayed the item for all to see. "This vial contains a poison which is so rare only a few could have the knowledge to produce it, fewer still would have the means and resources. It was found amongst the belongings of the one who, according to the reports we have been given, not only produced this poison but also administered it under the guise of treatment!"

Snorri's heart sank in his chest as he gazed upon the same type of vial he had seen within the lockbox in his friend's study. Remnants of a pale blue liquid could be seen within the delicate crystal. Worse still, the sealing twine and stopper were of the same make and design which his friend preferred for his creations. The dwarf cast a sideways glance towards his friend, the elf's face had drained of all color. Shock plastered across his features as though he had seen a phantom appear from the darkest corners of his mind come to life.

The king's face was drawn, emotionless as he spoke, "Sylvanus Chrystalan, High Sorcerer to the Throne of Maroth, I name you traitor of the crown and enemy of the kingdom. I place you under arrest, and you shall be taken hence from this place to the Black Tower, to await my judgment."

Before any protest could be raised, four guards appeared from behind the three companions seated at the table and, not too gently, grabbed the tall elf in their mailed hands and shuffled him out the door with little ceremony through the shocked crowd. Zulla and Snorri could only look on in horror as they watched the elf get dragged away through the throng of counselors and nobles and out the massive oaken doors to the long hall. The commander began to rise instinctively in an effort to follow his comrade, but Snorri held him back.

The dwarf slowly pulled his much taller friend back into their seat as he whispered, "Not here, and not now, my friend. There is nothing we can do if you are also locked in irons." But Snorri's gaze also followed his friend's departure through the doors, even until they closed, cutting off the last views of the flowing blue robes being dragged down the stone floor. It would be nothing short of a miracle if they saw him again now, his mind raced, there had to be an explanation, there certainly was a traitor, but who? He glanced around, taking note of all in attendance as he could, there were most but not all. Of course, most of the higher lords with holdings and lands were not in attendance including Firbank, Bardiche, and Heathridge.

Commander Zulla clenched his fist around the scroll still in his grasp, fingers turning pale from the strain as he stared at the table once more struggling to retain his composure. Taking a slow breath, the man slowly rose from his seat, brushing off Snorri's hand as he turned to face the king seated upon the throne of Maroth. "My king, I beg your grace when I ask, from where did this news arrive? And how certain are we in the validity of these claims of the heir's location?" Zulla could have almost sworn that the king's eyes were tinted with a hint of sadness before they spoke.

Merrick nodded slowly, "Your skepticism is understandable, but we have received word directly from our cousin, Lord Heathridge, that the heir travels to the western holdings near the Hinterlands. He has sent his envoys to escort the prince forthwith on our behalf. But in the meantime, more pressing matters must be attended to, we beg your leave counselors and leave you to other matters. May the gods watch over this council and this kingdom." With that, the monarch rose from his seat and made his way back from whence he had entered, flanked by his retinue through the great doors and down the passages of the palace. Zulla and Snorri, along with all others in attendance, rose and bowed once more as he made his way. Once the sound of the great doors closing shut echoed through the chamber, the two looked at each other with concern in their eyes. The shock of the loss of Sylvanus so suddenly was a blow they could ill afford at this time, along with the sudden developments in regard to the discovery of the heir's location they had yet to discover the man's name or identity as yet.

"It would seem that Lord Heathridge is more informed than we would have been led to believe in these matters, Commander." The old dwarf mumbled, his hand stroking the long wisps hanging from his beard thoughtfully.

Zulla shrugged, "He was just as aware as any of us that the heir lived, it stands to reason he would have the resources to conduct a search himself. He certainly has made a name for himself through commerce and trade, just look at how much he has done with his holdings through the years. And he has been a loyal friend to the crown in all things, even if his temperament is a little... rough."

"Rough would not be how I would characterize the man, Commander. Need I remind you that, until recently, Lord Heathridge was next in line for the crown until events as of late? Or his temperament upon learning of the heir? Did you not find it strange that he sequestered himself once this came to light? Or that he has, not even once, made any effort until now to further the king's wishes to bring the heir home? No, my friend, not everyone in a position of power uses that influence for the good of the realm. You seem to forget, at their core, people are selfish and will use that power and influence to further themselves before the benefit of others always."

Commander Zulla scowled at the prospect, "But that matters little for now, we have lost one compatriot. How long until we lose more? If what you are suggesting is true, then more are sure to follow him to the tower within the week."

The Black Tower was a squat, foreboding structure which stood surrounded by a deep moat in the northern side of the inner walls of the capitol of Maroth, from the battlements of the central keep one could look towards the ominous structure built of darkened stone carved from the great quarry. From a distance it resembled a giant chicken coop, with many barred windows and conical roof tiled in black pitch shingles. In the summers the interior became sweltering, and the winters had been known to cause prisoners to freeze to death before their trial could be set. To be marched over the deep moat through the wooden palisade and under the portulacas was as good as a death sentence for most depending on the season.

Sylvanus' hands were sore and raw from the shackles clamped tightly around his wrists as the shamed sorcerer now sat in the damp cell deep within the bowels of the tower. His feet were bruised and torn from the long walk through the crowded streets leading away from the castle. Crowds had looked on in shock at first, gawking at the sight of the blue-robed elf bound in chains and surrounded by guards. That had soon turned to animosity, jeers and shouts of 'Traitor' and 'Kill the elf' still echoed through his ears. His robes had been torn and splattered from the introduction of rotten fish and fruits, those who had been less kind endeavored to find the closest dung pile and deliver that instead. But the stones had been the worst, children seemed to have an innate fondness for throwing the hard projectiles, competing for who could throw the hardest or hit the most vulnerable target.

These people had cheered his name and sang his praises for years, decades even. If he had walked the street amongst them even a fortnight past, he would have been showered in praise. But this day all he had been met with was screams and threats of the most horrible deaths imaginable. A smoldering flame of rage took hold in the elf's heart, when the plague had ravaged through the slums he had saved hundreds with his potions. When the armies of Almach had encroached into their lands he had devised machines of war to defend their homes. When the drought had struck the land barren, he had provided the very aqueducts that now provided all the water they could ask for. He had built this city and saved it and her people many times over. He had served Maroth and her king all his life, and now he was to be cast aside with no word in his defense?

The prisoner looked about his cell, four walls with no windows save the small aperture set in the solid banded door at one side. He had enough space to lay his head on the floor, so long as he set his head in the corner. The dank stone floor was strewn with thin piles of damp straw which gave off a putrid scent. The smell was the least of Sylvanus' worries. If the axe didn't get him, the damp certainly would. He pulled his ruined blue robes close about him as he set about pushing as much of the dryer straw he could find into a solitary corner facing the door and resigned himself to the long wait ahead. He then set his mind to work, going over what he knew. Lost in his mulling, he hardly observed the silent scraping sound echoing from the stone wall beside him. Glancing over, expecting to find perhaps a rat or some other vermin companion, he could hardly contain his astonishment as he watched a portion of the wall sing inward and disappear into a dark void beyond. A cloaked, shambling figure crawled into his cell, a long wild beard dragging along the floor with a pair of wild green eyes clouded with age peered out from beneath the tattered cloak's hood.

The old man squatted at the entrance and stared at the elf with a crazed glint in his eye as he whispered low, "Well now, here we finally are then. A pleasure to finally meet you in person, Sylvanus Chrystalan, the mad elf of Maroth." A raspy chuckle like a rusty door hinge danced over the visitor's lips.

"If anyone is mad here, I can assure you it would not be me, friend," Sylvanus responded dryly, still trying to regain some sense of control over the rapidly declining situation he was finding himself in. He had half resigned himself to the headsman's kiss upon the block before having his mood so abruptly interrupted.

The old man shook with amusement, like an autumn branch in the breeze. "Oh, so we are friends already then, are we? I would like that so very much if you knew just what that entailed. But I will be kind and leave that for you to decide."

Sylvanus' eyes narrowed, this old man was quickly getting on his nerves, of which he had little supply at the moment. "Decide what?"

The old man cocked his head towards the small opening from whence he had appeared like a phantom. "You can come along like a good lad, throw your fate to the winds of the unknown. Or you can sit here in the damp and dark for what is certain." The old man then produced a black steel dagger, there was little ornamentation on the weapon, but it was clearly well cared for, unlike the one who wielded it. "But know this, a blade may also find your throat within. So then, friend, what are you going to choose?"

"My choices are the executioner's axe or your blade? I see little benefit for me in your offer, old man." Hissed the elf, his fists clenched within the manacles in rage.

The old man deposited the dagger beneath the folds of his cloak once more, his eyes still twisted in a crazed expression. But his face seemed as sober as any man one may meet anyplace else, "Death comes to us all, whether we wait for her or not. What matters is how we greet her when she does enfold us within her tender embrace. Some beg for mercy, the respite of a day or a month, others cry tears of joy. But a small few go kicking and screaming, fighting to the last breath against the inevitable."

Sylvanus pondered a moment, this strange man seemed to be far more than some crazed lunatic living in the walls of the Black Tower. There was a spark, some intrinsic draw that he felt towards the man squatted in his cell. He glanced once more at the maw leading to the void beyond, what could lie within he could not fathom. "Then who are you?"

The crazed man smiled, leaning in conspiratorially to the elf sorcerer bound in chains. "We are the inevitable."

*Chapter*

# TWELVE

# BIRTHRIGHT

Bart sat in silence at the long table set before him and his companions, the grouse on his plate untouched before him. At his side, Lorena drank slowly from her horn mug of mulled wine while they listened and observed the exchange unfolding before them. Having learned the identity of their companion, Lord Firbank had summoned his counselors and all persons of note within the city to feast with them in celebration and welcome. Ladies dressed in fine silks tittered like songbirds amongst opulently adorned guildsmen, merchants, advisors, and anyone of note who the lord of Twin Rivers could bid attend at such short notice.

Poor Armen had been whisked away shortly after the revelations and now sat alongside the lord of the castle, with Lawrence seated on the opposite shoulder. From where Bart sat, the three of them appeared to resemble a pair of nobles holding the poor man hostage. The bald warrior had been dressed again for the occasion, with sky-blue leggings and a doublet of green and black decorated with small silver bells. On his shoulders now sat a long green cloak lined in bear fur, the silver necklace now predominately displayed around his neck along with a gold chain that some merchant had gifted the poor lad. Bart almost found himself chuckling at the display as he watched Armen's wholly uncomfortable demeanor in full display as they fought to remain presentable.

Thrax had become something of a fascination for a few of the well-to-do gentry in attendance, as men and women alike reveled in fascination with their conversation. There had been some gasps of shock, of course, when the four of them had entered to take their places as honored guests.

One of the ladies seated opposite the serpentine warrior leaned forward curiously, her intricately braided red hair gliding softly across her shoulder, "Sir Thrax, I must say we are all so thrilled to meet one from the sand-swept plains of the southern deserts. These mountainous lands are filled with green, and our customs must surely be as foreign to you as your ways are to us. So, I do hope you would take no offense when I ask why you have forgone any, shall we say, conventional attire aside from that wonderful hat." Bart could have sworn he saw the woman's eyes dance greedily over the exposed chest of the Naga seated beside him.

Thrax tilted his head back, engulfing one of the boiled eggs topped with cheese euphorically. "My people have little need or understanding for the mammalian race's need to cover oneself, but since I have come to this land my companions have explained many of your customs. I do try to adapt, such as in the cold winters where I make use of a cloak or furs. But I find such things too confining."

The man seated alongside the red-headed woman nodded understandingly, engrossed in the grouse under his knife. "A fine sentiment, to be sure. To hold on to your own customs in a foreign land is a hard trial, but to expand your knowledge and learn more shows true strength I say."

The woman smiled, nodding in agreement, "Indeed, husband, I am sure Sir Thrax is quite strong to be sure, as you say." Lorena choked on a mouthful of wine, shaking as she tried not to drench the table or those around her. The woman looked over at the quaking elf, concern in her eyes, "Is the wine not to your liking, dear? I am sure we may have something more to your tastes if you wish."

The elf regained herself, smiling politely around the table, "Oh no, the wine is quite exquisite. I lost myself in the flavor of it and rushed too quickly. But as for my friend here, it is true his strength is quite unmatched with a sword in hand. There are few who could withstand his blade."

The woman blushed, fanning herself as she gazed back at the adonis seated opposite. "So then, have you a companion from where you come from, may I ask?" Her fork lazily brushed along the trail of peas upon the ridge of her plate before thrusting into the side of a roasted chunk of carrot which she then gracefully passed between her ruby lips.

Thrax shook his head solemnly, "My people have no custom of restricting ourselves to one another, when the time comes, we gather within one of the pits of Skash-Lomar deep within the heart of our sacred temples and partake of the rituals of the great egg. Because we are all nestlings, born of the same brood. We hold no custom of lineage or parentage; all are raised amongst the brood until we come of age then we embark on our own journey."

The woman's eyes widened, mouth agape as Thrax spoke. "So, the women of your species do they also, well, oh never mind." Her reddened face turned once more to the plate before her as she busied herself with the meal before them.

Bart leaned over towards Lorena; her expression uncaring at the conversation around her. "I have never seen a female of the serpent peoples, makes you curious, doesn't it?" He winced from the sharp jab in his rib from her elbow.

"And you are going to remain so, foul-minded fool. And if I ever find you trying to sneak your way into one of those pits, I am going to leave you to them, they can do as they please with you there if you survive." The mage flicked her short hair back with a huff as she lifted a slice of grouse on her fork.

Lord Timmon rose from his seat, tankard in hand, as he raised it high above those gathered at the long table set in the center of his great hall. "My friends, members of the great guilds of the Twin Rivers and the Northwestern Lands of Maroth. Nobles, Ladies, and Gentry, I thank you for joining us on this most auspicious occasion. As You now know, our prince has been returned to us after twenty long years." He waved his hand over Armen seated alongside, those gathered raised polite cheers of approval, some banging fists and tankards on the long wood surface in a muffled clatter. "You may also know that I had been named as successor by our King Merrick, gods save him and keep him, but those of you who have stood alongside me on the field or on the walls know I have never had such aspirations. My place is here, in the north with you, my friends!" cries of 'Here, here!' rose from a scattering of those seated around.

The Lord of Twin Rivers turned to face Armen, "My liege, I am thankful for your return and your presence here today. You have saved me from a most uncomfortable task, one which I do not envy in the least. But I swear to you, before the gods and all those here tonight, my sword is yours from here until the last. The Twin Rivers will stand firm against the Hinterlands as we always have, my Prince. May the gods save you and keep you in your graces, this day and all the days to come, to Prince Armen!"

Lawrence stood beside his father, raising his mug in salute to the bald warrior still seated in discomfort looking sheepishly about the room. "To Prince Armen, long may he shine in the light of the Father by the grace of the Mother and with the strength of the Warrior!"

At those words, all stood, raising their cups and tankards high in a rousing cheer. The baffled prince sat in muted bewilderment, humbled beyond measure by all that had happened. Slowly he stood, looking towards Bart, his closest friend and ally on their travels together. "I knew nothing of this until this day. I had always been raised as a Bardiche, to remain loyal to this kingdom, the crown, and her people. I beg your forgiveness if I appear incompetent and unprepared for such a role, all I can ask is that you have patience with me as I learn. And to my friends, Bart, Della, Lorena, and Thrax, I will always be your friend and ally. We have fought together against many foes and tackled every challenge before us without fail. I consider you my second family, I will always stand by your side, and I hope you will stand by mine."

Bart and the others stood. Before he could respond, the naga laughed jovially, his voice echoing through the halls without restraint. "Well, that is just stupid, friend Armen. Of course, we would never leave you alone just because of some small thing like that. We are sword brothers, you and I, my blades will always be here to get you out of any mess you find yourself."

The swordsman sighed, shaking his head as he smiled at the outburst he too looked up at his dear friend. "I always knew you had the potential for something greater than being a sell-sword, but this? I'm not too sure how well being a prince pays, but if you want to give it a go, I won't stop you." Lorena nodded alongside her lover, a tearful smile across her features as they both gazed proudly at their friend.

"You are always going to be that rabble-rousing troublemaker I saw beating two men with a stool," quipped Della, her eyes flashing with amusement from the memory of the broad-shouldered lad they had run across so many years ago. "At the very least, you were never cloistered in your upbringing, so as far as royals go, you are certainly amongst my favorites."

As the feast continued on in earnest those who had their fill began to meander about the room, cups in hand, gathering in small groups of mixed conversation under the music playing from throughout the room. Discussions on the future, and the past, but mostly centered around the new heir reached Bart's ear in snippets as he passed along the wall towards his friend who had been cornered by a sample of older gentry, their daughters in tow as they made their introductions and harangued the poor man like a cornered deer. Off to the side, young Lawrence stood leaning against one of the tall pillars lining either side of the long chamber. His attention was torn between the broad warrior surrounded by ravenous lords and the horn of mead in his grasp. Bart slipped in alongside, bowing his head curtly as he approached to join the young noble.

"You do not approve?" Bart whispered, hiding his lips from behind his mug.

Lawrence glanced over with a grim expression across his lips. "It is not that I approve or otherwise, Bart of Troutsmouth, I know my father had little aspiration for the crown, so I am pleased that his wishes have come to pass. What worries me now is if my cousin, or who I thought was my cousin, may be ill-prepared for the mantle so suddenly thrust upon him. I know he is a strong fighter; I've seen that for myself, but a good sword arm is not the only thing a future king needs. He does not seem to know anything of politics or intrigue, his humility brings the threat that those who have their interests may use their schemes to sway his mind and heart to align with their purpose." The young lord gestured towards the group of men eagerly presenting their daughters to the befuddled Armen, "These men know that by selling the hand of their daughters they will, in turn, buy access to the throne by way of marriage. Those who hold sway over the head wearing the crown may move the body of this kingdom."

The sellsword looked over at his tall friend, the poor lancer was desperately trying to hold his composure as best he could--the strain from conversation seemingly wearing down his defenses little by little as the gentry pressed their attack. "You might underestimate my friend, if I may be so bold, he certainly doesn't have the mind for the twisting games and shadow-play that the high houses seem to enjoy. But he has been on the other end of a coin purse held by men such as these for many years and knows the results of such plots and how they unfold. On our travels, we saw the worst side of humanity as well as the most blessed, it is his understanding of the people and those who rule over them which gives him a better understanding of the state of these lands. Given the right support and counsel, I believe he will do what is in the best interests of this land and the people."

Young Firbank smirked, casting a sideways glance at Bart beside him, "I don't suppose you have yourself in mind for such a role?"

"Gods, no!" exclaimed Bart, "I'm a sellsword, no more and no less. I have no business taking part in politics, pay me in silver and send me where you need my blade, that is all. Simple and to the point, but if he ever calls on me you can be sure I will come at all speed to stand by his side if the need arises." The two stood together watching the display unfold before them in silence. Armen looked over at the pair, his eyes pleading for rescue from his captors. "Looks like I will have to pull him from the mire once more, if you would pardon me, lord." Bart moved in like a snake amongst reeds, making his way to his friend's side and pulling him gently away from the grasp of would-be suitresses.

Amongst a gaggle of ladies Della and Lorena had caught the sight between conversations. The two could appreciate Armen's discomfort in these surroundings, thanks to the constant complementation and praise for their beauty in their current attire. They had little heart to tell these refined women just how rarely the two had ever worn such dress, let alone had themselves preened and pampered to the point of exhaustion.

Della fought to keep her smile as she whispered in the mage's ear. "So has Bart said anything about you tonight?"

Lorena's cheeks flushed brightly, "He did, I told him he best not get too used to the sight. Once all of this is over and done with, I don't want to see another corset for as long as I am breathing."

"Well, I am quite sure he will be more than happy to relieve you of that burden later tonight." Joked the elf, her lips gracing the rim of her cup which had yet to remain unfilled thanks to the stream of young men who flitted back and forth like bees amongst roses. She smiled, reveling in the renewed embarrassment on the mage's face, "If I can give you a bit of advice, enjoy the moments you can have together while you can. When opportunity for the new and unexplored passes near your fingers it would be best to grab hold and enjoy the small embers you can find in the cold winters on the road of life. Those memories are more precious than you can even imagine, and the pain of those not made is the deepest regret."

Lorena nodded understandingly, her eyes following her lover as he passed through the crowd with Armen. As the pair passed by an alcove set in the far wall, her gaze caught the figure of the old wizard from before, leaning in the door frame on his oaken staff, his hand fluttered subtly casting a faint green aura between his fingers. Within her mind, the woman felt his words as though they were a scribe's quill scratching on parchment behind her eyes. She turned to the elven warrior at her side who was currently deflecting the advances of a pair of twin boys with shockingly black hair dressed in fine red robes. "It seems someone wishes to speak with me, if anyone asks let them know. I will return once I may."

The elf looked over towards the alcove, the grey-blue hem of the wizard's robes disappearing down the passage beyond. "Try not to wear him out." She winked before returning to the pair.

"You are horrible, you know that?" spat the mage as she turned and followed the old wizard down the passage. As the sound of revelry and laughter dimmed behind her, Lorena made her way down the dimly lit hallway. The mounted heads of hunting trophies caught the sparse lighting provided by ensconced torches making it seem as though the dead glass eyes followed her steps as she followed the old man further along. Midway down the passage, an archway opened up into a small antechamber lined with tapestries that fluttered softly from a draft that had wormed its way through the ancient stonework.

Seated beside a small table piled with a collection of scrolls and vellum, Solon nodded in greeting as the younger practitioner entered. "It is most auspicious to find another student of the college in these trying times." He slowly stood, coaxing his old bones into motion. "But forgive my poor manners, my name is..."

"I know who you are, Master Solon, your infamy precedes you." Lorena kept her distance, watching the old wizard intently. "I don't appreciate having you intrude into my mind, if there was something you wished to discuss you could have just asked me plain." She kept her gaze locked on the older, and much more experienced, magician keeping special attention to his fingers which slipped partially out from beneath his flowing robes.

Solon bowed slightly, leaning heavily on his staff, "My apologies, Lorena of Kaelith-Oda, or do you prefer Lorena Red-Mist?" His eyes glinted as he stared back into the woman's scowling face. "Oh yes, I know exactly who you are. Your reputation might not be as well known, but I still have friends and resources even in my exile from the halls of the college. It is a wonder that your companions have never questioned you as to why someone of your caliber would decide to leave the sanctum of learning and travel the world as some sort of magic-wielding mercenary. Do you truly have such a taste for violence that you would defile the sanctity of the arts in the pursuit of glory and silver?"

Lorena felt her soul stir with fire, unconsciously reaching for where her pouches would normally hang had she not been forced to leave them behind. "That is none of your business, but if you must know, I have my own reasons for not locking myself away like some hermit surrounded by the ramblings of old men too distant from the world to understand how things really are outside of their high walls. If you don't have anything productive to discuss then I will take my leave." She turned on her heels, making for the open door.

"Someone has discovered how to perform the rites first developed by Hecktat." Said Solon, slowly easing his body back into the small, cushioned seat. As the mage stopped in her tracks and turned, the old wizard produced the black leather tome from under his robes and placed it on the table beside him. He tapped his palm on the cover, tracing the cryptic symbols embedded on the tanned cover.

The mage's eyes opened wide at the sight, "That cannot be what you are suggesting it is. All of that monster's works were destroyed, none exist." An involuntary chill coursed through her veins as the horrific book filled her gaze hauntingly.

Solon's voice was grim, "Yet here it sits, whole and untouched. But what should concern you most is if this book is here, then how is it that someone out in the world has managed to reproduce his results without the guidance found on these pages?"

Lorena's mind raced, her eyes dancing between the black book on the table and the man seated beside it. "Well, you are the one with the book. How am I supposed to believe that the person of whom you speak is not yourself? It wouldn't be the first time you committed the taboo of practicing dark magic in your pursuits. Isn't that why you now find yourself cloistered amongst the holy knights? So, they can keep you in check?" Her eyes narrowed as she pointed accusingly toward the frail old man who, despite his appearance, she knew held more than enough power and knowledge to level the city for miles if he so chose. "And don't you think for a moment I have forgotten you only mentioned Armen as one of the people listed on that letter Sir Walter brought with him, if you insist on keeping secrets then I don't know if I can trust another word."

The old wizard frowned disappointingly, "I don't suppose you would believe me if I said I was too weak to even begin to consider using this tome myself, or that I lacked the skill to do so. What I will say is that the magic I pursued was always with the intention of furthering our understanding of the art as a whole. You cannot have a full appreciation or understanding of a painting if you tear the canvas in half. There cannot be light without darkness, I sought to enlighten our understanding of this world and to further our knowledge as a whole. But those 'foolish old men' you mentioned were too blind to see my aims. But these methods," he lifted the tome and presented it to the wary red-headed mage, "are as close to true evil as I have ever found." His eyes rested heavily on the face of the red-haired mage before him, "As for the letter, I only said that they stood before us. I never mentioned your friend by name."

Slowly the mage approached, taking the book in her grasp with trembling hands she glanced at the wizard seated before her. "So, you have read this then? Forgive me if that does not put my mind at ease." She stared down at the tome in her hands, fingers gliding along the edges of the cover. But she could not bring herself to open the cursed pages herself, instead placing the book back on the table beside them. "So, what does it say, and how are these rites connected to our current situation? You hinted that you had knowledge of those creatures we fought on the road coming here, but you said little else."

Solon smiled coyly, "Well the news of the heir apparent suddenly appearing here in the furthermost reaches put a bit of a damper on the whole thing, did it not? But yes, I know what these creatures may well be." He leaned back, settling his weary bones into the soft cushions. "They are revenant, dead who are inhabited by the will of something not part of our natural order of the world or the realm of magic. From what I gathered reading that last surviving tome, these creatures must be formed from the bodies of the freshly dead or the greatly infirm. As you know from the legends, Hecktat forged a pact with a greater demon from the void between realms. But the price of his power was the souls of those who became revenant, sacrifices of men, women, and children from the kingdom of Almach. According to legend, he rose to such heights as there were those who began to worship the man as a god himself. There were whispers, for a time, that his cult remained hidden underground after his defeat at the hands of the united powers of the great ancient kingdoms. Maroth had not even been forged in those days over two hundred years ago, so our own histories depend on the writings of those long-lost lands. At the cost of near-complete annihilation, he was defeated, sealed with his dark master in the void. It was through that temporary alliance that two great orders were formed: The Order with their holy knights, sworn to the gods by blood and blade. And The College, home to the greatest practitioners of magic and the mystical arts. Since those days they have been the twin pillars holding the scales in balance across our continent."

Lorena slumped into one of the chairs nearby, pinching the bridge of her nose to fight off the ensuing ram battering down her skull. "Yes, yes, everyone from the college has recited the story as often as they draw breath. You would think the old masters believed they had some part in the victory from how they carried on when they told the tale. But that still does not answer the question of how someone can perform these rites without the text in hand." Her eyes grew grim, staring at the old man contemplatively, "Either there was another time that slipped through the fingers of the Magi Inquisitors, or they have returned to the source of that power themselves. If it is the latter..."

Solon nodded grimly, "Then the void has been opened, releasing the dark forces which Hecktat pledged themselves to all those years ago."

Meanwhile, amongst the revelry and merry making within the great hall, Bart, Thrax, and Armen once more found themselves together amongst the gathered crowd of nobles and merchants. Armen stood with his back to one of the columns, trying his best not to draw any further attention. The broad warrior seemed to have been drained of all life from the festivities, his tired gaze shifting slowly about the room as they spoke of long-lost days. As his eyes passed towards the main door to the hall, his gaze was met by that of one of the castle guards, dressed in chain mail with the grey tower of Lord Firbank emblazoned on his blue surcoat. The man made his way through the crowd, weaving his armored form through the clusters of conversation until he stood before the three.

"Prince Armen," The guardsman bowed as he spoke, "forgive the intrusion. You are acquainted with Sir Walter of the Cloud Knights, correct? If I may ask, have you seen him at all this evening? I have a message which must be placed to his hand."

Bart glanced about the room, as did his companions. The blond knight who had started this entire mess was nowhere to be seen in the room. The swordsman's eyes narrowed, that was strange, one would have believed the knight should be amongst them for this happy occasion. "We have not, I suppose this message you carry is of urgent business then?" He turned back to the guard, there was something not quite right, but he failed to put a finger on what.

Armen's exhaustion lifted from the news, "Well, I suppose we must take our leave and look for the man. Perhaps he is still in the guest house, we can start there." Shifting himself to make for the door, Armen's ears pricked at the sound of heavy footsteps rushing up the passageway. The sound was soon followed by the sight of two more guards hurriedly rushing through the doors and forcing their way towards Lord Timmon and his son who had now returned to their place at the head of the long table.

Bart strained to hear through the crowd as the two made their report to the Lord of Twin Rivers, his eyes widened. Quickly he turned upon the guard still standing close by, out of sheer instinct he shoved his friend to the side and jumped, placing himself between his friend and the armored guard just as a thin dagger whipped past where his friend had been standing. The swordsman faced the man who now wielded the hidden blade.

The attacker snarled, frustrated at the loss of his kill. "Nicely done, mercenary." The guard doubled over, driving his shoulder low and hard into Bart's hip, lifting them in one fluid motion before tossing him over their back and lunging once more toward the unarmed prince who had yet to regain his footing from the sudden movement. As his hand rose once more to drive the blade into his target, the would-be assassin felt themselves get jerked back in Thrax's tight coils.

The naga hissed menacingly, wrapping his coils tighter around the man in his clutches. "Be still or suffer." The scaled form squeezed slowly around the man, the sound of creaking muscle and popping joints echoing in Bart's ears as he picked himself up.

Bart lunged out grabbing the assailant's hand which still stood free from his companion's clutches, the dagger still tight within their grasp. Before the attacker could drive the blade down into the scaled form restraining him, Bart wrestled the blade away and drove his fist into the man's jaw as hard as he could. He felt teeth crack and heard their jaw snap from the blow as the man's face reeled back and drooped down, a trickle of blood and teeth escaping their lips as they slipped into unconsciousness.

Thrax gave a sudden cry of anger and pain, dropping the limp figure to the stone floor. Where the man's blood had dribbled over his scales, blisters quickly formed as though struck with hot oil. The naga grabbed the cup of a nearby lady and hurriedly splashed the contents over the wound, gritting his teeth from the pain as he pulled his coils free from the body on the floor.

Armen grabbed a knife from atop the table nearby, leaning down he placed the blade within the man's jaws and opened their mouth to expose the now blistering gums and throat of the attacker who had aimed for his life. "Poison." Armen spat, kicking the fresh corpse at his feet. "Bastard must have hidden a vial of it in his cheek in case he failed or was captured. A good thing you slugged him as you did, my friend, you must have shattered the vial."

Lord Timmon and his son had rushed towards the group with the two guards in tow, blades drawn, he looked down at the dead man wearing his colors in rage. "I was just informed that three of my guards were found dead in the south wing, their armor stripped and missing. When they searched, they found Sir Walter with his throat slit. It seems he may have seen the intruders and gave chase with my guards to capture them, but they were overtaken."

Bart and the others made their way from the hall filled with gawking onlookers who now fluttered about the room like hens. Following the guardsmen, they made their way down the hall and turned towards the south wing on the same floor. Passing the libraries, armories, storerooms, and guest lodgings, they found the huddled forms of the two deceased guards where they had been found; both had been stabbed multiple times under the armpit and in the nape between shoulder and neck. A third lay further down the hall, partially dragged into a small antechamber, all three had been stripped of arms and armor.

Bart crouched down, examining the wounds which had been inflicted on the two corpses. Off to the side lay the blond-haired body of Sir Walter. The knight's wounds deviated from the others, the man had been stabbed in the chest multiple times possibly puncturing the heart at least twice. Their hands and forearms were slashed as well, tearing the sleeves of the long blood-stained tunic. He had also been slashed deep across his throat, the pool of blood on the floor along with traces of gore across the walls and alcoves led him to believe the man had been slain here where he stood. Bart was suddenly taken aback, "I hate to ask, but were the throats of your guards slit as well?"

One of the guards leaned over his fallen comrades shaking their head, his sword still free from their scabbard. "No, sir. Only Sir Walter seems to have had his throat cut, in addition to other injuries he sustained. The three guards were dispatched by other means, only the knight received such attention from whoever they pursued."

The mercenary leaned in close to Lord Firbank, his voice lowered as he passed his gaze about the room. "Lord, it would seem that this man did not come alone. There may be at least two others, perhaps dressed as your guard who now roam the castle free. The threat may not be over."

Lord Firbank glowered in silent rage as he turned to one of the guards, "Sound the alert, search this castle from root to stem. I want them found, question everyone. No room untouched or stone unturned. Capture if you can, kill if you must, but I want answers."

*Chapter*

# THIRTEEN

# BLADES

Bart sat within the bed chamber within the northern wing facing the door, sword in hand, as his friend donned the steel plate behind him. Lord Firbank had refused all offers of aid from their party, insisting that no further risk could be afforded to the safety of their prince. The swordsman and his friends had been moved from the separate guest house and now had rooms along the northern hall. It would have been an honor to have such accommodations, but given the circumstances, they found little comfort in down-filled pillows and silk sheets. Even the decanter of wine sat untouched along the far wall near the writing desk. A tremble had taken hold in one of Bart's legs, rattling the leather and steel scabbard resting on his lap with a rattling tempo.

Armen walked up from behind his companion and placed his hand on the man's shoulder. "Nothing more we can do, Bart. We have to trust they know what they are doing and move on."

Bart lifted himself and switched places with the tall warrior, leaning his sword against the bedpost as he began donning the steel breastplate and leather greaves over the finery he still wore from the party. The refined silk shoes found themselves tossed aside in favor of his heavy leather boots still stained with mud from their journey. "You haven't been a prince more than a day and already someone is trying to kill you, sounds like you got the worst end of this deal."

"From what Lawrence has said, I am under the impression they have been looking for us since before we arrived." Replied Armen, his eyes still fixed on the door leading to the hallway. A knock on the door drew both of the men's attention, slowly the taller warrior raised the short sword and glanced over at his companion stealthily making his way to the side of the door. "Who is it?" he challenged, adjusting his grip on the leather-wrapped hilt. The faint familiar voice carried under the door and eased the tension in the pair's shoulders.

"It's Della, I have Lorena and Thrax here with me as well." The elf slowly pulled the door open, glancing about the room as the red-haired mage marched in ahead of her. Thrax stood further behind, his scimitars strapped across his back once more as he gazed down both ends of the hall behind the three. Bart sheathed his blade, embracing Lorena as she entered and pulling her to the side away from the door in his arms.

The swordsman looked down into her blue eyes, his face scarred with worry, "Where have you been? We looked for you in the hall, but you had disappeared, Della said you were speaking with someone and stepped away."

The mage smiled soothingly, her hands reaching for his worn cheeks as she soothed away his pain. "Master Solon had insights he wished to share with me, but I will explain what I know." She led him to the others, her soft fingers entwined in his calloused hands. Together they listened to the mage's account of what she had learned from the old wizard, the nature of the creatures they had met on the road, the history from centuries past which seemed to connect to the present day, and the twists and turns which had transpired far from their own travels.

Armen sighed, leaning against the bedpost from his seat on the carpeted floor. "Well at least we know they cannot breed amongst themselves, but from what you are saying this is some sort of high magic, surely this means there is some sort of balance that they need to achieve to make these things or some limit to what can transpire. But even with all this, do you think we can trust the old man?"

Lorena nodded in agreement, the elf's fist clenched under her chin in thought. "He could be leaving something out or exaggerating the facts to his own ends. You said he possesses the only book known to exist detailing the spells required. For all we know he could still have a hand in all this."

The mage's shoulders shrugged, "That's possible, I cannot deny that, but he doesn't have any reason to lie about what we discussed. After all, he is forever shamed and ostracized by the elders within the college and banished from the halls of magic. There is nothing for him to gain by withholding what he knows, much less divulging what he has. Either way, Master Solon remains as he is, an outcast in the circles of magic."

Bart still had his doubts, they shone clear as the afternoon sun on his face. "He is an outcast, yet you still refer to him as 'Master' Solon, if he is truly shamed then does he not lose such respect?"

"Some would say yes", replied Lorena, "But I believe that he has done more than enough to retain his title, as do some others within the college. He is eccentric, to be sure, but his accomplishments and contributions to our understanding of magic as a whole are without denial. Even those who spit at the mention of his name still use his research and writings as the foundation for our understanding of this world and the mystic arts. He may not be referenced in any official capacity, but it is acknowledged in secret that he has been instrumental to our practice. I even have a few of his original spells within my own tome, not any of the forbidden spells of course." She gestured assuringly at the gawking faces around her.

Thrax had listened in silence from his post by the door, one ear proffered towards the conversation while the other focused on any sound which may carry from the door. Silently the naga raised his hand towards the room, gesturing silence. The others quickly cut off any further conversation. Thrax slowly leaned back from the wooden door, motioning with his fingers as though they were walking along the air like a marionette.

With as much silence as they could manage, the five readied their weapons and staff, eyes peeled towards the door. Bart blew out one of the candles nearby while Della did the same, cloaking the corners in darkness, the only light within afforded by the small window set at the center of the far wall facing the door. In the stillness, all could now hear the soft patter of footsteps closing in on the room where they lay in wait, a slight shadow passed quickly from under the door cast by the torches in the hall outside. Suddenly the light from without also dispersed. Whoever was on the other side of that door had snuffed out the nearby torches, as Bart's eyes finally grew more accustomed to the blackness, he saw the signal from the reptilian sentry, two fingers followed by a third.

So, two, maybe three of them were out there, Bart readied his sword, casting his gaze about to take stock of their positions. Lorena was close by, as she met his gaze the mage nodded, pulling out a small pinch of sulfur and a shard of glass from her pouches. The swordsman's ears pricked up at the sound of metal scraping against itself, lock-picks, these people were good. He most likely would not have heard them if he had not been listening for the sound. Thrax had seemed to hear the noise as well, the naga turned towards Bart, a knowing look in his glowing orange eyes in the darkness.

With a nod from Bart, the reptilian fighter reared back from the door and drove his tightly wrapped coils against the wooden frame driving the door violently outward. Wood splintered and exploded into the hallway, catching the two cloaked figures by surprise. The red-haired mage muttered under her breath, crushing the glass in her palm and drawing blood before throwing it towards the opened door. There was a violent crack as the magic mingled and twisted mid-air in a display of sparks followed by a brilliant white light burst into the once-still darkness illuminating the two outside and blinding the one who had been forcing the lock, her tools still in hand. The smaller figure reeled back from the shock, clasping her hands to her eyes which were covered in trickles of blood from the fresh wounds on her face, and fell back into the hallway. The other crouched back, drawing a pair of knives they threw both blindly into the room in a single motion. One clattered against the bedpost, flinging off into the room at a wild trajectory, the other embedded itself deep into Bart's leg.

The swordsman gasped from the pain, grasping his thigh as he doubled over to catch himself against the wall. Armen charged out of the room, sword lowered in a thrust as he drove the point of his blade deep into the chest of the knife-throwing figure. Together they hammered into the stone floor of the north wing's hallway, locked in a struggle over the blade which slowly forced itself deep into the assassin's chest. Armen leaned his full weight down, driving the tip of his sword into the man's ribs, he could feel the bones crack against the steel, and with one final lunge, he sank the blade further through the assassin's chest until he felt the tip strike the stone floor beneath them. Simultaneously, Della leaped through the doorway past the bald warrior, twin daggers drawn as she closed the distance with the female still bleeding against the wall. The elf brought both blades down into the woman's shoulders pinning her in place beneath the elf who straddled the figure beneath. Thrax followed close behind, forcing his hand into the woman's mouth and prying the small glass vial from her cheek.

"Your friend already pulled that trick, miss, but my friends are going to have questions for you." The naga hissed menacingly, his predatory gaze close to the woman's face. Thrax's coils squeezed tightly around the struggling woman, restraining her arms and legs deftly within his scales as his tail slipped around the woman's neck, slowly cutting her off from the realm of the conscious.

Armen rose from the crumpled, bloody, corpse beneath him. Blood smeared across the battered breastplate and dripping from his face. He wiped his sleeve across his lips trying to clean away the crimson, further ruining the fine silk tunic now sodden and hung heavily on his shoulders. The bald warrior turned towards the struggling woman caught in his friend's coils, leaving his sword lodged in the chest of his opponent impaled on the stone floor now pooling with blood.

Hand still pressed against his wounded leg, Bart felt a shiver pierce his soul, the look on his friend's face was one he had never seen. Never before had he seen Armen's face twisted with such rage, a visceral hatred. The bald warrior's dark eyes seemed to sink into pools of infinite darkness, he watched as the armored form of his companion trod across the stone floor, staining the stones with each bloody footstep. Gripping the blade in his thigh, Bart pressed his palm down and pulled the knife free from his flesh. He winced, feeling the hot flash of pain renewed as it came free. In the dim remnants of light from the window he looked down at the bright crimson flowing through his breeches, a lucky turn, if it had been the color of dark wine he would have had some serious trouble. The swordsman turned the blade over in his palm, sniffing the blade, he couldn't find any hint of poison. He tucked the knife into a pouch, no point wasting a good knife.

Lorena stood short of the hallway, her hands pulling out a small crystal which, with a whisper, she held aloft with a soft glow in the darkness. The mage turned her gaze back towards Bart, leaning against the wall, "Are you alright?" Bart nodded. Relieved, she turned back towards the scene in the hallway. "I think she is out cold, Thrax, she is more useful alive."

The naga slowly loosened his grasp from around the woman's throat, dropping his prisoner to the floor in a crumpled heap. Together, he and Della stripped the assassin of the belt and pouches strapped around her waist, searching for any other little tricks or tools they may still hold. Ripping the belt free of the pouches and scabbard, Thrax twisted the rough leather deftly around the unconscious woman's wrists and bound her, arms locked behind her back.

The elf cocked a quizzical look at her reptilian friend, "You seem to have done this before, where did you learn that neat little trick?" She leaned over, admiring the intricate binding.

Thrax glanced up, "Oh, this? Bart showed me this trick back in that brothel a few months ago." He turned his attention back to the prisoner still lying unmoving at their feet, shallow breaths escaping her lips brushed ripples across the thin pools of blood trickling across the floor. He never noticed the knowing glance Della shot over at Lorena, nor the bashful turn of the mage's face away from the matriarchal elven warrior.

"It is a nice knot, isn't it Lorena? Looks very sturdy." The elf whispered to her friend holding her illuminated crystal.

Before the mage could reply, Armen had grabbed the unconscious assassin, hoisted the small frame up by the collar of the dark hooded robes, and began dragging her down the hallway towards the main halls. "Well, we aren't going to get any answers standing around here, but I think Lord Firbank will have some idea what to do with her."

Tying a strip of the bed sheets firmly over the wound in his leg, Bart quickly followed close behind. The others did the same, Thrax leaned down and tossed the corpse over his shoulder, pulling Armen's sword free and handing it over to Bart as he passed. Together the five made their way down the long hall until they reached the staircase, following the large bald figure of Armen towards the keep's central chambers on the first level. A pair of roaming guards were locked with shock at the sight of the bloody companions carrying two bodies as though they had returned from a hunt in the glen with fresh game. Armen shouldered one of the doors leading into the banquet hall, startling the occupants within. Most of the guests had evacuated the castle after the first attempt made on the prince's life, but some had remained to lend their support and counsel to lord Timmon who sat at the head of the long table which still held remnants of the feast from before.

Bart followed his friend as they passed by the shocked faces and gawkers scattered around the hall. Off to the side along the columns at the edges of the room, the swordsman noted that the servants had already cleaned away the blood from before. The body of the first assassin lay covered by a tablecloth atop a small table nearby illuminated by a standing candelabra. They certainly were not making any friends amongst the staff, he inwardly groaned at the thought of the servants who would have yet more to tidy up on the north wing.

Thrax slid over to another table by the first body, depositing his burden on the wooden face with a thud. His sharp gaze could make out the first body still wearing the guard attire beneath the sheet stained with blood on the nearby table. The second wore the dark robes and hood of an assassin, the naga's brow furrowed in contemplation as he inspected each in turn.

Approaching the head of the table, Armen tossed the still form of the woman at Lord Firbank's feet. She groaned softly from the impact of stone against her limp frame, stirring the assassin from her stupor. "I think we have found our friend's accomplices, Lord Firbank. We managed to take this one alive," His eyes glowered down at the hooded figure bound between them, "for now. If you have any wish to extend your time amongst the living, I am sure that can be arranged. But it makes little difference, you tried to kill me. Worse, you hurt one of my friends and killed another."

Lord Firbank rose, attended by Master Solon stroking his grey scruff contemplatively. "Well done, my prince. My men can take it from here, no need for you to further soil your hands with this wench." The lord sneered down his nose at the bound figure beneath him, "There are ways to extract the truth from those such as her."

The wizard shook his head, doubt furrowed his features mostly hidden beneath the grey brush. "Those who are pledged to the Shadow Guild are notorious for never divulging their secrets, I fear you are wasting your time, my lord. Better to cut her throat and be over with it."

Young Timmon leaned back in his seat, arms crossed. "Still, no harm can come from some time below, for us at least."

Bart could have sworn a flash of fear crossed over the young woman's face as she listened to her captors. She wasn't that much older than Lorena or himself. Her face was bronzed from the sun, much like those he had met during his travels in the southern borders. A streak of freckles dotted across her cheeks and under her amber eyes which sat unmoving now that she had regained her senses. As two of the Twin Rivers guards shuffled their prisoner off to what Bart could only assume was the deepest, darkest place within the estate, he found his view blocked by the face of Lord Timmon.

"Don't waste your pity on that one, young man. She, as with all the others, knew exactly what they were signing up for when they joined the shadows. Capture or death is only a question of when, not if, for their kind." Lord Timmon turned on his heel, walking over to the two corpses still kept in his hall. His hands clasped loosely behind his back as he turned from one to the other. "Strip them of anything we can use to see who hired these cutthroats, once that is done, dispose of them they are stinking up my halls."

The doors to the hall slammed forward like the crack of thunder. Bart turned, drawing his blade swiftly, his heart beating against the inside of his chest as though it could break free and run from him. The mud-coated figure collapsed halfway into the room, gasping for breath as they fought to stand. Bart could see from their garb the man was some sort of rider or scout, beneath the mud and dust of the road he could make out the faint grey tower emblazoned on their leather gambeson.

"The Red Horse!" The rider gasped between breaths, "Creatures have crossed and attacked the villages to the north, those who were able have fled to the mountains. But they are headed this way, Lord."

Lawrence rushed forward, helping another guard lift the messenger to his feet, "How many? How long do we have, soldier?"

The rider struggled to meet the young lord's gaze, all his strength had been spent on the road to Twin Rivers. "Two days, maybe less. They struck like demons or beasts possessed by demons. At first, we thought them to be orcs and goblins painted with ash. But there were others, elves, and humans even. But the way they moved, lord, they were like nothing we had ever seen. Me and my fellows were garrisoned at the outpost north of one of the fishing villages along the river, I was awake on watch when they crossed. By the time my friends had been roused it was too late, they swept over everything like a wave of corpses, I was lucky to escape. But the others..." the man broke down into a blubbering mess, unable to continue.

Young Firbank turned to his father, "There would have been twenty men at the outpost along the river. The same for the other four we have between here and the mountain pass, I doubt we can withdraw everyone and evacuate the villages in time."

Lord Timmon frowned, collapsing in his seat at the news, "Including soldiers and the villages, you are suggesting I leave more than two hundred souls to their deaths? No, we will send riders to the closest villages and hold the gates until as many of those which can be saved are within these walls."

The quaking guard looked up at his liege through the tears streaming freely across their cheeks, "I raised the alarm as I passed southward, my lord, as I rode hard through the night, I could see the signal fires light up from the other outposts. They should be gathering those who remain and be headed this way to the castle. I tried, lord, I..." The man fell consumed once more by his grief.

A sigh of relief flowed through Bart's shoulders, two days was little time to prepare for a siege. But these creatures had been frightening enough as a dozen, but the thought of hundreds more chilled his soul like a winter's breeze.

In the hours that followed among the preparations to repel the impending siege, riders and pigeons were dispatched. All carried the same call for aid and warning of attack from the Hinterlands. The flutter of wings and clamor of hooves filled the night air, rousing the populace from their slumber. The dust from the eastern gate's road filled the horizon for miles as each made their way to every town or village with the call.

From his chambers, Solon sat watching the message-laden flock rise ever skyward. The two knights who had accompanied him thus far stood at his back.

One broke the silence hesitantly, "Master Solon, if we are to depart then now would be the time. You have no reason to remain, the news you wished to convey has been passed, and we may not be able to guarantee your safety in the coming battle. If what you have said is true, these abominations are but the first wave of a greater force." The other knight nodded in agreement.

The old wizard sighed, feeling his age all the more in these dark times. "I thank you for your concern, but should Twin Rivers fall, then not even your garrison will be able to withstand the tide on our shores. No, I will remain, there are yet some things I must see to before my time comes. And it would seem the gods have generously made arrangements for this old fool."

—⁂—

Deep below the streets of Maroth, Sylvanus was slowly making his way through the dark and winding tunnels close behind the crouched figure of the crazed old man. The elf's shoulders and neck ached from having to crouch so low in the blackness, keeping his hand against the rough stone woven with moss. At least, he hoped it was moss, the smell made him dread otherwise. Here and there the floor had dipped, pooling with stagnant water that seeped into the tattered hem of his stained robes and soaked his feet which burned from the sores and bruises on his soles. Every time it seemed he would begin to dry off, another pool of water rose up in his path to begin the torture once more. Even with his keen vision, the elf had no source of light to guide his steps, only the faint sound of his guide's steps provided any measure of awareness. A silent panic welled within his troubled heart, is this where he would meet his end? Alone in the dark with only this wild-eyed lunatic to bear witness to his final moments? A part of the sorcerer's soul yearned for the headman's axe. At least in the public square, there would be sunlight and fresh air before he met the block.

Sylvanus suddenly found himself halted as he bumped into the figure before him, his hand instinctively reached out before his face in the darkness, grasping for answers. He felt his hand grasped by gnarled fingers, and a gasp escaped his lips, inwardly the elf cursed at his own fear. Here he was, the wisest and most influential practitioner of his time, whimpering in the darkness like a newborn. The elf bit his lip, drawing blood, forcing his mind to calm itself before fear took any further hold.

The old man cackled silently, "Hush now, we have arrived." With a deft motion obscured by the darkness of the tunnel, his fingers met a small metal ring set into the ceiling. With a twist he pulled it down suddenly, yanking the hidden chain which caught the gears of some unknown mechanism foreign in sound to the elf's ears.

Light streamed into the darkness, blinding the elf who shielded his gaze with the sodden and tattered blue robes of his former office. Blinking slowly, he followed his guide through the opening into a torch-lit chamber. As his eyes grew accustomed to his surroundings, Sylvanus gawked at the room he found himself in. The chamber was massive, shaped in a solid dome of brick and stone that reached high overhead. From the center of the dome hung an immense chandelier lit with a multitude of oil lamps. Along the walls hung more oil lamps, their flames flickering from the sudden gust of wind that followed them from the tunnel. Between each lamp, shelves lined with books and random objects filled the walls, dark cloaked figures flitted to and fro across the gallery adhered to their own purposes. The elf could make out other doors along the walls amongst the shelves and alcoves, as well as a long curved staircase that reached upward along the far wall leading to a second level also lined with yet even more books and scrolls on shelves. At the center of the room, tables were laden with beakers, glasses, vials, and other tools and equipment he knew by sight. Even his collection, the pride and joy of his years, seemed an amateur assortment in comparison to what these people had. The elf forgot for a moment the fear which had frozen his heart just moments before, his soul leaped at the thought of what he could accomplish with such a collection.

"Impressive, is it not?" whispered the old man standing alongside.

To Sylvanus' shock, he watched as the doddering old human stretched and straightened his frame. Muscles creaked and groaned, joints popped back into place. The wild look on the man's face was gone, replaced by smug humor. As the grey-tattered robes fell away, the elf now looked upon a man wearing dark robes and blackened chain mail, a white sash was wrapped about their waist under a thick leather belt lined with pouches and knives. A hood hung by the man's shoulders, embroidered with white thread around the trim.

Waving his hand over the scene before them, the dark-robed man spoke with a voice far stronger than his years would suggest. "Welcome to the Hall of Shadows."

The sorcerer, who an hour past had resigned himself to death or imprisonment, felt as though his entire world had spun out of control. Leaning heavily against the wall, Sylvanus collided with the edge of one of the tall bookshelves nearby and slumped to the floor in a trembling heap. "Why?" He mumbled, his head clasped between his trembling hands, "Why did you bring me here? Why pull me away from the axe and show me all of this?"

The bearded assassin crouched beside the quaking elf, his voice was calm, as though he were speaking to a child, regardless that the elf before him was easily more than twice his age. "You and most others only hear of us and think we are bloodthirsty and cruel, that we have little regard for who we work for as well as the pay is good. While money is always a great motivator, there is more to the Guild of Shadows than murder and espionage." The man rose, lifting Sylvanus alongside and leading him to the array of tables filled with the intricate assortments of alchemical tools and supplies. "You are more useful to our needs with your knowledge intact. No more, no less. You may yet find a purpose here amongst us in the dark corners of society, finding the answers to the questions long sought for millennia. If you agree to stay, we will provide you with as much freedom as can be found to pursue your own ambition. All we ask is that, from time to time, you solve little problems for us."

"And if I refuse?" asked the elf, his lips tightened in a grimace in anticipation of the answer he knew must follow.

The assassin turned, twirling that same thin blade in his palm between his deft fingers. "I already told you, the headman's axe wasn't the only blade that may await you." The man stowed the dagger, then turned to the table and lifted a small vial from amongst its contents. The elf's eyes widened in horror, then narrowed with rage as he looked upon the small crystalline vial filled with a viscous blue liquid. The man smiled knowingly, "I don't suppose I have to tell you what this is. After all, we stole it from your own chambers." He lifted his hand before the elf's lips, "Before you ask, the vial which was given to the king of Maroth was a forgery. This is the vial which contains the poison used to kill Queen Eliza, so in a way, you were right on the money with your suspicions of our hand in her death."

Sylvanus shook with rage, "You just said you didn't serve money, that you had some sort of higher purpose. What purpose can be justified by the killing of innocents?" He would have liked to choke the man standing there before him, but the elf was more than certain he would perish long before he could grasp hold.

The man tossed the vial to the elf sorcerer's hands, turning away as he spoke. "That is not what I said, merely that money is a motivator. Let me answer your question with a riddle, show me the intellect that turned you from the hero of the common people to the most hated official in the courts." The man halted before a giant mounted map of the continent, drawn and detailed with an exactness not found even in the Solar Temple in the Far East. "What drives civilization to progress in medicine, topography, revenue, and technology?"

The sorcerer furrowed his brow, looking down at the small vial that had become the bane of his life, "Problems. Solving those which were unknown before and therefore had no need of a solution. New diseases need new cures, new lands, and the routes to meet them require new maps, New lands mean resources and the technology to harvest them and put them to use."

A boisterous chuckle rose from the man still turned towards the map, "It is so simple, my friend. You over-think the question and therefore misinterpret the answer." The assassin turned back to Sylvanus, arms spread. "War, my good elf. War is what drives the machine of knowledge forward. They have stronger armor, so you create a crossbow capable of defeating it. You have higher walls around your castles, they create siege craft to tear it down or dig beneath. They have faster horses, so you tame griffins for your knights to ride into battle. The cycle is never ending so long as one thing never comes to pass." The assassin's eyes glinted with that same madness the elf had first seen back in his dank cell beneath the Black Tower, "When you helped the king bargain for it and marry one of the royal daughters of Almach you halted the very thing which gave you purpose. Peace kills progress, my friend, it is a cancer that stagnates the drive of nations and the furtherance of civilization. That is why she died, to begin the cycle anew, soon the war which has been delayed between the powerhouses of the continent will once more draw steel against one another and the march of progress will be heralded by the drums of war."

*Chapter*

# FOURTEEN

# 'INVASION

As the early dawn of a new day rose behind her back from atop the massive griffin, Captain Eliza's eyes watered from the gusts of wind as she and her command screamed toward the distant mountains ahead. The snow-capped peaks of the Giant's Spine glinted with amber and gold like a dragon's horde in the distance. Further beyond she could make out the grey blur of the walls of Twin Rivers. The mounted knights around her darted between clouds on their approach, masking their numbers and direction as best they could now that they had lost the cover of night. To her left, one of Eliza's knights picked at the remnants of blood and feathers from a pigeon they had collided with mid-flight in the darkness, grey-white feathers rippled on their chest and glided off as they sped ever onward. The captain shook her head, she well knew the feeling, they would be lucky if only a few ribs were broken. It was yet another casualty within her command, and this one had not been dealt by any enemy.

The commander gauged the distance once more, rolling the numbers over in her mind. Right about now her lieutenant should be arriving at Twin Rivers heralding their arrival, to arrive in force without warning might have resulted in the garrison opening fire on her retinue before any explanation for their presence could be relayed. Now the only cause for concern should be whether Lord Firbank would cooperate, he had always been a stalwart ally of the crown and the kingdom, but the

Border Lords were notorious for also being aloof in a way thanks to the constant vigil they held across the borders of Maroth. As the sun rose ever higher behind and the imposing castle loomed ever closer, her eyes caught the gleam of steel from the battlements. With a wave of her hand, the company of mounted knights dove low towards an open clearing east of the city just across the southern banks of the Tsere River which marked the eastern borders of Lord Firbank's domain. Arrayed around the open field, the advance party had been joined by riders bearing the tower of Twin Rivers. Dismounting short of the cluster, she joined her lieutenant who saluted at once, a grim cloud hanging over his usually bright demeanor.

"Captain, news from Twin Rivers, there is a horde of creatures making swift pace upon the garrison from the north. They seem to have come from the Hinterlands, crossing the Red Horse in the dead of night. Multiple villages have already fallen as well as at least one outpost along the border." He looked about the arriving knights surrounding the field where they stood. "It may not be feasible to enter the city in force, might I suggest we encamp here in reserve? Should any come through the mountain's pass, they may seek to encircle the castle from the North and cut off support from the east and south."

Captain Eliza looked at the map held by the soldier from Twin Rivers, "It is a good plan, save one problem, we are here on orders from the High Commander as an escort, not to support an open battle against an unknown enemy. We do not have the supplies or forces for which they seek."

The soldier nodded, "Understandable, Ma'am. My lord has dispatched requests for reinforcement in the night, we hope to receive word within the week. The surrounding provinces have already begun gathering what supplies and manpower we can muster, and they are moving to within the walls as we stand here."

The commander nodded, "That would explain the pigeons. Very well, for now, my lieutenant and I with a few others will enter the city to meet with your lord in regard to our own orders, the rest will remain here in reserve for the time being on orders to hold the flank and report any movement." She turned to Lieutenant Frig, her slight frame rushing up to meet the others as they spoke. "You will remain here, hold this ground and I want patrols along the mountains, any movement is to be reported to the garrison immediately. I will send more details once we determine the current state. See if we can secure lodging at the town nearby, we may be able to use it as a base."

Lieutenant Theodoric nodded, "That would be River's Pass, Captain, from what I have learned they are almost evacuated. But the mayor should still be there directing his people, he may oblige."

Preparations having been made to her satisfaction, the captain and her retinue made their way to the Eastern Gate via the wide dirt road. As she passed through the thick walls of the outer city, the group fought their way through the bogged streets of the inner city through the crowds which rushed back and forth in chaos. Merchants were loading what wares could not be sold onto wagons and rushing out any avenue available. A siege was bad for business, looters even more so once the fighting began, they would be taking their chances elsewhere. Breaking free of the mob, the riders hastened up the street towards the main keep. All along the walls and within the blue-tiled towers, soldiers stood at watch with spears and bows at the ready. Passing through the gates the captain caught a glimpse of more soldiers and a group of what looked to be mercenaries, including a large naga with two blades strapped across their back, handing out pikes and spears to the citizenry which were now conscripted into the defense of their home.

Dismounting her steed by the stables and guardhouse, her eye caught the familiar shape of another griffin already within. The golden coat tinged with red was unmistakable, "That's Ginger, Sir Walter's mount!" She pointed out to Lieutenant Theodoric.

The dark-haired officer nodded, "I suppose he has already made it then, if he is still here then the heir must also remain." He noted with a glint of hope in his eyes. From behind the pair another voice cut in above the commotion.

"Indeed, we have kept her well cared for and fed, Captain." Lawrence Firbank called out as he approached the group of knights, nodding to the soldier in his family crest, dismissing them from their charge. "I assumed you would make your way here, our scouts picked you up at first light. We are grateful for your presence, yet I fear you find us in no condition to greet you with proper honors. I am sure you understand."

The Knight Commander saluted, hand over chest as she spoke. "My Lord, I am Captain Eliza Daughter of Zulla, Commander of the Second Cohort of the Order of Cloud Knights, The Emerald Dragons. And this is my aide, Lieutenant Theodoric. If you have met Sir Walter then I am certain he has apprised you and your father of our mission, however, I swear we will do all we can give the circumstances." She looked about the courtyard, seeking each face in turn. "If I may ask, where is Sir Walter?"

The young noble frowned, shaking his head. "This is not the place for such a discussion, please come with me, my father can explain what has happened. And as for the one you seek, he will join you in due course."

Outside the guardhouse and armory, Bart handed over another of the steel-headed pikes to Armen who, in turn, passed the weapon off to a burly man whose better summers had long passed. The swordsman kept a watchful eye on the new arrivals dressed in shining plate as they left their griffins and followed the Firbank heir into the keep, their captain had looked their way as they entered but Bart saw no hint of recognition in her face when she did. With a shrug, he returned to the task at hand. Rows of pikes, spears, and crossbows stood awaiting the hands of men and women whom the guards had sorted according to age and fitness to fight. At first, he had been surprised at the number of women who had answered the call, but from the looks on their faces it had become clear that this was their home as well, and they had just as much to lose should the city fall.

Armen had forgone the regalia offered by Lord Firbank, preferring to wear his old plate armor. Still, the news of his arrival had made its way amongst the populace, and on more than one occasion he had needed to play the prince as peasants, tradesmen, and spinsters bowed before him as they arrived to retrieve their weapons and armor. A few had needed to be dragged away, gently, by nearby guards lest the line be bogged down further.

Della looked over, as yet another supplicant was drawn away, bowing profusely. "You are going to have to get used to this sooner or later, Prince Armen." The elf chided as she handed over a crossbow to a lad no more than thirteen summers.

Thrax nodded from behind the group, his arms laden with piles of armor sewn from boiled leather and sealed with oil. "Well, I think it does them good to see you, friend Armen. They may draw some courage knowing the future king stands with them in their time of need."

"Don't even start with that, Thrax." Groaned the bald warrior, "Ever since people started saying prince this, prince that, I have seen nothing come of it but death. In less than a day, there has been murder and torture all because the people who raised me aren't even my real parents." He turned towards Bart, leaning closer as he took another pike to pass along. "If it is all the same, I would rather go back to just being me. Forget the crown, forget politics and all that nonsense, I'm no leader."

Bart shook his head, patting his tall friend on the shoulder. "Well, nothing to do for it now, fate has a funny way of putting you in places and times we would rather not be." The mercenary stared over the gathered masses flowing ever onward before them, "Twin hells, I never thought I would be back this way, but here we are. If there really are gods, they hate us."

From beyond the crowd, Armen's attention was caught by the waving figure of Lawrence, followed by the arrival of two guards who saluted as they approached. "My prince," said one, hand over heart, "Lord Firbank requests your presence on a matter most urgent. If you would accompany us, we shall escort you hence."

Lorena elbowed the tall man, a thin smile across her lips. "Go on, Your Highness, we have this sorted out. You and Bart go along, remember to behave yourself." Armen shot a scowl back, then turned to follow the pair.

Bart fell in alongside, hand on his hilt as the four made their way through the crowd and up the steps leading to the keep. Making their way through the corridors towards the hall, Bart cast his gaze about the bustle of soldiers and guards posted at intervals. Since the recent attempts on his friend's life, Lord Timmon had stepped up security all about the castle. This was completely understandable, regardless of the threat approaching from the Hinterlands, it would have been a black mark on his reputation if the heir to the crown were to die will in his care. Yet Lord Firbank had allowed Armen and his companions the freedom to exercise their own initiative and assist with the preparations and defenses, albeit under the ever-vigilant eye of his guards.

Upon entering the hall, Bart once more saw the armored knights who had just arrived. The long table had been cleared of the remaining remnants of the feast before, replaced by the array of charts and maps dotted with small statuettes carved from wood and painted with an array of colors like game pieces on a game board. At the head of the table sat Lord Timmon himself, the captain of the newly arrived knights close at hand. She turned her head upon their arrival, her features while grim still held a martial poise which clearly let Bart know this was a woman not to be taken lightly. The swordsman could see the medallion Sir Walter had presented clasped in her hands as she rose to meet them from her seat.

"So this is him, the lost prince of Maroth." Captain Eliza spoke as she marched towards the pair, her piercing gaze hammering into Armen's features. Stopping short of the tall warrior, she examined the face before her. Satisfied, she drew her sword and knelt before him. "As Captain of the Second Cohort and Knight of Maroth, I swear my sword and those of my command to your service, my prince." In the accompaniment of their commander's oath, the other knights present drew their swords as well, kneeling where they stood. The ringing of steel almost caused Bart to draw his blade as well, the swordsman's body tensed, ready to fight. Only the reassuring hand of Armen halted his friend's reaction.

Turning to the kneeling captain, Armen bowed his head in return. "Please, Captain, if you would stand. I am not used to this whole turn of events myself, but I thank you all the same." the tall warrior frowned, sadness and regret in his eyes. "And you have my sincere regret for the death of Sir Walter, he was a good man, even if I only knew him for a short while. I am truly sorry for his loss."

Eliza stood tall before her newfound prince, the man for whom two of her knights had lost their lives in the effort to find. "Sir Walter knew what his oaths meant, I am sure he died with honor knowing he served the realm and the crown."

Bart frowned as he listened, thinking back to how they had found the blond-haired knight. Honor? The man died in the dark, slain by assassins, his throat slashed like an animal led to slaughter. Where was the honor in such a death? He wanted to yell as much, yet bit his tongue.

Captain Eliza continued, "My father, Commander Zulla, dispatched us to find you. We must get you to the capitol at all haste so that you can attain the crown. King Merrick, or should I say your father, will be abdicating the throne by the harvest. I suggest we send word to the capitol with all haste, to let them know of your arrival."

Lord Firbanks shook his head, "There is too much risk for that now," the lord interjected, "there have already been at least two attempts on the prince. Our guest in the dungeon has found her tongue, it would seem that the one who has orchestrated this affair provided two names for the knife. Sir Walter apparently was one of them, whoever they are, their client has known of your identity far longer than us. I would suggest caution, my prince, until we know who our friends are."

"With all due respect, I have no intention of leaving Twin Rivers until the danger has passed," Armen said, looking over the charts and maps spread about the table. "If I am this lost heir that everyone has been looking for, then what sort of prince would I be if I tucked my tail and ran leaving the people here to fend for themselves? Do whatever you think is necessary, Captain, but I am not leaving just yet. And I am sure Lord Firbanks would be more than grateful for your aid, should you stay as well."

Bart watched on in shocked silence. In less than a few days he had watched his large mischievous companion be heralded as the heir to the throne, fight ghouls from the gates of hell, become adorned in finery and wealth from the hands of nobles, and now they were discussing politics and war like it was second nature. The swordsman felt a small swell of pride as he watched his friend, it did not matter if Armen was royal or not, he was sure that the man would always be the same carefree brawler that had joined him on the road.

Armen looked up at his friend, catching the slight smile etched into Bart's features. "I don't suppose I have to ask if you and the others will stay? I may be a prince now, but I have no clue as to what sort of payment you can expect should you all choose to fight with us."

"I'm hurt," Bart scoffed, "you know as well as I that we would never leave you alone to have all the fun by your lonesome. Besides, Della would tan my hide if we didn't keep an eye on you."

From the main corridor, another armored figure marched into the chamber. Plated boots hammering into the stone floor, the Holy Knight saluted before speaking. "My Lords, scouts have reported dust on the northern road, along with the creatures last seen crossing the Red Horse. They will be here by nightfall."

Bart chuckled silently, drawing a glare from Captain Eliza, "Looks like even if we wanted to leave it would have been too late anyway, my friend." He patted the tall warrior on his broad shoulder, "I guess we will just have to stick around and kill more of these bastards for you, how does that sound?"

In the waning hours towards dusk, the dim last rays of day glinted across the walls of Twin Rivers. Spears bristled along the ramparts of the outer walls, archers tested their bows and checked their quivers. Back and forth along the parapets, the voices of sergeants and officers cut through the still air, calling out commands and reports as they once more made the rounds. Above the gatehouse facing the northern road, Bart found himself once more surrounded by his long-time companions. A breeze slowly flowed in from the mountains, his nose caught the foul scent they had first encountered along the road near Kaelith's Pass. They were close now, those fiends from the deepest pits of hell, if he could smell them then soon, they would see the foul beasts. Along the walls, outside of the swordsman's view, torches and braziers began to spark into life. From atop one of the towers set into the wall, a horn called out with a single long note. Hands pointed northward along the battlements at the growing dark mass rumbling from around the foot of the mountains along the road headed straight for them. Even now Bart and his companions could hear the mass of guttural, snarling voices echoing through the silence. The swordsman stared out at the mass of writhing forms lurching and stumbling towards where he and his companions stood. He could feel the cold hand of dread grasp at his heart, for as the mob came closer into view, he could recognize the familiar shapes of the massive orcs amongst the undead.

Della squinted, gaging the distance before nocking one of the shafts to her bow and drawing back. The ashen limbs creaked from the strain, urging for the sweet release that would send its feathered charge onward in flight. With a sharp crack, the elf loosed upon her distant target, the grey-fletched shaft screamed upward on its fatal flight out into the open sky before slowly arcing down towards the rumbling mass of potential targets. With a grunt of satisfaction, the elf watched as one of the mottled, screaming creature's heads snapped back and collapsed with the arrow sprouting from their forehead like a sapling.

"Oh good," mumbled Armen, "only a few hundred more to go. Would you like the rest of us to join you or do you have this covered yourself?"

Della smiled, "Oh I don't mind at all, your highness, if you would like to kill a few that would be just fine. There seems to be plenty for everyone." She loosed another shaft into the approaching mass which shut the howling maw of one of the thin humanoid beings into silence.

Bart drew his blade, a tremor passing through him as the horde drew ever closer. In the time Della had fallen two of the creatures they had crossed well more than a third of the distance. Now they had fallen well within range of those who lacked the inherent skill of the elf. Along the wall, the call went up for the rest of the archers. Arrows and bolts filled the darkness like deadly rain as they plummeted into the mass of bodies charging toward the walls. With a cry of feral rage, they lunged forward, picking up speed. To the horror of the defenders, many bristled with arrows that had failed to slay their targets outright, wave after wave of missiles plummeted into the crowded forms below. Those who fell were trampled underfoot without a care from the flood which crashed against the high stone walls and thick iron-banded gates. The swordsman could feel the tremor beneath his feet as the bodies slammed against the defenses. It reminded him of an earthquake, now it seemed the earth shook once more from the tremendous force.

Lorena glanced down over the battlements, the torchlight only reached so far but she could just make out stains of blood on the stonework from where the skulls of the rushing mob had smashed into the walls. The mage lifted her staff out and over, whispering in the tongue known only to those of the craft. The crystal embedded atop her staff glowed blue, then green, and swirled together before flashing with a shuddering crack as a bolt of lightning flashed from the clouds swirling overhead. Screams and howls of rage filled the air as charred bodies flew from the impact. A smoldering crater remained where the spell had struck. A cheer arose from those who had witnessed the spellcaster's blow, but she could only grit her teeth in disappointment.

"How many more of those do you think you can manage?" Bart called out, looking over at the destruction wrought by his lover. It always surprised the swordsman just how powerful some of her magic could be, one of the many reasons why he had always avoided arguing with the hot-tempered redhead.

The mage turned back, stroking the wood shaft of her staff contemplatively. "Not as many as we would need to finish them off, unfortunately. I don't have many spells that could help, and if I were to use fire it might burn the gates, they are so packed in, that the flames would spread." She loosed another bolt of lightning further along the wall, flinging more smoking corpses into the night air. "If that damn wizard would get out here maybe it would be a different story."

Bart looked about the walls, it was true, neither the old man nor the two holy knights he had barely seen since their arrival were anywhere to be seen. "What's the point then? Why would they show up, warn us of what is coming, then sit back and do nothing?"

Armen chucked a javelin down into the swarming mass below, smiling grimly as it impaled an orc-like fiend grasping at the walls. "Oh, you know how those religious fanatics are, thumping their shiny breastplates and spouting all that rhetoric about how the gods are on their side and all that right until the battle is almost won then they swoop in and steal the glory."

A panicked cry broke out further down the wall, drawing the companion's attention. "Ladders!" shouted one of the soldiers, "Ladders on the wall!"

Bart sprinted down the wall, sword on his shoulder as he hugged the far side of the battlements to pass behind archers and spearmen arrayed along the battlement. It was true, the rough wood frame of a ladder clambered against the parapets and shook as something clambered its way up rapidly. The swordsman grabbed one of the bill hooks from a nearby rack along the wall and jammed the curved catch set into the blade along the rung. Shoving with all his weight, Bart felt the timber lattice heave outward until it stood vertical then slowly plummeted back into the gathered masses with a sickening crunch. His eyes darted along the walls, ladder after ladder clattered into place, rising up from the swarming masses. In the gloom he could barely make out the armored forms which had been hidden amongst the swarming, grasping hands and bodies of the undead.

"There are orcs down there!" Cried out Thrax, the naga's scimitar hammering down into the exposed skull of a tattooed orc clasping a wicked, curved blade between their teeth. Blood and bits of skull scattered across the stones as the heavy blade sparked against the steel dagger that had been held between its fangs. In the distance a haunting call blew from a ram's horn, heralding the arrival of a new enemy. In the waning tones of that call to war, a faint whistling buzz could just be heard cutting through the darkness.

Bart dove against the wall, instinct taking over, just as a swarm of the black shafts clattered against the walls and pierced through the limbs and armor of the scattered defenders. One woman wielding a crossbow fell back choking from the shaft lodged into her throat. Choking on her own blood, her hand twitched, releasing the loaded bolt which flew wildly off into the night. The swordsman lunged for the weapon, grabbing the quiver strapped around the dead woman's waist, and began making his way back towards the gatehouse. Screams of the wounded filled the air amongst the calls for arrows and aid. Crouched below the battlements, Bart heard the ladder clamoring against the wall to his side. Shoving himself from the wall, he pulled back on the bowstring and notched it under the metal catch set into the trigger of his crossbow, fumbling for one of the bolts remaining in the quiver he had scavenged. Raising the weapon up, ready to fire, he was greeted with the green-skinned form of a snarling goblin poking its long-eared pointed face over the edge. Bart loosed the bolt, adding another piercing to the goblin's collection as they flew back from the ladder into the open air.

Armen rushed to his friend's side, pulling Bart up to his feet amongst the chaos quickly overwhelming the wall. "We have to do something about those ladders! The bastards keep catching them and sending them right back up!"

Bart nodded in agreement, "No choice then, fire it is." The two rushed along the wall, joining the rest atop the gatehouse. The swordsman, handing his crossbow off to Lorena, reached for one of the torches set within the brazier. Armen was close behind as they left, carrying a wood bucket filled with the stinking, black pitch that bubbled softly. Reaching one of the ladders, Armen upended the sticky, scalding liquid over the edge, coating the wooden limbs and rungs and burning the skin from the screaming goblin that had made it halfway up the structure. Bart reached over, lighting the tar which whooshed in a plume of smoke and flame. It lit up the darkness greater than any torch along the wall, falling back in a fiery arc as it fell back, once more, into the masses below. Along the defenses, the word spread as more buckets and torches set to work lighting as many ladders as the defenders could reach, engulfing the attackers below in the choking fumes and flames.

Leaning over the edge of the gatehouse wall, Della released another arrow into the snarling masses clustered before the gates. "This is taking too long, Armen. We are going to run out of arrows before they exhaust themselves."

Bart nodded, peeking out over the walls into the newly illuminated darkness below. With a start, he searched to and fro amongst the scene, eyes wide in the flickering gloom. "Where are the corpses?"

Peering up beside the swordsman, Lorena searched the chaos below. What Bart had said was true, there were far too few bodies to be found amongst the charging figures. "Look!" cried the mage, pointing out past the rear of the horde below. To their horror, the defenders could see the teams of goblins sprinting back and forth from the throng, dragging away the bodies into the darkness beyond.

Across the Tsere River and east of the dense forests sitting in the open plains south of Timberview, the high garrison of The Order resounded with the call of bells from atop the high towers within. Columns and rows of knights clad in full armor, squires alongside, sergeants and garrison soldiers adorned in the black tabards of those who had not taken the full oaths of their brotherhood stood in silence. The order had come in the middle of the night, torches filled the air illuminating the silver edges of spears, lances, pikes, and halberds bristling like a forest of steel. A balcony overlooked the formations awaiting the word of their Grand Master, from the edge, a rolled banner unfurled under the guiding hand of two knights adorned with golden eagles across their chests. The broad red cloth flowed heavily down into the space below and fluttered lazily in the gusts of wind. Those who had a full view of the banner knew what it entailed. The red banner, emblazoned with the eagle of The Order clasping a sword betwixt its talons was the deceleration of open war on the enemies of the faithful. No quarter would be given, none expected, and any who marched did so with the certainty of death on the horizon.

Grand Master Bernard marched solemnly to the edge of the balcony, his pure white armor adorned with a red sash across his polished breastplate. At his hip hung the Sword of Masters, the blade passed down to every Grand Master since the founding of their chapters under Grand Master Kraxus, the Blade of the Morning. "Brothers and Sisters, as some of you may know, a short time ago I dispatched two of our Order along with the wizard Solon in response to a grave and ancient threat. This enemy has not been seen since before the founding of Maroth, but once more it has turned its dark gaze upon the realm of the living. We are the light, we stand before the gates that lead into the darkness, against the forces that would seek the destruction of the faithful. And now we are called, once more, to preserve the faith and stand against the tide. Father, guide us! Mother, preserve us! Warrior, lend us your strength!"

The words echoed back from the myriad of voices below, resounding from the walls. With a wave of the Grand Master's hand, horses were mounted, and foot soldiers fell into step as they exited the open gates leading into the night. Onward they marched, arrayed in all their glory into the open plains to the west. Amongst the heavy cavalry at the center of the column, Grand Master Bernard rocked in the saddle alongside his senior commanders. Lifting his gaze to the starry night, the small pinpricks of light pulsed within the infinite darkness of the heavens. The banners of his order fluttered in the breeze, wafting the steady cloud of dust rising from the footsteps of soldiers, horses, and wagons marching onward toward their destiny. Three thousand brothers and sisters, the greatest force The Order had ever raised, now made the journey north towards the impending battle.

A scout sped up from the column's rear, saluting as he reared his horse alongside. "Grand Master, all forces have cleared the road. And the wagon train is at hand as well, the rear guard reports no sighting of any movement to the rear or flanks. But that may well change come the dawn."

Bernard nodded approvingly, dismissing the young rider who galloped back to rejoin his fellows. He motioned for one of his aids alongside, "Once we are in sight of the Tsere, I want scouts dispatched along The Spine to find a forward camp. We must assume the city will be well under siege by the time we arrive. The wagons and rear guard will remain on the eastern side of the river, I will not risk them being caught up as we cross should there be an ambush."

From beneath his gauntlet, the old veteran pulled the missive he had received in the night. Although he could no longer read the words for lack of light, he remembered each detail from blistering memory. That old wizard had been right all along, but he had delayed any action. Now not only would he have to risk a forced night march, in the dark over rolling and unpaved terrain, but he would also have to face that old man and eat crow. By his reckoning, it would take two days to reach the northern reaches, but the battle may very well have been underway by now. All the Grand Master could hope for was that the city would hold long enough for his reinforcements to arrive. Aside from the rear guard, he now fielded one thousand foot soldiers, half as many archers, six hundred mounted sergeants, four hundred heavy calvary, and the rest comprised his personal guard. All their years of training would now face the ultimate test.

Deep amongst the shadows of the pines, a pair of figures clad in black watched in silence before slinking back to a pair of waiting horses. One scribbled a quick note, sliding the message into a tube banded to the leg of a grey pigeon. Letting the bird loose, they once more mounted their horses and rode off into the night. One turned east, along the winding road that would take them towards Lakeshore, then north to Harvest and beyond. The other rode south, driving hard for Crossings and the capitol.

# FIFTEEN

# FLOOD

Marguk's eyes gleamed in the darkness as he and his fellow chieftains watched the swarms of ghoulish creatures hammer against the defenses of the soft skins. He could feel his blood boil deep within, the rush of anticipation for battle, to deal death on his enemies and hear their screams of terror and pain. The massive orc's eyes rolled back, breathing deep of the smell of burning flesh and smoke, this was the scent of battle. No other sensation could compare to how much it stirred his soul. The warlord opened his eyes once more, surveying the remainder of his gathered forces still waiting for their chance to join in the fray.

Most of the tribes had fallen into line following the aftermath of the 'disagreement' between the Wolf Clan and the Long Fangs, those who had mumbled in derision now found themselves amongst the shambling horde piling against the walls which stood in his way. Even the dead have a use in the eyes of the Far-Seer, perhaps more than they ever would in life. The screams and yowls from the ensuing battle in the darkness echoed from the sheer rock faces of the mountains to the east, filling the air with their haunting chorus. Arrayed at the front of his army, lines of archers readied their bows once more, sending wave after wave of the obsidian and iron-headed shafts skyward into the darkness towards the upper ramparts lined with the cowardly pink skins.

Horka Dead Crow whistled at the sight of one of the ladders bursting into flame and crashing down into the milling swarm. "You gotta admit, brother, those little cowards do know how to liven up a party." He chuckled, watching the small figures dart back and forth with torches along the edge of the walls.

"They only know how to whimper and hide," growled the hulking war chief, "soon they will sing a different tune as we break down their precious walls and set their city to their own torches." Marguk watched on, impassively, as teams of goblins swooped in amongst the carnage and began dragging the dead and wounded away from the field, piling them beyond the range of the archers arrayed atop the stone walls of the city.

Gamona and Sula watched on from behind the gathered chieftains, the female dwarf now clad in furs along with the armor she had been gifted by her master. The orc priestess had donned a shirt of chain as well over her flowing robes. Sula's eyes hardened, the flow of bodies never ceasing their procession back from the battle unfolding at the base of the wall. More than a few times it had seemed that their forces would gain a foothold atop the wall, but each time the humans had driven them back, lighting the wooden ladders and throwing them down amongst the attacking mob below. She understood that the undead creatures now bolstering her brother's forces were viewed as expendable, but they had once been their brothers and sisters in the eyes of Gog. This black magic chilled her heart to its core, and violated every belief she and the priesthood held dear, was there even honor to be found for those who had turned?

The branded dwarf turned up towards the one who had once led her by the slave's chain from the temple, "Mistress, are you troubled by this as well?" Had she not been granted her place amongst the warriors, the question may very well have been greeted with a swift blow from the priestess' hand.

Sula's hand clenched around her staff, flesh digging into the rough fibers of the wood. "There are some things in this world, dwarf, that should never see the light. The dead are to remain in their slumber, not rise time after time to serve the will of the living. I do not know which god that woman draws her power from, but the Far-Seer would never condone such atrocities." The priestess watched on as the rows of bodies grew before the feet of the black-haired witch. Since they had departed the plains, leaving the temple and sacred places of Korb behind, that woman had seemingly entwined her tentacles into the hearts and minds of not only her brother but many of the other chiefs as well. It felt as though the sorceress was turning every sacred belief they once held into ashes, that haunting power that seemingly breathed new life into the slain drew the awe and reverence of many who saw it. Many now openly proclaimed she may be a prophet sent by Gog himself, to lead their people into the new fertile lands once promised in the ancient prophecies.

Marguk turned to the pair nearby, "Sister, Beast-Slayer, attend Susalla and make sure she has everything she needs for the ritual. It will soon be time to drive fear into the hearts of our enemies atop their precious walls." As the two bowed and departed in obedience, the warlord motioned towards another chief nearby. From head to toe, this warrior was covered in deep scars, each earned with pride after many long years of raiding. "Take your shield warriors along with them, be ready to advance on the wall, I want to be in that city before the dawn. Do not let any harm come to the sorceress."

The warrior nodded, "And what of your sister and the champion?"

The warlord breathed deeply, gazing upon the walls which stood in his way. "If they fall, they fall. Should they be needed, Susalla can raise them once more to serve my will, now go." As the chieftain turned to follow the priestess and the warrior dwarf, Marguk waved forward a thin-limbed goblin adorned with brightly-colored strips of cloth in a rainbow of colors. "Sound the charge, let these humans hear the death cries of their city."

The goblin chattered with glee, sprinting forward to meet his fellow harlequin-garbed friends. Each carried a large horn made from either brass or bone. Jumping and screeching in wild glee they bellowed out the haunting tones into the night sky. A crescendo of chaos called out to the armies gathered away from the fight who answered the horns in turn, howling into the sky, beating their shields and spears, rattling bones atop great banners adorned with skulls of beasts and enemies alike. As a solid mass, they charged the city walls, trampling any who stumbled or were too slow to keep pace. Goblins astride crocottas howled with glee, waving their spears, urging the great beasts forward. Their fangs dripped with anticipation of fresh kills as their heavy paws dug deep into the earth propelling their powerful forms onward into the darkness.

At the center of the charging horde, four hulking trolls, their tough grey skin painted with swirling blue and green paint, ambled amongst the smaller orcs and goblins. They towered over them, ten to twelve feet tall, and between them swung the gigantic tree trunk of an ancient oak capped with sheets of patchwork iron.

The war chief smiled in grim anticipation, the opening waves had served their purpose. The archers atop those high walls had spent much of what he knew would be a dwindling supply of arrows, and they had openly avoided using fire near the gates. Now he had found their weakness, he would smash those gates open, crack the city open like a ripe melon and his army would pour within like locusts. Of course, the masses of thralls raised by his sorceress would bolster the main force, there was no greater advantage to be had than an army that refused to remain dead. It almost felt like he was a yearling again, cheating at games for the simple joy of winning at any cost.

From his vantage point within a tower set high amongst the inner defenses of the castle itself, Lord Firbanks watched the fires rising from beyond the walls of his city. The old wizard sat nearby, watching the battle unfold with grim eyes. Behind the pair of observers, aids and messengers darted two and fro relaying news from the battle. Movements of the enemy, reports from scouts set within the mountains and along the eastern ridge on their flank, and the status of the wounded which now flowed into the makeshift hospital with the help of litters and wagons manned by those who could not fight.

"What do you think, Master Solon?" asked the noble, now clad for battle in scale and chain, the proud crest of his family emblazoned boldly on his chest. "Is this truly all our enemy can manage? To throw themselves blindly against our walls like wheat to be chaffed? From what you had preached, I would have thought our odds less favorable."

The old wizard sighed, shaking his head as he looked out over the northern walls. "I pray you are right, Lord, if we can hold them here and crush their numbers before they reach the open fields then all the better. The terrain of your domain is certainly an advantage, funneling their numbers into a single front and restricting their movement. What concerns me, still, is that if they were under the control of someone from the Hinterlands, surely they know they could have avoided us and swept around to the north through the pass? If they are being driven here against your walls, then there must be some alternative goal in mind, as to what, I cannot say."

Timmon Firbank turned away from the opening, "Has there been any word from Captain Eliza and her knights in the south?" he called out.

One of the aids amongst the maps shook her head, "None, Lord, they are still posted along the Tsere keeping watch for anything that may approach from the eastern passes. So far there has been nothing to report."

The lord of Twin Rivers nodded, "All the same, send a request for them to scout the rear of our enemy to the north. If our enemy is planning something, it is sure to launch from there." Saluting, the aid rushed from the room to see to the request. Lord Firbank returned his attention to the battle stagnating along the outer defenses of his city.

"Does something concern you?" the old wizard asked, his hands stroking the long grey hairs of his beard.

With a shrug, the master of Twin Rivers gazed out towards the dark horizon of the north. "We have fought off invaders before, but on all those occasions we had warning of their approach from the outliers along the Hinterlands. This feels too sudden to be just another raid from those cursed lands, no, there is something else at play this time. Even without the threat of these creatures you and the others described, there is something I feel I am blind to, and I do not plan on being surprised again." Hearing the old wizard gasp, he turned to see the aged magician trembling like a leaf at the height of autumn. A faint yellow glow shone from their eyes, welling with tears. "What?"

Master Solon's voice cracked, any moisture driven from his tongue with fear. Gazing out into the darkness he whispered, "The corpses, they are standing up." He turned, ashen-faced towards the castle lord, gripping the black tome in his pale, trembling grasp. "The necromancer is here."

Along the banks of the Tsere River, the Cloud Knights encampment sprawled north of Rivers Pass. Most of the townsfolk had already evacuated into the city, leaving only a few of the few obstinate residents behind, the town mayor among them. Captain Eliza and her staff had been provided full use of the town center, including the mayoral long house and a nearby temple for their use. Knights passed to and fro amongst the buildings whence they had been billeted, taking turns keeping watch or on patrol along the river and the northern flank of the defense. All was silent, save for the sounds of distant battle ringing from the city to the northwest. Eliza sat with her back resting against the smooth timber walls of the Mayor's home, her eyes sought the high battlements for any sign, a signal that could give cause for the captain to bring her forces to bear. They had finally made it this far, found the heir, and secured the tentative safety and future of the kingdom only to now sit back from the front. Lieutenant Frig's hurried footsteps from within pulled her attention from the western horizon.

"Word from one of our scouts captain," the shorter officer whispered, "the enemy is calling up their reserves. It seems they plan to make a concentrated push on the gates, and their archers will soon be forced to advance lest they strike down their own."

Captain Eliza nodded, lifting herself from her seat, she entered the mayoral residence and walked over to a long table set with candles and the large map of the Northern Lands. "I would do the same, it is likely they wish to breach the outer defenses before the sun breaks. From their position, they would risk becoming blinded with the dawn." Worry drew deep ridges across her disturbed face as she spoke.

"You seem worried, Ma'am" The junior officer noted.

"That's just the thing," said the knight commander, her eyes fixed upon the inked outlines of the chart before them. "It is precisely what I, or any other commander, would press. The longer this battle draws out, the more I am becoming convinced that this is no disjointed horde of barbarians, raiding and plundering like a blaze caught upon the breeze. They are disciplined and there is strategy at work here. Have you ever known the hill tribes from the Hinterlands to display such? I certainly have not, so that means there is some reason as to why they crossed the Red Horse and turned south to engage Twin Rivers, they could have easily taken the northern pass and swept around to continue raiding the defenseless towns and villages further inland."

The two women examined the map together, searching for some hidden revelation amongst the lines and markers dotting its face. Black disks along the westernmost river of the Twin Rivers domain clearly noted the line of villages north of the city that had fallen to the creatures as they made their way south. Yet there were several that had not been touched, according to Lord Firbank's scouts, further north along the Red Horse.

Lieutenant Frig traced her finger along the trail, "It almost seems as though they purposefully have avoided coming near our border with Almach further north. If all they sought was riches and plunder, surely it matters little from whence they pilfer their goods and slaves. Almach has little in the way of natural defenses once you cross the river, and there are more than enough villages near the mountains for them to provide a tempting bounty."

Eliza studied the area with interest, what her junior had said was true, so why the focus on Twin Rivers? She bit her thumb, chewing the nail softly. "Where is Theodoric?"

The lieutenant pointed along the eastern line of the Giant's Spine to their north, "He should have a forward outpost here, short of the bridge west of Timberglenn, he would have full command of the area and observe any movement without discovery from here. It was his scouts who scouted out the rear of the enemy line." Frig looked up at her commander, "Should we reinforce his position? But if we do, we would be splitting our forces."

"Even if we split our forces," Captain Eliza tapped the map before her, southeast of where her regiment now waited, "the Garrison of The Order is at our rear. By now they must have sent some reinforcement, if they are not headed this way already then surely following the dawn they must show signs to the south. Lord Timmon sent word prior to our departure, I have all faith they will respond, their oaths demand it." Reaching out her hand, the captain collected a few of the blue stones piled around Rivers Pass which denoted her forces and placed them north along the mountains. "Send half our forces to support Theodoric, if we are called into support then our main body here will swing in from the south. That will provide the opening for him to attack from the mountains on the east and north. We have the advantage from the air, and by attacking from two sides we can crush them against the walls should it come down to that. But if the enemy tries to come around our flank via the mountains, we will have a strong enough buffer to hold the flank until we can support him."

In little time, the air filled once more with the sound of strong wings driving north through the night sky. The two remaining officers stood watching the dark shadows disappear amongst the scattered stars above. Their force of eighty mounted knights was hardly ample reinforcement, and there would be little to no defense against archers if they risked an open assault. But Captain Eliza knew her forces would be of little use locked within the city, maneuverability was key to their doctrine, and it was the one thing she could exercise to hopefully dwindle the invaders. A cry from the western edge of the small town drew her attention with a snap of her neck. There atop one of the open-topped watchtowers set into the south wall blazed a signal pyre, flames spiraling upward against the star-filled sky. The gates had been breached.

Commander Zulla stood amongst the gathered lords and nobles before the throne. The summons had come without warning, and many of those gathered murmured amongst themselves in hushed tones. Having been roused from their beds even before the break of dawn, it was with good reason many found themselves nervously glancing towards the exits. In the wake of the arrest of Sylvanus, more than a few nobles and ministers had come to question the current state of affairs with a wary eye. Until now the king had been so far removed from the day-to-day workings and policies of the kingdom that it had become commonplace for the council to govern without oversight.

Snorri fidgeted alongside his human friend, no word had come from the Black Tower, and the guards whom he had contacts with could provide no word as to the state of his long-time companion. The pounding of spears announced the arrival of their monarch, the dwarf looked on in suspense as the old king slowly ascended the throne and sat to face his gathered subjects.

"We have gathered you here on matters of the greatest urgency", King Merrick's voice echoed through the room with a strength and boldness none had heard since the days he rode at the head of their armies. "We have received tragic news. Our cousin, the Lord of Twin Rivers, is now besieged by a great force raised from amongst the Hill Tribes. While the defense of our lands is of the greatest importance, so too is the loyalty of our lords and nobles." His eyes cast about the upturned faces gathered in the throne room, "The crown prince, whom our cousin had taken in, and assured us of his safekeeping, has been slain through means most foul!"

Snorri turned quickly towards his armored friend, the commander's face was twisted in a scowl. It would seem they had no knowledge of this either, but this was the second time in as many days that the king had knowledge unbeknown to his nobility. Taking a deep breath, he steeled himself before stepping out in plain view of his king. Kneeling before the throne, Snorri fought to keep his voice as calm as he could manage, "My king, I pray your indulgence, but from where have you received this news? I find it hard to accept such a thing, your good cousin has been a noble and steadfast ally to your reign. And his loyalty has been praised from shore to peak as being second to none."

King Merrick nodded, "We would remind you, Snorri Hammerstone, that we have another cousin. One who, despite the whispers behind his back, has been in constant communication with us since we commanded our heir to be found." He glowered over the gathered assembly, "Unlike some of those who stand here in silence! You who stand here before us and gawk like fools, lips still save when you vie for personal wealth and favor! These clucking hens, pecking about for scraps to gorge themselves!" The monarch stood slowly, "I name Lord Timmon Firbank, and his kin, Traitor of the Realm. We strip him of his lands and his titles, and decree that whoever brings him bound in chains before us to face judgment shall be given the domain of Twin Rivers and all the properties therein! Now, leave us!"

Slowly, the throng of nobles and counselors made their way from the throne. Stooping to pull up the trembling form of Snorri, Commander Zulla glanced up towards the throne. Any sense of the calm, wise king he had served all his life now seemed absent. The man who now sat atop the throne, pulsed with rage from beneath the golden crown. Neither said a word as they pushed their way through the crowd, out the throne room, and down the wide halls before turning down a passageway leading to the dark recesses of the castle.

"I fear our king has truly lost his reason," Snorri softly whispered. "The slippery words of his cousin have tainted his ear. If that man achieves his aim unhindered, the kingdom is lost."

Commander Zulla nodded. "But what are we to do about it? Duke Rolfe has a stranglehold on the king, no other will be able to break through the deception to enlighten him now."

The dwarf bit his lip before answering, "We must march on Twin Rivers with all haste then, I believe the heir still lives and Heathridge hopes to claim the crown for himself by defaming his only opponent. I never did like that man, he always struck me as a snake amongst roses."

"Even if we were to march at once, we would never make it in time." sighed the veteran knight with a shrug. "What's more, if we were to marshal my forces and join the defense of Twin Rivers, it may lead to us both being named traitors as well. If we stand with the king, blinded by his faith in his cousin, we defy his will to defend and support his heir. If we stand with the prince, we defy the king, who has ordered that Lord Firbank be taken." Zulla paused, turning to the senior counselor, "Duke Rolfe has played us from the beginning, he must have known once the king commanded that the heir be found I would send our most elite forces forth to find them. Now my forces are scattered, leaving him room to manipulate other lords to support his claim. With the heir declared dead, and Lord Timmon named a traitor, which leaves him to inherit the crown. Any who might claim the prince still lives would be viewed as a rebel, leading the nation into civil war."

—⁓—

Far from the flames of battle or the comforts of the capitol, an army marched along the roads weaving along the borders of Maroth. The steady trod of boots and hooves kept pace with the drums as banners flapped in the breeze. The double-headed axe of Heathridge set on green and white fields stood proudly above the martial parade, along with the crests and banners of other houses and companies who had joined in the campaign. There was the red fist of Sir Oralla of Krot, and the anchor over blue waves of Sir Trenton from Bayhome. The mercenary companies of the Grey Eagles, Silver Swords, and Free Brothers supplemented the force. But amongst the banners and pennants there also waved the Black Eagle of Almach set on a field of crimson. Those who had seen the banner in passing found themselves risking a second.

Duke Rolfe, Master of Heathridge, smiled from astride his horse. The lines of troops he had carefully gathered over the course of his time rebuilding his domain marched along the road winding westward. Soon they would pass Falmat and reach the edges of the Timber Glenn, the thick woods would slow their march but there was little need for haste now. A cloaked rider spurred his black steed alongside, his gleaming breastplate catching the morning rays of the sun tinting it as crimson as his beard. The pair watched on as the lines of spearmen and men-at-arms trod lock-step along the dusty road in the dawn.

"When they write the annals of your reign, this shall be the morning they say it began." Said the bearded rider, a thin smile peeking out.

Shaking his head, Duke Rolfe's eyes followed the column. "Under my reign, the scholars will write whatever I command them to. Do you think my cousin, the old fool of a king, allowed the chroniclers to mention how he failed to overcome famine, plague, and invasion time and time again? How his reign was born on the shoulders of his counselors, leaving him to squander his waning years as a puppet king? He was handed a prosperous and strong kingdom, and he squandered the treasury on the pet projects of his friends instead of looking after the people. Any lord who had built their domain from the ashes faced the possibility of losing those lands to a favorite of the crown, he even sent his own flesh and blood to the wastes of the north to defend his borders so he would not have to muster the courage to face his enemies on the field." Spitting on the ground, the lord steered his horse to follow alongside the army.

Following suit, the bearded warrior pulled back his hood to let the warming rays seep into his scalp. "And so now, for the first time in history, the forces of Almach and Maroth march side by side against a common enemy. All in the name of preserving peace and tranquility for their peoples from the clutches of darkness. Quite the romantic tale, I must say."

"A darkness of your own making, General." Chuckled the Duke.

The man laughed, "Oh no, not mine good Duke. I simply encouraged the pursuit of knowledge, and if that just so happened to align with our goals then all the better." Ducking his head to avoid the outstretched branch of an old beech tree near the path, he gazed upon the countryside stretching south. The distant hills and scattered leafy sentinels glimmered with morning dew, catching the first golden rays from the horizon. In contrast, the stony reaches of his homeland sliced into the northern sky across the Niend River like jagged teeth, foreboding and cold. "It is moments like this I remember why my people have always sought to reclaim the southern lands of our kingdom. The earth here is rich and green, a rarity once you cross the Tsere. These lands are ripe with seed and sprout, while my own flow with iron." A soft chuckled rippled from the general's throat, "But one cannot eat stone, were it not for you expanding trade across your lands and our borders, I imagine many of our children would have departed for the lands of eternal spring with empty bellies."

Rolfe cocked his head, casting a sideways glance at the Almachian General. "Hunger is no stranger, even in lands such as these. While these people toil in the heat of the sun, the rich and fat lords who attained their position through inheritance of blood instead of shedding it, grow ever more so on the fruits of the land. Many of them have never even seen their holdings, much less worked them. And while they gorge themselves on wine and meat, embellishing themselves with finery and lofty titles, the people suffer. But once I hold the crown that will all change, I will purge the nobility and cut out the cancer swelling in this kingdom root and stem so that our children may never know such misery. Still, what was your daughter's name again? The one who you sent out to stir up our foes."

Stroking his rusty beard, the General gazed west. "Susalla"

—◊◊◊—

Bart clung to the battlements, fighting for his footing as the gatehouse shook once more from the impact of the massive battering ram wielded by four gigantic trolls. They had appeared without warning, charging from beyond the darkness and striking the iron-banded gate like a thunderbolt. Only a handful of archers had even managed a shot at the beasts before it was too late. Screams of fear and pain echoed up from below as splinters sprayed inward from the force, a gaping hole quickly forming in the thick timbers. Iron strained to hold purchase, as though even the gate itself knew it must hold for as long as it could save the tide of death stream through unabated.

Armen grabbed his friend roughly, shouting over the din. "We have to fall back now! The gate will not hold!"

The swordsman shook himself, what his friend said was true. Already there were lines of defenders streaming along the ramparts and down the stairs, making their way to the second line of defense. A few remained, mostly those who were too wounded or stubborn enough to withdraw. "We must set a rear guard, delay them as long as we can so our forces can regroup at the keep! Otherwise, we will be cut down amongst the city streets!"

"I will stay, friend." Hissed Thrax.

Bart turned to protest, halting his tongue as he looked upon the bloody form of the scimitar-wielding warrior from the southern sands. Their scaly lower form was strewn with bloody gashes, blood seeped into the stonework and mortar at his feet.

"You go ahead, I will not let them get past without a fight. Just get Armen to the castle." Nodding with a weak smile, the naga made his way down the stairs at the back of the gatehouse and joined the gathering rear guard facing the creaking gates.

Della and Lorena rushed forward, pulling Bart away as he tried to follow his friend below. "We have to go! He knows what he is doing, we all knew what staying might mean!" cried the elf, her voice fighting to remain stoic, even as tears fell from her eyes. Together, the four ambled along the wall behind the steady stream of defenders making their way to the inner defenses. With a terrible crash of iron and wood, Bart could hear the gate explode inward far behind. As he glanced back toward the gatehouse, he caught a glimpse of the reptilian warrior lunging forward into the swarming masses, twin blades spinning through the air shimmering in the flames and moonlight. He could almost swear he could hear laughter, a raspy strange tone, human yet not.

Marguk stepped over the scattered remnants of thick timbers, weaving between the rush of bodies flowing into the city. Strewn about the entrance within, disembodied limbs and bloody corpses of humans, elven descendants, and revenants mingled together like autumn leaves. The strange body of a half-serpent being still wielding a pair of curved blades caught his eye as he passed. That one had been an annoyance, they had fought like a demon possessed, even from a distance he had seen those twin blades mow down line after line of his warriors as they charged the open gate. They would have made a fine addition to the horde, but now their body was so torn and mangled he doubted Susalla could even raise the steadfast defender in their current state. Pushing his way into the weaving stone-paved streets amongst the buildings and houses, the warlord took stock of his surroundings. Even as the weak soft skins had abandoned the outer defenses and run back to the supposed safety of the high walls of their castle, many were now cut off. Now the horde would need to fight street by street, clearing the buildings of any survivors as they were found.

"We should just burn it, Great Chief, smoke out the little rats and cut them down!" Growled one of the chieftains nearby.

Turning to the one who had spoken, Marguk returned the tone in kind, "Our people will be claiming this city. It will become our foothold in the green lands. The more I can claim for our people the better."

The one who had spoken up turned away with a sneer, spitting on the ground as they did. "Sounds like someone is having second thoughts then, going soft already?" Any further thoughts were cut off by the axe blade burying itself in their skull. A few who had stopped nearby shrank back in fear as Marguk pulled his weapon free, kicking the insubordinate chieftain's corpse in disgust.

Grabbing a burning timber from the rubble, the axe-wielding leader of the horde tossed it atop the twitching body at his feet, "Burn that." Satisfied, he once more turned down the streets of his latest conquest, eyes set on the castle's high walls on the great city's northern side.

The trails of destruction swept amongst the once vibrant city, screams of death and rage echoed from the plaster and timber of homes which had housed generations of residents. Those who had not made it to the castle either fought however they could or cowered in the shadows praying to their absent gods. Gamona followed along with the flood of warriors, her sword drawn yet unbloodied. As she turned the corner of what had once been some sort of mercantile district, amongst strewn piles of silk and bolts of cloth, she saw a trio of humans surrounded by jeering orcs and goblins. From their garb, the dwarf could tell the three were guards, blood smeared across the grey tower which was their sigil. They stood backs to each other, swords facing out into the growing mob inching ever closer. Now and then one of the warriors surrounding the battered trio would mockingly lunge forward, drawing whoever was nearest to react. Each pitiful defense met with yet more raucous laughter and howling mockery from the exuberant horde. An arrow sprouted from the chest of one of the soldiers, who slowly crumbled to their knees clutching the quivering shaft as they fell over in a pool of blood. All at once, the mob charged in, wrestling the remaining pair to the ground and beating them mercilessly. The dwarf turned away, those two would be lucky if the horde decided to end their lives. Alternatively, they would be taken as prizes as she had.

*Chapter*

# SIXTEEN

# HERO OF ORIA

Moans of pain and anguish filled the hall which had once resounded with music and joy. Bart looked about, numb from the scene, as he held the untouched wooden cup filled with water in his blood-stained hands. Darting to and fro amongst the bodies of the wounded, those who had any knowledge of wounds or herbalism fought their own battle amongst the field of dead and dying. With each loss, another sheet draped over the still forms in passing. Their numbers had been few, to begin with, but now they were slowly dwindling beyond hope. At the main entrance to the keep, the defenders hurriedly piled anything that could barricade the door. Chairs, tables, and desks piled up against the inner frame.

Pulling themselves away from the scene on the first floor, the remaining companions climbed spiraled stairs leading to the upper floors of the castle and made their way to a large chamber which, via a balcony, provided a commanding view of the city below. Lord Timmon and his son stood there amongst archers posted alongside. Now and then one of the bowmen would draw back, aiming at the distant targets streaming down the roads below, and let fly onto the rushing horde. Master Solon sat at a small table near the fireplace along the wall, the black leather book open in his hands, his eyes darting back and forth as he searched the pages within.

Patting Bart's shoulder, Lorena made her way over to the fellow magician. The swordsman looked on, helpless, torn. The screams and cries from the city streets below echoed through his ears, tugging dark memories he had once kept locked deep within. Della had joined the archers along the edge of the balcony, her bow sang as she fired any arrow she could get her hands on down into the approaching mob of bodies. Tears burned in the elf's eyes, the pain lessening little by little with each orc or goblin she sent hurtling into the dirt, her arrow protruding from their lifeless husks. Armen pulled up a chair to the map-set table lit with small candles and set his silent friend on the soft cushions before joining the two lords observing the attack below. Bart sat there cut off from the world, lost in his own thoughts and regrets. The myriad of voices around him sounded as though he were underwater.

"Bart! Can you hear me?"

The swordsman shook himself, blinking as the freckled face of Lorena hovered at his side, her hands grasping his, shaking him awake. "What is it?" he mumbled.

Lorena forced a weak smile, tightening her grasp on her lover's hand. "Master Solon believes he might have found a way to stop the revenants. If we can keep them from resurrecting their dead, then we can hold out until reinforcements arrive."

The old wizard nodded from his seat, "It is possible, however, the solution itself is not written within these pages, it is only a theory."

Armen and the two lords approached from the balcony, along with Della who rubbed her sore fingers. Lord Firbank shook his head with a sigh, "At this point, Master Solon, I would welcome theories and guesses as warmly as a hundred armored knights." Pulling a crumpled note from his robes, he continued. "It would seem my family has been named 'Traitors to the Realm' by our gracious king, for the death of the heir apparent. Someone has told the counsel of lords the prince was slain on my order, so we should not expect any assistance from the army."

Bart glanced up, confused. "I thought you said Armen was the heir?" he pressed, cocking his head towards the taller warrior. "Looks pretty alive to me, with all respect."

"I assume that someone is using the death of Sir Walter as an excuse to defame me," explained Firbank, eyes downcast into the flames, "And should we not survive, the truth dies with us. An elegant plan I admit. That leaves our survival in your hands, Master Solon."

The wizard held up the book that had been the center of his attention, "Everything I have read within these pages seems to indicate two key factors essential to perform most of the rituals within; an innate connection to the dark forces once sealed with the fall of Hecktat, and whoever uses the secrets within must provide the essence of life. I have seen no signs of a rift between our worlds, which leads me to believe what we are seeing is a shadow of the necromancer's true potential power."

Lorena nodded along, "And the other key element, 'essence of life', is something any who practices the arts draws upon. Simply put, kill the caster and we end the spell. If we consider the revenant as a curse, then we can break their forces by focusing on the one who raises them. And thanks to Master Solon we know the identity of the woman responsible for these creatures."

Marguk cursed the fates, glaring up at the castle gates mocking him. Thanks to the layout of the city, buildings pressed together in an intricate maze of timber and brick, his army now hindered any advance of the four trolls which had smashed the first gate open with impunity. And the slope rising up to the castle walls provided no purchase for his ladders. Each time they lifted the timber frames it would slide back, crashing to the ground.

The warlord turned away from the siege, grabbing one of the brightly-garbed goblin trumpeters. "Find the troll-master, tell him when I want those gates down now!"

"But, my chief, the path is not clear. They would crush our own if they..."

The hulking orc lifted the stuttering creature by its throat to face him, "You do as you're told, or I will use your skull to hammer down the gates myself!" Tossing the goblin aside, Marguk grinned darkly as he watched the rainbow-clad messenger scramble away. A sudden tremor on the back of his neck caused him to jump back, impulsively, just as a steel-headed javelin clattered off the stone road where he had been standing. His attention was pulled upward into the waning night, astonished at the sight of a score of winged beasts high ahead in the dim light. Griffins soared above the city, their riders hurling spears and javelins down into the packed masses strewn throughout the city. Caught by surprise, warriors hurled themselves under any cover they could find. A few lifted their shields, seeking protection from the hail of missiles. But the heavy shafts slammed into the crude defilade, piercing plank and flesh with impunity. The revenant did not so much as react, hurling themselves forward mindlessly into the heavy gates before them, clawing at the timbers with bare hands, tearing the flesh from their fingers with unfeeling abandon. Archers darted from cover, aiming at the flying beasts, trying to knock them from the sky. But the thin shafts seemed to glance harmlessly off the dense feathers. Howling with rage, Marguk ripped one of the javelins from the writhing body of an orc nearby and hurled it back to the sky-borne foe. Laughing with satisfaction he watched the griffin spiral mid-air, the terrified scream of its rider ending with a crunch as they were thrown from the saddle and smashed into the tiled roofs of a house far below. It did not take long for others to follow their leader's example as they scampered to and fro gathering anything they could use to hurl at the new threat above.

Gamona ducked back under an overhang just as another needle-headed javelin screamed downward, catching a bow-wielding goblin through the shoulder and sending them spinning to the ground. The orc priestess huddled nearby, blood staining her robes from the pools and rivers strewn throughout as they had made their way through the winding buildings. The pair had followed the sorceress from the gates, through the surrounding carnage amongst the horde, stopping only for Susalla to perform her ritual on the piles of bodies scattered about. The army of revenants now teemed with not only goblins and orcs, but now humans, beast-kin, elves, and Gamona's fellow dwarves had been added to their ranks. The groaning, shambling masses lurched together with a singular purpose up the winding roads toward the castle gates. The female dwarf's stomach turned at the sight, the guilt panged deep within.

A weak groan caught the dwarf's ear, turning towards the remnants of a shattered door nearby, her eye caught sight of a wounded human lying in the shadows of a ruined house. A deep gash crossed the man's face, the skin of his forehead peeled back exposing the white bone beneath as they lay in agony. Gamona, glancing about to see if any were paying any heed to her movements, slowly made her way to their side. Finger raised to her lips, she pulled a heavy tarp from amongst the rubble and draped it over the wounded soldier.

"What do you think you are doing?" growled a voice from behind the dwarf's ear.

With a start, Gamona turned to see the scowling face of the heavily scarred chieftain who had been ordered to escort them as they moved through the city. He and his warriors each bore a heavy-planked shield banded with leather and studded with iron nails. Words caught in her throat, unable to find her voice as she stood alone before the hulking warrior. Sula appeared from behind them, making her way between the two fighters caught in the stand-still.

The priestess turned to the shield-bearing warrior, "What harm is there in letting one human die from its wounds? There is no need to waste our steel on a corpse."

"Then it should be brought to the Raven-Haired one, to join its fellow corpses under the glory of Gog!" growled the scarred orc, venom dripping from his lips.

Sula had heard enough of this, sneering back, "The Far-Seer has no hand in this! This is dark magic, twisted and reviled. My brother, your overlord, has been deceived by this foul witch! She invites our destruction! Look at how many have died in the name of her own ambition, the fall at the hands of our enemies only to rise as slaves to her will! Our people are being slaughtered, for what? Promises of glory and riches. Fertile lands to hold and keep for our children? There will be no such thing because none will live to enjoy the riches or fruits of our conquest!" The priestess turned to join Gamona, she never felt the sharp blade across her throat until the warm flow draped the collar of her robes in sweet crimson.

Gamona gasped in horror, staring up at the black-haired human standing over the fading, lifeless body of the priestess. The blade in her hand was still dripping from her kill. "You bitch!" Screamed the dwarven warrior, drawing her blade and lunging at the sorceress with a leap. Her blade thudded against the thick shield of the nearby warrior, a hideous grin plastered across his fanged maw.

"I've been waiting for this, little one." Mocked the orc, his yellowed fangs inches from her face. Pushing the smaller warrior back, the orc lifted the iron-headed mace banded with leather and brought it down towards her head.

The dwarf stumbled back, parrying the blow wildly, trying to regain her footing in the tight space. Her foot slipped slightly in the thick blood beneath her sandals as she slid around the outside of her opponent's reach and brought her sword down at the back of his dark-skinned wrist. She could feel the bone chip on the edge of her blade, but the strike seemingly had no effect as the orc swung the shield in his left hand, aiming the steel-banded edge at her throat. She ducked, feeling the air pass over her as the wood shield slammed into the wall behind her. Gamona rolled forward, pulling the sword free as she aimed for the orc's loins hoping to catch an artery or something else in passing. The air was hammered from her lungs as his giant green foot slammed down on her back, she could feel the bones in her spine creak and snap, and her chest burned as she felt the rib snap inward. Blood shot from her throat and lips, writhing in pain as she felt the air escaping her lungs inside, it almost felt as though she was drowning, air failed to ease the pain it only made it worse. Fear gripped Gamona's heart as the towering orc leaned over her, dripping the thick blood from his wrist over her upturned face.

"I already saw that trick, little wolf." He laughed, spitting on her trembling, gasping form before turning to the sorceress watching the exchange with little interest. "It's all yours, mistress."

The dark-haired woman approached slowly, dark tendrils of smoke seeping from her outstretched fingers. Gamona cowered, tears in her aching eyes as her vision slowly faded, the last words she heard before slipping into the darkness tore her soul asunder. "What Sula said was true, I don't give a damn about the hill tribes. They are merely flesh to be consumed by my master, and I don't mean your precious Marguk."

With a heavy flutter of wings, the griffins landed one after another and trotted out of the way making room for the others. The Cloud Knight's losses had been too great, of those who had charged under Captain Eliza's command, only six remained. Now the bedraggled knights left their steeds to join the defenders on foot. Atop the castle walls, archers fired unceasingly into the roaring horde pressed against the gates. It would not be long before they exhausted their supply, others hurled javelins and stones down into the fray in hopes of dwindling their numbers. From a blue-tiled tower set into the perimeter, Bart and the others peered out into the city. Master Solon stood alongside, his hand stroking the black leather tome in contemplation.

Della's hand shot out, "There! By the fountain in the square." cried the elf.

Her companions followed her finger, and sure enough, there was the black-robed figure. She was pacing back and forth at the rear of the army. As they followed her movement, the woman halted. A shudder passed through their collective spines as they watched the figure raise her arms towards the castle gates, streams of black tendril smoke flowed out like a pit of vipers amongst the charging horde. The smoke plumed and billowed beneath their feet, weaving up the stone walls and through the courtyard. Instinctively, those atop the walls and in the courtyard covered their mouths, eyes wide in horror as the strange ether rippled and pooled across the ground before dispersing.

With a start, Solon clutched at his robes. Something was burning against his skin, burning like a hot poker. The tome fell at his feet, the same eerie smoke bellowing softly from its pages. The wizard crouched down, waving his hand over the black leather and whispering softly to himself as a faint black aura surrounded his palm. A flash of sparks flung him back, driving the air from his body as he slammed against the stone walls of the tower.

Bart stared on in horror as corpses slowly rose up from amongst the screaming throng below, those eerie white eyes glowing in the early dawn. Screams ripped out from the inner keep, pulling his attention to the open doors behind them. A woman, clad in blood-stained robes of a healer, collapsed on the stair leading up to the keep. A pair of snarling, howling creatures clawing at her throat.

Armen was the first to move, bolting towards the stairs leading to the courtyard he shouted, "They are inside!"

Captain Eliza and her knights, who had stationed themselves behind the gates, turned just in time to see the flood of revenant pouring towards them from the inner castle. Steel flashed in the morning light meeting flesh and bone in a frenzy. One knight fell back, tackled by three of the creatures who clawed frantically at their steel plate, trying to find purchase at their face and throat.

Della took aim at the writhing pile, setting loose her eagle-fletched arrow, it streaked behind the captain's head and through the skull of one of the creatures lunging at the fallen knight's neck. Armen bolted across, driving his shoulder into the other two and rolling through the impact to stand over one of the creatures. He brought his heavy boot down, smashing the screaming face beneath him. Bart followed close behind, cutting the legs out from under two as he followed his bulky friend across the courtyard and leaping, sword raised, atop the third. His blade slammed home with a crunch, splitting the jaw open in a silent scream.

"Where the hell did they come from?" screamed Eliza, blood dripping from a gash across her face, a bit of nail embedded above her eye, she pulled the grotesque spur free and spat the ichor from her mouth.

Armen plunged his short sword through the spine of a screaming creature that had once been one of the Twin Rivers guardsmen. "The witch out there doesn't need to see who she raises, it seems." His eyes rose toward the open keep at the other end of the courtyard, there were potentially dozens or hundreds more within.

Lorena shook the old wizard, his breathing was labored. A small trickle of blood escaped the corner of his mouth as his eyes stared blankly up at the timber ceiling. "Master Solon! What happened? What did you do?" The unseeing eyes turned towards the sound of her voice, a weak hand beckoning her closer. As she leaned in, his trembling lips pressed against the mage's ear as his hand caressed Lorena's red hair. The words came softly, draining the old man with each syllable before slumping heavily in her arms. She stumbled back, palms pressed against her temples as the throbbing pressure built up and rang like temple bells inside her skull. Flashes of images, sounds, faces, arcane symbols, and flowing script intertwined with each other and hammered into the backs of her eyes before fading to white as she collapsed opposite the dead wizard, gasping for air.

Having seen the flash, then the collapsing mage nearby, Della turned her attention from the courtyard to her young friend. The mage was groaning softly, her eyes shuttered tightly against the dawn, but she was alive. The old wizard, however, seemed to have passed from his worries. The elf bowed her head in a silent, brief prayer which was shortly interrupted by the bellowing of horns and a thunderous roar down in the city streets. Peeking through one of the arrowslits, her stomach turned at the sight of the four trolls preparing to charge from beyond the market square, it was a straight line from there to the small outer gate for the castle walls.

"Take down those trolls! Leave the others to the spears!" cried Della, her bow drawing taught alongside the other archers on the wall. A cloud of shafts and bolts flew out from every tower, wall, and barricade within range of the four hulking beasts, wave after wave of missiles thudded into the thick blue-painted hides. Without any regard for their fellows underfoot, the four ram-wielding giants charged down the city streets, smashing through bodies and buildings alike. Brick and plaster filled the air in a choking cloud, the earth rumbled as pave-stones and bodies were smashed into rubble.

Aiming at the closest troll, Della drew back once more, taking her time as she lined up her shot on the ugly painted face lurching towards them. The arrow sped forward with a sharp hiss, plunging deep into the troll's eye as arrowhead, shaft, and fletch disappeared into its skull. Fluid and blood spurted from the wound as the massive beast lurched and twisted, dropping their hold on the ram and grasping their face before collapsing sideways onto a crumbling ruin. A cheer broke out along the wall, weapons raised at the sight of the small victory won. Unbalanced, the front of the ram dug into the torn-up cobblestones, sending the troll behind the slain bearer flying over their comrade's corpse headlong into a nearby building sending timber and brick flying in a cloud of destruction. Screams of panic filled the streets below as the chaos unfolded, sending more of the green-skinned horde to their deaths. As the dust settled, the elf's sharp gaze caught sight of the black-robed woman beyond. Her breath halted, waiting for the distant figure to lift their arms once more and send those tendrils forth to raise the dead, but it did not come.

"It seems they cannot cast the spell with impunity," said Lorena, having regained her senses, "this is our chance. We strike now!" Together, the two women rushed down the stairs into the courtyard. Finding those below standing against the ebbing tide of revenant rushing from the inner keep, they rushed in amongst the fray. The mage rushed through the crowd to the swordsman's side, Bart was side-by-side with the armored captain and Armen, catching their breath in the brief respite as the remaining knights and a few guards formed the defensive line. In hurried words, she appraised the three of what had happened, and the sorceress' delayed act.

Armen nodded, "But we cannot get out the gates, how are we supposed to reach her?"

"My griffins!" The knight captain shouted with a point of her sword, "Eight remain for the gamble. I will bring three of my men with you." She called forward three of her knights and turned to her subordinate, "Lieutenant Frig, you have the command." The junior officer turned and saluted with her wide smile, and wild eyes matted with blood before turning back to face the screaming creatures.

At a sprint the eight made their way into the stables, the beasts had remained harnessed save Ginger. With the aid of Frig and another, Bart managed to ready the creature. A sense of calm seemed to come over him, he looked into the beast's eyes, golden as the sun cresting the eastern sky and filled with a passion he had never felt. He patted the thick plumage and climbed into the saddle, ducking his head under a crossbeam his gaze caught the engraved 'W' on the pommel inlaid in silver. The eight riders formed up before Captain Eliza, wings twitching and eager to take flight.

With a salute of her sword, Captain Eliza looked over them. "Glory for Maroth! Death to our enemies!" and with a kick of her boot, they rose in unison spiraling around the inner towers of the keep and crested the walls diving downward above the cries of friend and foe alike.

Gripping the reigns tightly, Bart crouched low in the saddle. This was nothing like the horses he was used to, the wind bit at his face and tore rivulets of tears from his eyes as the powerful wings pulled them to even greater speeds over the battle below. Buildings blurred to either side and below as he fought to keep his focus on the distant figure beyond, near the merchant's square. The red-furred griffin lurched sideways, spinning like a bolt from a crossbow, dodging a hail of missiles from the screaming horde below. The swordsman clung, pale-faced to the creature, praying to any god or devil that would hear him to spare him from flying off into the open air. Righting itself, the beast rejoined the others in a wide arc over the sprawling city as they rose ever higher into the dawn. For a moment, Bart reveled in the view; snow-capped mountains, sprawling green fields, and the rushing waters of the Red Horse River. Forcing himself to focus, he unstrapped the heavy lance from beside the saddle and tucked it under his shoulder, bracing himself to join the downward charge onto the small cluster below. With a sharp whistle from Captain Eliza's Griffin, they dove, talons and lances outstretched. Predators from above now hunted the horde below, braying for blood, eager for the kill. A will thrill filled Bart as the ground rushed closer and closer, he lined up the point of his lance on the shape of an orc bracing a massive oaken shield before him. Riders and mounts alike, cried out in shrill unison, shaking the air with their battle song as they smashed into the shields and bodies below.

Talon tore into flesh, lances pierced shield and bone. The battle joined, riders leaped from the griffins and rushed in amongst the startled defenders at the rear of the horde. Armen, wielding his halberd in a wide arc, mowed down a pair of brightly-clad goblins scattering before him before they could raise their horns to their lips. Eliza and her knights charged shoulder to shoulder with their prince, steel ringing as they cut down any who came close to the heir. Lorena's voice called out amongst the din, twisted in the spidery tongue of magic as roots sprouted from the ground and engulfed startled warriors, dragging them screaming beneath the earth. Lorena had tossed set her bow, drawing her daggers as she ducked around shields and bodies to slit exposed throats.

With Lorena at his side, Bart searched the mele for the black-robed figure lost in the chaos. Bodies mingled in the violent struggle, slipping in blood and gore beneath their feet. Movement from the corner of his eye made him turn sharply, sword raised, barely deflecting the axe blow from the howling orc that had charged from behind. He continued the arc, slashing from right to left across the orc's throat. The green-skinned warrior ducked back, swinging the axe inward against the steel blade, trying to disarm the swordsman or pull them off balance. Bart felt the force of the blow pull at his shoulder almost opening him, fighting to reposition he spun with the blow and stepped forward, following the momentum until he was behind the shocked orc warrior and drove the point of his blade through the back of their neck through to the hilt. Blood spouted over the silver steel as the swordsman raised his boot, kicking his enemy free from the blade.

With a bestial cry, the hulking war chief lunged at one of the steel-clad knights. Axe raised, he cleaved his foe from shoulder to hip, steel crumbled like paper beneath his blow as the man screamed in dismay and collapsed like a child's doll writhing in pain nearly cleaved in twain. Reaching down with a tattooed arm, Marguk grabbed the screaming face, held the armored knight aloft, and hurled them toward a charging griffin, knocking the beast unconscious. Turning on his heel, the war chief of the hill tribes leaped towards another of the winged beasts that were clawing at a fallen warrior and brought his black-steel blade down hard on the back of the blood-stained plumage, separating the beaked head from the lion's body. Standing over his kill, the great warrior surveyed the scene. The soft-skins had charged from the sky, a brave feat, but now they were more trouble than they were worth. And that tall bald one with the halberd surrounded by knights looked important, if he could kill him, then he could break these pathetic humans.

Armen leveled his halberd at the howling, axe-wielding orc. At his side, the steel-clad knights stood their ground, shields, and swords raised, doubtful that it would provide any more defense against such a blow. An arrow hissed past Armen's ear, the orc ducked his head out of the way with a wide grin before hefting his axe over his shoulder. Gritting his teeth, Armen slid forward his grip on the haft of his weapon, judging the distance, he knew what was coming, it was always the same; they would charge with as much power as they could to try and bowl them over, best to hold him back and keep the distance between them.

With a howl it came, Marguk charged, axe raised straight for the bald warrior flanked by knights. Armen braced his shoulder, planting the butt of his halberd under his boot and leaning hard on the haft of his weapon ready for the impact. With a thunderous roar the great orc's flesh met the steel spike at the end of his weapon, and snapped the oak shaft with a crack, driving both to the ground in a pile of dust and flesh. The wind was driven from Armen's lungs as he felt his spine groan from the impact. His hand fought to reach the small dagger at his waist, but he could not reach it. He could feel the foul breath by his ear, the warm blood pooling over him.

Teeth bared, Marguk leaned in, eyes bloodshot from battle-rage. "Your little twig is broken, human! Next, I will break you!" grabbing the bald warrior's throat in both hands, the orc chieftain squeezed hard, rearing back his head to strike down on Armen's face.

Sword level, Bart charged in screaming. His body moved on its own, pushing him forward towards the hulking, tattooed figure atop his friend. He felt the blade dig deep into the green shoulder and snap under the weight. The orc howled dropping his grip on the bald warrior and swung out against the annoyance, catching the swordsman across the jaw. Bart felt the bone crack, his neck snapped awkwardly to the side as weightlessness overtook his body and he sailed across the cobblestone and landed against the crumpled form of a dead griffin, the lifeless wings shading his form from the sun above.

The knights, seizing the opportunity, plunged their blades deep into the howling chieftain, drawing the warm blood from his scarred body until he finally fell back never to rise again.

"Fine work! More fodder for my master's horde." Mocked Susalla, the black tendrils rippling from beneath her robes and around her feet as she approached, hands clapping together softly.

Della drew back, taking aim at the raven-haired skull, and loosed the shaft with a twang. A tendril rose up like a serpent and glanced the missile away, as though swatting a fly with a dismissive flick.

Susalla's eyes were wild with euphoric release, arms raised, as the corpses surrounding the market square slowly began to rise and groan in a symphony of death. "This day has been two hundred years in the making! My master will have his due, and there is nothing any of you can do to stop him! I am a daughter of Hecktat, servant of the voiceless ones, and this world will be theirs!"

Stumbling from beneath the griffin's wing with a groan, the stumbling figure of Bart emerged. Lorena's heart sank, waiting to see the pale glowing eyes where her lover's had once been. His eyes rose, meeting hers, then turned towards the sorceress and beyond. At a crouch, the swordsman bolted, every last bit of strength he had left in his body now spent on one final act. Crying out in rage he drove his shoulder hard into the sorceress's stomach, picking the woman up and slamming both of their bodies against the point of the protruding end of a lance, still upturned in the air. She screamed angrily, the black mist surrounding the pair as she clawed and kicked at her attacker, desperate to fight free of the impalement. Pushing himself free, Bart stumbled from the skewered sorceress, collapsing on the blood-strewn streets.

Screams of rage echoed from the throats of the undead creatures teaming throughout the city as they rushed towards the scene, trampling any who stood in their path. Clawing, biting, and slashing as they focused solely on reaching their mistress. Her screams called out to them, a siren song for the undead. Blood pooled in the ears of those closest to her voice, deafening them from the screams. Black mists pooled around them, threatening to choke off nostrils and throats, blinding them where they stood as it blotted out the dawn.

A voice, silent and calm echoed within the mage's mind, easing her spirit. With tears in her eyes, she raised her staff above the clawing hordes of creatures swarming towards them. "Kulasie" she muttered, a spark shuttered from the tip of her staff followed by a swirling inferno that engulfed the sorceress below, locked in her deadly embrace. A shrill scream filled the air as the orange flames twirled below and intertwined with the black tendrils of smoke consuming all within the inferno. As the flames died down, the corpses that had been lurching and charging amongst the living suddenly stopped and turned to ash where they stood, flowing into nothingness, flowing along the breeze without any sign save the memory of those who had witnessed their passing.

A great cheer arose from the defenders of Twin Rivers, they had survived, and the living had prospered. But Lorena did not hear them. Eyes swelled red with tears, she collapsed at Bart's side, his lifeless eyes staring skyward into the dawn he would never see again.

In the true fashion of The Order, they had entered the city of Twin Rivers with much fanfare and ceremony. Horns and drums announced their presence, and one would have thought they had been the saviors of the day from the way they carried themselves. With their pristine armor and rich adornment, untouched by the ash or blood of battle they marched on parade through the city in full array with their banners gleaming in the sun.

From atop the castle walls Captain Eliza, Armen, Lord Firbank, and his son watched on dismissively. There had been little they could do to keep them from entering the city, even less to prevent them from reveling in their glory. At the very least, they might help secure the city against further incursions. Better to have reinforcement at the end of the battle than none at all. Down below, the wounded were collectively gathered in any structure that could hold them. The supplies that had been brought by The Order had been most welcome if nothing else. They had brought medicine, healers, bandages, food, wine, blankets, and prayer books. If receiving aid meant letting the holy order march around like strutting peacocks, then so be it.

Carts flowed through the city, driven by teams of oxen and horses laden with the bodies of slain goblins and orcs which were dumped into deep pits covered in lime and burned outside the city walls. Those who had survived had run from the city back across the Red Horse into the Hinterlands, pursued by the riders under the command of Lieutenant Theodoric. His riders now kept watch from the clouds above, wary of any further movement. The only sign of the creatures known as 'Revenant' were the telltale piles of black soot scattered through the streets like ash from fires run rampant. Their horrific memory scorched the minds of the ones who had faced the onslaught.

As the day gave way to dusk, torches gathered along the city walls and around the pyres that had been raised in the squares and courtyards for the fallen. Prayers were offered by the warrior priests from The Order, garbed in the white robes of the clerical faith. In the castle's training ground, a pair of stone monuments adorned with wreaths of flowers had been erected.

Grand Master Bernard stood; hands raised in solemn prayer before the gathered crowd. "May the Father ease their burden, the Mother hold their hand, and the warrior shield them from any harm. We who remain will remember them now and always, from this day until the final dawn." Bowing his head, the warrior priest stepped aside.

Armen, now clad in the finery suited to his station. His purple robe adorned in silver buttons and white silk trim on the hem and sleeves, gazed down at the only remaining remnant of his friends. Placing his hand on the smooth gray stone, he knelt before the memorial and bade his final farewell. Close behind, Della and Lorena gazed down at the pair of stones, tears in their eyes as the three read the words.

'Here lies Thrax, Warrior of the Southern Sands. Friend of Armen, Prince of Maroth. Defender of the Northern Gate who slew a hundred foes.'

'Here lies Bart of Troutsmouth, Friend of Armen, Prince of Maroth. Who, by sacrificing himself to rid the continent of darkness, stands as Hero of Oria'

# Chapter

# SEVENTEEN

# EPILOGUE

Commander Zulla stared down at the map covered in small wood figures and paper flags on the table. Along with the officers he had gathered, they examined the disposition across the landscape as though they were planning their next move in chess. But in this game, each piece may represent hundreds or thousands of lives of their countrymen. One of the junior officers continued reading from a list held in their hands.

"House Firbank, along with their Minor Lords, still holds the lands across the Tsere. They are joined by the marshaled forces gathered by The Order under Grand Master Bernard, as well as Lords Olbrecht, Bertolf, and Gisko. House Bardiche has also proclaimed their alliance, drawing Duke Hugo and Lady Priscilla to their aid. Together they have declared themselves as 'The Central Principality' claiming they are beholden to the one true heir of Maroth." The speaker pointed along the span of central mountains running from Hills Reach south to Hammerpeak. "The armies under Duke Rolf have encamped along the Tsere River, with the aim of cutting off reinforcement from the Garrison of The Order and to suppress any potential dissent from the towns and villages who may join the rebellion. He has also garnered the support of General Jehan of Almach, who has supplied not only troops but relief aid to the northern reaches."

The old knight nodded, "We are all knights sworn to the crown and the kingdom. This war will be unlike any we have fought since the founding of Maroth. We face not some foreign invader or adversary but our friends and, in some cases, our own families." His eyes passed over the gathered faces, all solemn at the prospect in silence. "I will not command you to stay, nor will I pursue those who wish to join their families. But know this, any who departs after the first snow will be branded as a deserter and a traitor. Just as my own daughter now stands against us, bound by her own brand of honor. Make your choices, and should you choose to leave go with honor."

Across the land, word of the impending conflict spread as fires through the villages and towns. This winter would be overshadowed by the threat of war come the spring, and a time that normally heralded the beginning of new life would be fed with the blood of the slain. And with the first spring dawning, banners of the scattered houses would bloom in fields of steel.

The story continues in
*Banners of Oria*